Praise for **Starship: Pirate**

"Through these now many years the collected works of Mike Resnick have given me more pleasure per capita than those of any other writer; I read *Soul Eater* in manuscript in 1980 and pronounced that if he carried on Resnick would in a decade be viewed as the most important science fiction writer to emerge in the decade to come. An easy call as the rocket ships then accumulated. *Starship: Pirate* is a wonderful novel, an expanse of color, light, and wit; its splendid rogues in space as fetching as they are wickedly memorable. It is a privilege to have lived and worked in science fiction during Mike Resnick's quarter century."

—Barry N. Malzberg

Praise for **Starship: Mutiny**

"Resnick's writing is effortless, full of snappy dialogue and a fast-moving plot. . . . This is high-quality work. . . . There's a veneer of quality and above all believability that makes this heads above many space operas. . . . [I]t's damn good fun."

—*SFCrowsnest*

"An action-packed romp through a science fiction funhouse complete with bizarre aliens, breathtaking escapes, space battles, and the biggest battle of all, trying to do the right thing when everyone around you is beyond caring."

—*SFSite*

STARSHIP: PIRATE

ALSO AVAILABLE BY MIKE RESNICK

STARSHIP: MUTINY
BOOK ONE

NEW DREAMS FOR OLD

MIKE RESNICK

STARSHIP: PIRATE

BOOK TWO

an imprint of **Prometheus Books**
Amherst, NY

Published 2006 by Pyr®, an imprint of Prometheus Books

Inquiries should be addressed to
Pyr
59 John Glenn Drive
Amherst, New York 14228–2197
VOICE: 716–691–0133, ext. 207
FAX: 716–564–2711
WWW.PYRSF.COM

10 09 08 07 06   5 4 3 2 1

Library of Congress Cataloging-in-Publication Data

Resnick, Michael D.
    Starship—pirate : book two / by Mike Resnick.
        p. cm.
    ISBN-13: 978–1–59102–490–3 (hardcover : alk. paper)
    ISBN-10: 1–59102–490–0 (hardcover : alk. paper)
    1. Space ships—Fiction. 2. Piracy—Fiction. I. Title. II. Title: Pirate.

PS3568.E698S737 2006
813'.54—dc22

                                                              2006027555

Printed in the United States on acid-free paper

To Carol, as always,

And to the rest of the Catalunya gang:

Jack McDevitt

Kristine Kathryn Rusch

Robert J. Sawyer

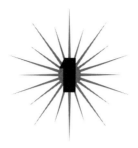

The broad, burly, three-legged alien spun slowly down the battered, shopworn corridor, muttering to himself. He growled at a junior officer who didn't get out of his way fast enough, glared at another who quickly stepped into a room to let him pass in the narrow corridor, and finally reached the small, cramped mess hall of the *Theodore Roosevelt*. He spotted his captain sitting at an oft-repaired table, nursing a beer, spun across the room in his surprisingly graceful gait until he reached the table, and then seated himself.

"I hate these chairs!" he muttered in his deep guttural voice.

"I'm glad to see you too, Four Eyes," said the captain pleasantly.

"We have to get more furniture designed for Molarians if I'm going to continue to serve on this ship."

"Maybe we'll just jettison you into space," replied Wilson Cole. "It's probably cheaper than buying new chairs, and it would certainly be easier on everyone's nerves."

"You'd be lost without me."

"Who needs *you*? I think we've been lost for the past three days." Cole took a sip of his beer. "At the very least, we're in uncharted territory."

"Damn it, Wilson!" snapped the alien. "What the hell are we doing here?"

"I don't know about you," said Cole. "As for me, I'm drinking beer and listening to you show off all the new Terran words you've learned." He paused and stared at the alien. "Are you going to keep it up, or would you like to tell me what's really bothering you?"

"I don't know," said the alien. "When we decided to become a pirate ship, I thought life was going to be romantic and filled with adventure."

"You want adventure?" replied Cole with a smile. "Go back into the Republic. They'll give you all the adventure you can handle, or have you forgotten why we're out here in the middle of nowhere?"

"I know, I know. The last time I checked there was a ten-million-credit bounty on your ugly head."

"I hope you're not feeling ignored," said Cole. "As of last week they're offering three million for Commander Forrice as well."

"I can't tell you how flattered I am," muttered Forrice.

Cole laughed aloud. "I've said it before, and I'll say it again. What I love about Molarians is that they're the only other race besides Men who share our speech patterns and our sense of humor."

"Only one of us is trying to be funny," said Forrice. "We've been clear of the Republic and traveling the Inner Frontier for almost three weeks. Isn't it about time we went about the business of pirating?"

"Soon."

"What are you waiting for?"

"I'm waiting to feel safe."

"You've been safe for three weeks," said Forrice. "No one's come after us."

"I don't know that, and neither do you," replied Cole. "Look, I was the Navy's first mutineer in more than six centuries. It doesn't matter that they know I saved five million lives by taking over the ship. Once the press got the story and ran with it, there was no way I was going to beat the charges—and then the *Teddy R* made the Navy look like fools when the crew broke me out of jail. If you were the Republic, would *you* give up this soon?"

"They're fighting a war, Wilson," the Molarian pointed out. "They've got better uses for their assets."

"I agree—but if they were that reasonable, I wouldn't have had to take over the ship in the first place. The fact that we haven't spotted any pursuit for the last few weeks doesn't necessarily mean they've called it off. That's why we're in the emptiest sector of the Frontier we could find; it'll be easier to make sure no one's tracking us. And once I know they're not pursuing us, I'll buy you a cutlass and let you maim and pillage to your heart's content—always assuming that Molarians have hearts."

"You really think they might still be looking for us?" asked Forrice.

"If I'd killed Fleet Admiral Garcia or blown up a friendly planet by mistake, they might have given up by now." Cole smiled ruefully. "But they'll never forgive me for escaping while the press was gathered on Timos for my court-martial."

"All this running away is getting on my nerves."

"I didn't know you had any."

The Molarian stared at him. "I'm getting so bored that I even tried some of that stuff you're drinking."

"You mean beer?" asked Cole. "I wouldn't think it would do much for the Molarian digestive system."

Forrice made a face, which would have seemed hideous to anyone who was unacquainted with his race. "What it did was totally clean out the Molarian digestive system," he admitted. "I was sick for a whole day."

"We don't have days out here," noted Cole. "Just three eight-hour shifts of night." He paused. "What else is bothering you, Four Eyes?"

"We're running short of food."

"We'll synthesize some."

"And fuel."

"We don't need fuel except for accelerating and braking," answered Cole placidly.

"And there are no Molarian females left on this damned ship!" exploded Forrice.

"Ah," said Cole with a smile. "Now we come to it."

"You'd feel the same way if you didn't have half the human females fighting for the right to cohabit with the great galactic hero!"

"Do I detect a note of jealousy?"

"Jealousy, envy, frustration—it's all the same when you're stuck on a ship without the opposite sex."

"And I'm told Molarian females are about as opposite as they come," said Cole.

"Enough," said Forrice. "If anyone's going to make crude remarks about Molarian females, it's my prerogative."

"By the way, I thought Molarian females were seasonal."

"*They* are!" thundered Forrice. "*I'm* not!"

"There are two other Molarians aboard," said Cole. "Go swap dirty jokes with them. But when you're through, we've got some important things to discuss."

"We have?" asked Forrice quickly. "You mean you and me?"

Cole shook his head. "The whole ship. But we'll start with what passes for the senior staff, which means you, me, and Sharon Blacksmith."

"So it's a Security matter?"

"No."

"Then why include the Chief of Security?"

"I value her opinion."

"And you share her bedroom," said Forrice bitterly.

"Actually, she shares mine," replied Cole with no show of embarrassment. "It's bigger. Why don't you meet me there at 2200 hours, ship's time?"

Forrice nodded his massive head. "I'll be there."

He lumbered off, and Cole finished his beer, stood up, stretched, and wandered out into the corridor. *We really need to do something to modernize this ship*, he thought; *I'll bet it hasn't been touched in fifty years. Most of it looks like a cheap spacehand's dive on a trading world, and the rest looks even worse.*

He wanted to go to his cabin and relax, perhaps finish the book he'd been reading, but he decided it was more important to maintain the illusion that the captain was involved in the mundane day-to-day business of running the ship, so he took an airlift up to the bridge instead.

Lieutenant Christine Mboya, a tall, slender, grimly efficient woman in her late twenties, sat at a computer complex, studying screens, whispering commands and questions that neither Cole nor anyone else could hear.

Malcolm Briggs, an athletic-looking young man, also wearing a lieutenant's uniform, sat at the weapons station, watching a holographic entertainment that was being transmitted to his gunnery console from the ship's library.

Overhead, floating in a transparent pod attached high on the wall, was Wxakgini, the only pilot the ship had had for the past seven years. He was a member of the Bdxeni race, a bullet-shaped being with insectoid features, curled into a fetal position, multifaceted eyes wide open and unblinking, with six shining cables connecting his head to a navigational computer hidden inside the bulkhead. The Bdxeni never slept, which made them ideal pilots, and they formed such a symbiosis with their ships' navigational computers that it was difficult to tell where one started and the other left off.

"Captain on the bridge!" announced Christine, jumping to attention and snapping off a salute the moment she saw him. Briggs followed suit a few seconds later.

"Cut it out," said Cole. "How many times do I have to explain that we're not in the Navy anymore?"

"Maybe so, but you're still the captain," said Christine stubbornly.

"I am an outlaw," he said patiently. "You are an outlaw. Outlaws don't salute each other."

"*This* outlaw does, sir," she replied.

"So does this one, sir," added Briggs, saluting again.

"I think when we finally update this ship, the very first piece of new equipment I'm going to install is a mainmast, so I can tie insubordinate officers to it and flog the hell out of them," said Cole wryly. He looked up toward the ceiling. "Thanks, Pilot."

"For what?" asked Wxakgini, staring endlessly at some fixed point in time and space that only he and the navigational computer could see or comprehend.

"For not paying any special attention to me whenever I come onto the bridge."

"Oh," said Wxakgini tonelessly, all thoughts of Cole and the rest of the bridge's personnel seemingly vanished from his mind.

"Now that we're all through greeting each other and ignoring our Captain's wishes," he said to Christine, "is there anything to report?"

"Still no signs of pursuit, sir," she replied. "We've passed eleven habitable planets during the last Standard day. None of them have been colonized or show enough neutrino activity to suggest any sign of industrial civilization."

"All right," said Cole. "Four Eyes is feeling ill-used. It'll be a shame to spoil his snit, but I think it's safe to say that the Republic has decided we're more trouble than we're worth, at least for the moment. They need every ship they've got for the war against the Teroni Federation."

"What now, sir?" asked Briggs.

"I guess we wear eye patches and practice saying 'Avast there' and 'Shiver me timbers.'"

Christine couldn't repress a giggle, but Briggs persisted: "Seriously, sir, what do we do now?"

"Seriously, I'm not sure yet," answered Cole. "I have a feeling there's more to the pirating game than meets the eye."

"I always thought it was simple and straightforward," said Briggs.

"Okay," said Cole. "Pick a target."

"I beg your pardon, sir?"

"When's the last time you or Christine spotted a luxury ship?" asked Cole. "Or even a cargo ship?"

"Eleven days, sir," said Christine promptly.

"And the last planet worth plundering?"

"There were diamonds on two of the worlds we passed yesterday, and fissionable materials on three more."

"But no industrial civilizations," noted Cole.

"No, sir," said Briggs.

"I thought you wanted to be a pirate," he said. "But of course, if you'd rather be a miner, we can drop you off and come back in a couple of years to see what you've uncovered."

"I think I'll stick to piracy, sir," said Briggs.

"If you insist, Mr. Briggs . . ." said Cole, unable to keep the amused tone from his voice. "As for ships," he continued, "a lot of them will be better armed than we are, and some will have Republic escorts."

"You're the most decorated officer in the Republic," said Briggs. "You'll figure out the best way to go beat them, sir."

"I am no longer an officer in the Republic, and none of my medals was for excelling at piracy," said Cole. "This is as new to me as I hope it is to the rest of you."

"But you've been thinking about it since we escaped," said Briggs with absolute certainty. "I'm sure you've got it all doped out by now."

"You confidence is appreciated," said Cole. *And don't buy any bargain real estate*, he added mentally. He turned to Christine. "I suppose you might as well start mapping out the most populated worlds on the Inner Frontier, and see if you can dig up any information about the major trade routes. There's no rush on this; we're probably days away from any of them, and to tell the truth I don't know if I'll use anything you manage to find. But on the assumption that I might need it, it wouldn't be a bad idea to begin gathering the information now."

"Is there anything I can do, sir?" asked Briggs.

"See if you can find out the schedules and routes of the largest spaceliners that travel to the Inner Frontier. They probably don't hit more than a dozen worlds—Binder X, Roosevelt III, a few others—but see what you can learn. And be subtle."

"Subtle, sir?"

"We are outlaws with prices on our heads," he explained patiently, wondering how long it would be before the crew started getting used to the idea. "Don't let anyone trace your queries back to the source."

"Yes, sir," said Briggs, offering a snappy salute.

Cole stared at him, considered explaining yet again that saluting wasn't necessary, decided it would be an exercise in futility, and left the bridge.

"You're going to break that poor young hero-worshiper's spirit," said a familiar female voice.

"You were monitoring that?" Cole asked of the empty air as he traversed the corridor on his way to the airlift.

"I like to snoop," said Sharon Blacksmith's disembodied voice. "It's my job."

"If you were snooping earlier, you know I want you in my cabin at 2200 hours," said Cole.

"You *always* want me in your cabin at 2200 hours," replied the voice.

"With your clothes on."

"What fun is that?" asked Sharon.

"Fun time's over," said Cole. "It's time we got down to the serious business of plundering the galaxy."

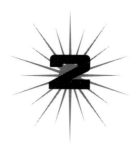

Sharon Blacksmith showed up in Cole's cabin at 2200 hours. She was small and wiry, and her uniform efficiently eliminated such curves as she possessed.

"This *must* be an important meeting," she said. "This is the first time you've made your bed since before the mutiny."

"I figure if I keep you busy enough criticizing my housekeeping, you won't have time to criticize my performance," he replied. Suddenly he smiled. "Besides, my office is a mess."

"I know."

Forrice arrived a moment later. Human chairs were not made for his physical structure, and he lowered himself gently to the bed.

"All right, we're here," said the Molarian. "Now what?"

"Now we discuss the future," said Cole, seated at a desk. "Not the far future," he added. "The immediate future."

"What's to discuss?" asked Forrice. "We can't return to the Republic. We have a whole ship and crew at our disposal. It's time to go to work."

"True," said Cole. "But we have to start considering just what *kind* of pirates we plan to be."

"What are you talking about?" demanded Forrice. "A pirate is a pirate."

"Before we begin," interjected Sharon, "are we waiting for anyone else?"

Cole shook his head. "No, there's just the three of us—the ship's senior officers."

"Then I shouldn't be here," she said. "I'm not a senior officer."

"You stood up for me when I took over the ship," said Cole. "You were charged with abetting a mutiny. As far as I'm concerned, that makes you a senior officer."

"But I'm not," she said. "I'm Chief of Security."

"The Captain says you are," said Cole. "We're no longer a part of the Navy. We're no longer in the Republic. We're an outlaw ship with no rules to guide us." He paused. "Now, under those circumstances, whose word is law?"

"Yours," said Sharon.

"Until someone decides to lop your head off," added Forrice. "After all, we're pirates."

"I'll count on the Chief of Security to protect me," said Cole.

"While we're on the subject of senior officers," said Sharon, "I assume Forrice has been promoted from Third to First Officer. But shouldn't you be appointing a Second and a Third Officer?"

"We haven't needed them up to now," answered Cole. "All we've been doing is running without any sign of pursuit. Pilot, whose name I will never learn to pronounce, was able to handle that without any help. When we embark on our campaign, I'll fill those positions."

"Then let's get on with whatever you called us here for," said the Molarian.

Cole nodded. "We have some decisions to make, and as I said, the most important concerns exactly what kind of pirates we intend to be."

"The kind who get rich," said Forrice.

Cole touched a spot on his desk and made instant contact with the bridge. A pretty young woman's holograph instantly appeared in front of him.

"Ensign Marcos," he said, "send me a view of the nearest habitable planet."

"Habitable by humans, sir?" asked Rachel Marcos.

"By humans."

Suddenly the holograph of a green and gold world began revolving above Sharon's head.

"Thank you, Ensign," said Cole. She smiled and her image vanished. "There it is, Four Eyes. Ripe for the picking."

"All right, there it is," said Forrice. "So what?"

"Let's say there are six families living there. Originally there were thirty, but eight fell to native predation and sixteen left during a three-year drought. There are currently eleven adults, and fourteen kids ranging from three months to sixteen years. They're farming it. What do we do?"

"What do you mean, what do we do?"

"Let's say we need to resupply the mess hall. Let's further say that somehow, perhaps through Sharon's good offices, we know beyond any shadow of a doubt that they've got an aggregate of eighteen thousand credits and some very valuable gold and platinum family heirlooms. It would take ten minutes to send a party down in a shuttle and rob them of everything they have. Of course, even if they put up no resistance and we didn't kill them, we'd have to destroy any subspace radio we found so they couldn't report us—"

"This is the Frontier," interjected Sharon. "There's no one to report us *to*."

"I stand corrected," said Cole. "All right, we'll steal the radios—they must be worth something on the market—and we'll certainly disable or destroy any ships they have so they can't pursue us." He stared at Forrice. "Sound like the kind of thing you had in mind?"

"You know it isn't," growled the Molarian.

"Let me give you another example. A Republic ship is racing through the Frontier. Lieutenant Mboya or Ensign Braxite charts its course and tells us that we can alter our own course and confront it in five hours. The ship has some weaponry, but we can outgun it. And I'll give you one more thing to consider: its cargo is worth ten million credits."

"That's it?" asked Forrice.

"That's it," answered Cole. "A ship from the hated Republic, poorly armed, and carrying an incredibly valuable cargo. What do we do?"

"We attack, we disable it, and we plunder its cargo."

"Do we kill the crew?"

"Not if they surrender," said Forrice. "We set them down on the nearest oxygen world."

"But they can identify us."

An alien smile crossed the Molarian's face. "How much more can the Republic hate you?"

"Point taken," said Cole. "So we disable the ship and take its cargo."

"Right."

"Want to know what the cargo is?" asked Cole.

Forrice shrugged. "Why not?"

"Very rare, very unstable vaccine, valued at ten million credits. It's being shipped to a colony world where a new plague has broken out. If it doesn't get there before it spoils in three Standard days, a couple of million colonists will die. And so it won't seem like a loaded example, the colonists aren't Men or Molarians—they're Polonoi. And every last one of them is as stubborn and wrongheaded as the Polonoi captain I deposed a few weeks ago."

"You can't let two million innocent beings die," said Forrice. "Even Polonoi."

"I'm sure our three Polonoi crew members would agree," said Cole. "But we don't have to let them die. Once we disable the ship, strand the crew, and appropriate the vaccine, we contact the Republic and offer to deliver the vaccine before it goes bad—for thirty million credits. Oh, hell, why think small? For two hundred million. That's only a hundred credits a colonist, and now if they die we can say it's the Republic's fault. Let's further hypothesize that I was killed while we were taking the Republic ship, and now you're in command. What's your decision?"

"You know what it is," said Forrice.

"If I didn't, you wouldn't be on board," said Cole. "But now you see why we need to know what kind of pirates we plan to be. It sounds like a contradiction in terms, but we need to create something akin to a Pirates' Code of Ethics, even if it applies to just the *Teddy R.*"

"You know," said Forrice, "you're exactly the kind of hero I hate." He rumbled deep in his chest. "Whatever happened to heroes who didn't think everything through, but just walked in with weapons blazing?"

"They're buried in graveyards all across the galaxy," said Cole.

"I've got a question," said Sharon.

"Go ahead."

"I asked it before: What am I doing here? You obviously know what kind of code you want to operate under."

"I gave Four Eyes some loaded examples," answered Cole. "But saying that we won't kill a few innocent families for peanuts, or that we won't hold two million lives hostage, is not the same as saying what we *will* do, and that's what we have to discuss. Who and what *is* fair game, and who and what *isn't?* Under what circumstances will we use deadly force and under what circumstances won't we? Will we stay on the Inner Frontier, or will we make forays into the Republic? The Republic's at war with the Teroni Federation. Until a few weeks ago, so were we. If we chance upon a Teroni ship, do we give it safe passage or engage it?"

Forrice sighed deeply. "You know, piracy was a lot simpler when it only had me thinking about it."

"Well," said Sharon, "we're here because of the Republic. Not its citizenry, and certainly not the Teroni Federation. So I think that unless we have cause to attack someone else, we should limit our activities to those things and ships belonging to the Republic."

"That's a start," said Cole.

"What about your hypothetical medical ship?"

"Of course we're not going to attack a medical ship," responded Cole. "But we still need to decide what *is* fair game. Any suggestions?"

"Anything of sufficient value to warrant our risk," replied Sharon. "And the plundering of which will not cause undue harm or suffering to innocent people, whether they're Republic citizens or not."

"Go back to my first example," said Cole. "Doesn't the loss of an heirloom cause suffering? And if the person we take it from isn't a member of the Republic's military or government, wouldn't you call that suffering undue?"

"If you put enough restrictions on it, you're going to limit yourself to robbing only heavily insured banks on Deluros VIII," said Sharon. "We need some flexibility. How can we know at this moment what the effect of attacking a ship nineteen days from now will be? What kind of ship is it? Who's on it? What's it carrying?"

"I'll give you something else to think about," said Forrice, who had been silent for a few moments. "Let's say the ship is a military ship. So were we, until the mutiny. Let's say that they defend themselves against what they've been told is an outlaw ship. *We* would have." He paused. "Do we really want to kill a crew that is doing precisely what we spent our whole careers doing—following orders and defending their ship?"

"It's something to think about," agreed Cole pleasantly, as if to say: *It took you long enough to think of that.*

"It's something to avoid," said Sharon.

"Actually," said Forrice, "the truth of the matter is that the *Teddy R* should have been decommissioned half a century ago. The odds are that we'll be outgunned by any Republic or Teroni ship we come across."

"I don't know about that," said Cole. "This is the Frontier. The only way a souped-up warship is going to come here is if it's in hot pursuit. I think the *Teddy R* is precisely the kind of military vessel we're likely to come across here."

"Which means we're likely to kill some young officers and crewmen who are guilty of nothing more than protecting their ship," said Sharon.

"I agree," said Cole. "Where does that leave us?"

"Perhaps—" began Forrice.

"Oh, shut up!" said Sharon wearily. She turned to Cole. "Why don't you simply tell us, since you obviously had your mind made up before calling this little meeting."

"It never hurts to have the people who work with you draw the same conclusion," he replied without denying her charge.

"Well?" she said.

"I should think it's obvious," said Cole. "We don't want to kill or even rob innocent civilians. We don't want to kill military personnel who are just carrying out orders and defending themselves. We don't want to get into a pitched battle with any Republic or Teroni ship that might outgun us. We don't even want to get into a battle with one we can beat. After all, there's no economic reward in destroying a military vessel; all it does is cost us casualties and ammunition."

"What's left?" asked Forrice.

Cole smiled without answering.

"Oh my God!" said Sharon a moment later. "It never occurred to me!"

"It *still* hasn't occurred to me," complained Forrice.

"Pirates!" exclaimed Sharon. "We're going to plunder pirates!"

Suddenly the cabin was filled with thunderous hoots of alien laughter. "I *like* it!"

"We don't want to rob or kill innocent victims," said Cole. "If they're pirates, they're not innocent. We don't want to get into a pitched battle with warships from either side. If they're pirates, they're not in a warship. We want the reward to be commensurate with the risks. If they're pirates, it figures to be." He paused. "Another consideration is that we've been running shorthanded since we left the Republic. Who better to recruit than pirates who know how our rivals operate and where they're likely to be?"

"Sounds good to me," said Forrice. "When do we start?"

Suddenly Rachel Marcos's image appeared above Cole's computer. "Excuse me, sir," she said. "But I thought you should know that we've spotted a ship."

"Republic?" asked Cole promptly.

"No, sir," replied Rachel. "A class-QQ ship of Taborian origin, unarmed. Chlorine atmosphere, which is what Taborians breathe. I'd say it's a colony ship, sir."

"Thank you, Ensign. Keep tracking it, but don't hail it or alter course. If they send any radio messages, let me know."

"Yes, sir," she said, flashing him a sharp salute and a smile.

Her image vanished.

"She still hyperventilates at the very sight of you," noted Sharon dryly.

"You'd prefer she hyperventilated for Four Eyes?" asked Cole with a smile.

"For someone who's not old enough to be her father, anyway."

"I hate to interrupt," said Forrice, "but let's get back to this ship she spotted."

"There's something like four hundred and fifty billion sentient beings in the galaxy," responded Cole. "That we know of. We couldn't expect not to come across some of them out here sooner or later."

"You're not worried that they'll report our presence?" persisted the Molarian.

"To whom?" he replied. "We're in a vast No Man's Land. Let's take it at face value and assume they're looking for a chlorine planet to colonize. And even if we're wrong, by the time the Republic could get here we'll be a few thousand light-years away."

"I thought we were all through running."

"We are," said Cole. "But we're not going to just stay in this empty sector. Tomorrow we start searching."

"Searching?" repeated the Molarian. "For pirate ships?"

Cole shook his head. "For all the things we need," he answered. "We've been traveling without a doctor since we escaped. We need at least one, probably two—one who specializes in humans, one who can work with the non-human species we're carrying. We need a safe haven, some port that we can use as our headquarters."

"Why not just use the ship?" asked Forrice.

"Because it can be pretty damned hard for a fence with a warehouse to find us when we're hiding between engagements. And since he'll almost certainly be operating inside the Republic, we don't want to get anywhere near his world, let alone touch down on it."

"It'd be nice if we could trade the first shipload of plunder for some better weaponry," suggested Sharon.

"I wouldn't hold my breath," said Cole. "Who trades in the kind of pulse and laser cannons we're looking for?"

"You pass the word and flash enough money, and *somebody* will," said Forrice with certainty.

"Anything's possible," admitted Cole. "But if I were you, I wouldn't hold my breath until it happens."

"Well, that's that," said Sharon. "May we assume that this Pirates' Code of Ethics was a bunch of bullshit?"

"Not at all," said Cole. "Every member of the crew put his life and career on the line for me. They deserve to know what our policy is, since they're going to have to abide by it."

And the next morning there was a message posted on every private and public computer aboard the *Theodore Roosevelt*:

CODE OF ETHICS

1. The *Theodore Roosevelt* will not attack any innocent individual of any race.
2. The *Theodore Roosevelt* will not attack any innocent ships, even military ships, that are going about their business.
3. The *Theodore Roosevelt* will not plunder any innocent individual's or group's property.
4. Pirates are not innocent.

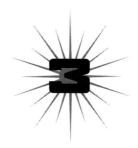

Cole stood at the entrance to the Gunnery Section of the *Teddy R.* The sole crew member stationed there amidst the laser and pulsar cannons was a large, heavily muscled man who snapped to attention and saluted.

"Good morning, sir," said Eric Pampas.

"Good morning, Bull," said Cole. "And I keep telling you that you don't have to salute or call me sir."

"It just seems natural, sir," said Pampas. "By the way, sir, I saw the ethics code you posted."

"And?"

"I never liked the thought of holding up civilians or colonists at gunpoint. This sounds a lot more like what we've been trained for— our ship against other pirate ships."

"Is that pretty much the general attitude among the crew?" asked Cole.

"Well, among the gunnery staff anyway, sir," answered Pampas. "I haven't spoken to anyone else today."

"Which brings up a question," said Cole. "Now that you and Four Eyes have had a chance to train them, how many crew members would you say are qualified to work in this section?"

"Eight, maybe nine."

"That's a lot better than it was when I was transferred to the *Teddy R*," said Cole. "Starting tomorrow, you're relieved of duty."

"Sir?" said Pampas, frowning.

"You can choose your own successor as chief of the Gunnery Section," continued Cole. "You know each of their capabilities better than I do. We have enough Men heading other sections, so try to pick a non-human."

"With all due respect, sir," said Pampas, "nobody knows these weapons better than I do."

"I don't doubt it."

"Have I done something to offend you, sir? Or broken some regulation?"

"We're a pirate ship," said Cole. "We no longer *have* any regulations. Until I create some new ones, anyway."

"Then why—?"

"It's not a demotion, Bull. I have a more important job for you."

"More important than manning the weapons?" asked Pampas.

"Think about it, Bull," said Cole. "We want to plunder pirate ships, right?"

"Right."

"If you blow one up with one of our cannons, what's left to plunder?" asked Cole. "From now on these weapons are strictly for self-defense, not attack, and the gunnery crew's job is simply to make sure they're functioning. Christine or someone else on the bridge will program their targets into them."

"I hadn't thought of that, sir," admitted Pampas. "Of course we can't annihilate the ships we plan to rob."

"I'm glad we're in agreement on that," said Cole dryly.

"But all I've done since I enlisted seven years ago is work on weaponry," said Pampas. "It's what I know."

"You know a little more than that, Bull. You put four crew members into the infirmary for using drugs, remember?"

"You told me to stop them," said Pampas defensively.

"I'm not castigating you, I'm *reminding* you," said Cole. "One of them was a warrior-caste Polonoi. You damned near killed him."

"He was endangering the ship. We couldn't allow him around the weapons in that condition."

"I don't disagree. But any man who can beat a warrior-caste Polonoi with his bare hands knows how to use them."

"They *are* a little different from normal Polonoi," agreed Pampas.

And indeed they were, reflected Cole. All Polonoi were heavyset and muscular, but what differentiated the warrior caste was that their sexual organs, their eating and breathing orifices, and all their soft vulnerable spots—the equivalent of human bellies and midsections—had been genetically engineered so that they were on the warriors' backs. They were built to win or die. For a warrior-caste Polonoi to turn his back on an enemy was to present that enemy with all his vulnerable areas, whereas their fronts were heavily armored with bony plates and were practically immune to pain.

"Still, it was a lucky blow, sir," continued Pampas.

"I hope to hell you're being modest," replied Cole, "because I want a man with what I take to be your physical prowess on our boarding team."

"Boarding team, sir?"

"If we're not going to blow the enemy out of the sky, and we want to appropriate its cargo, sooner or later we're going to have to board it," said Cole as if explaining it to a child. *They can't really be this dumb,* he told himself; *they just haven't started thinking like pirates.* "Would you have any problem killing a pirate with your hands or your weapons?"

"Not if he wanted to kill *me,* sir."

"What if she weighed a hundred and ten pounds and looked as young and pretty and vulnerable as our Ensign Marcos?"

"Put a weapon in her hand and Ensign Marcos can squeeze the trigger just as easily as a five-hundred-pound Torqual can, sir. I don't have a problem with defending myself."

"Okay, you're hired," said Cole.

"I could stay on duty here until we spot a pirate ship, sir," suggested Pampas.

Cole considered it, then shook his head. "Who the hell knows when that'll be? I want you fresh. Besides, if the weapons are working now, they'll be working when we come across a pirate ship. I'm sure anyone you've trained can handle any minor adjustments that are needed." He paused. "I wish we had a gym for you to work out in, or a target range. But the *Teddy R* has barely got enough room to turn around in, so just keep yourself in shape as best you can in that tiny exercise room."

"Yes, sir," said Pampas, sensing that the interview was over and saluting.

"And try to get out of the habit of saluting."

"Like I said, sir . . ."

"I have my reasons, Bull," said Cole. "We've gotten rid of the Republic insignia on the ship. We've already jettisoned all our military uniforms. If we board a pirate ship, and they've got someone hiding out of sight, waiting to take a couple of potshots at us, there's only one way he's going to know who to kill first—and that's whoever it is that everyone else salutes."

"I hadn't thought of that, sir," said Pampas. "I'll do my best not to salute, sir."

"Or to call me sir," added Cole. "I *ask* it of the bridge personnel, but they're not going anywhere. I'm going to *demand* it of the boarding parties."

"Yes—" He stopped himself just in time.

"Fine. Pick your successor, clear the name with me or Forrice, and kiss this section good-bye at the end of your shift. And make sure all your hand weapons are in working order."

Cole turned before he could see if Pampas saluted him again, and walked to an airlift. He rode it up to the bridge, where Braxite, a Molarian, and Vladimir Sokolov, a tall blond man, were on duty.

"Captain on the bridge!" shouted Braxite, jumping to attention. Sokolov, who was working the computer consoles, stood up and saluted.

"Knock it off," said Cole wearily. "Has anyone got anything to report?"

"Lieutenant Mboya left orders that I was to continue the charts she started making," said Sokolov. He uttered a brief order to one of the computers in a language that seemed to be all numbers and formulae, and a moment later a three-dimensional star chart filled the space above his console. Another order and seventeen stars glowed a bright yellow and began blinking on and off.

"Each of these systems has one of the most populated worlds on the Inner Frontier. Fourteen are oxygen worlds, two are chlorine, and one is ammonia. The distance separating the two farthest apart is about three thousand light-years."

"That's not much, given the size of the Frontier," noted Cole.

"People tend to congregate together, sir," said Sokolov. "Especially out here, where there are so few of them."

"What about trade routes?"

Another incomprehensible command from Sokolov, and some seventy-five flashing purple lines popped into existence, each leading from one world to another. More than half the lines went directly from major mining worlds to unshown worlds of the Republic.

Cole turned to Braxite. "Anything on spaceliner routes or schedules?"

"Just what's posted, which anyone in the galaxy can access," answered the Molarian. "But I can't find out which ones travel with Republic warships as escorts, and each ship has so many fare levels that it's impossible to figure out which has the most affluent set of passengers. The luxury cruise ships, the ones with gambling and entertainment, never venture outside the borders of the Republic, and while they don't have military ships protecting them, they each hire mercenary ships for protection. Most of them also hire former police and military officers to patrol the ship itself. All incognito, of course."

"Of course," said Cole. "Well, we didn't want to rob any innocent parties on spaceliners anyway."

"An observation, sir?" said Sokolov.

"Yes?"

"If they're amusing themselves on a gambling ship during wartime, how innocent can they be?"

"I don't know how innocent they are, Lieutenant," answered Cole. "But if they've got mercenary ships and police guarding them, they're too well-protected to interest us. We'll stick to pirate ships."

"There figure to be a few thousand ships in this general area"— Sokolov waved a hand toward the seventeen flashing systems and about half the trade routes—"at any given moment. How will we pinpoint the pirate ships?"

"We won't."

"Then how will we—?"

"We'll let *them* find *us*," answered Cole. "Tell Slick I want to speak to him."

"In person, sir?"

"No, that's not necessary."

"In private, then? I can have him transmit his image to your quarters."

"Right here is fine," answered Cole.

"Coming right up," announced Sokolov, and suddenly Cole found himself facing the full-sized holographic image of the *Teddy R*'s only

Tolobite. It was a squat, shining, bipedal being. Its skin, smooth and oily, literally glowed. Its upper limbs were thick and tentacular, more like an elephant's trunk than an octopus's legs. There was no neck; the head grew directly out of the shoulders, and was incapable of turning or swiveling. Its mouth had no teeth, and seemed equipped only for sucking fluids. Its eyes were very dark and wide-set. No nostrils were evident. Its ears were mere slits at the sides of the head. It actually did possess most of the features that seemed missing or inadequate, but it possessed a unique one as well: a Gorib—a living, thinking symbiote that functioned as a protective second skin that filtered out all germs and viruses.

Cole found its name unpronounceable, as he did most aliens', so he had dubbed it "Slick" because of its shining false skin, and as far as he was concerned, Slick was the most valuable member of the crew, because its Gorib enabled it to function for limited durations in the vacuum of space or on the surface of chlorine and methane worlds, without any chance of an equipment malfunction, because except for the Gorib Slick wore no protective suit.

"You wished to speak to me, sir?" asked Slick in heavily accented Terran.

"Yeah. Remember when I had you climb outside and replace the ship's Republic insignia with a skull and crossbones right after we escaped?"

"Yes, sir."

"We were celebrating, and I wasn't thinking clearly," said Cole. "In the cold light of day, it's obvious that the very last thing we want to do is advertise the fact that we're pirates."

"Do you want me to just remove the skull and crossbones, or replace it with something else?" asked Slick.

"You'll be replacing it."

"What with, sir?"

"Hold on a second." He turned to Sokolov. "You're of Russian descent, right?"

"God knows how many centuries ago, sir."

"Can you give me a Russian name or location?"

"How about Stalin?"

"No, New Stalin's a major Republic world," responded Cole. "Try another."

"Samarkand?"

"That'll do." He turned back to Slick's holograph. "Wherever you remove a skull and crossbones, I want you to replace it with a logo for the Samarkand Cargo Lines."

"A logo, sir?" asked Slick.

"Mr. Sokolov will create a batch of them for you. I'll want it on the front and back of the ship, and you might as well put it on all four shuttlecraft as well. Can you get it done today?"

"Probably," said Slick.

"If it's a strain on your Gorib, you can do it over two Standard days," said Cole.

"The Gorib can handle it, sir. It just depends on how long it takes me to remove the skulls and crossbones. The old Republic insignia was partially worn away from the handful of occasions the ship had entered various atmospheres to land—but the skulls and crossbones have never been subjected to that kind of heat or friction."

"Well, get started as soon as possible, and let the bridge know when you're done."

"Yes, sir," said Slick, ending the transmission.

"Remarkable being, that Slick," said Cole admiringly. "Give me fifty like him and I could conquer any chlorine world in the Teroni Federation."

"Or the Republic," added Braxite.

"Or the Republic," agreed Cole. "They're peas in a pod."

"Whatever a pea is," said Braxite. "And whatever a pod is."

"Sir," said Sokolov, "I take it you want me to create a logo or an emblem for something called the Samarkand Cargo Lines?"

"Yeah," said Cole. "Once you've got it done, make it up in a dozen different sizes, each big enough to cover the skulls and crossbones just in case traces of them remain. Slick will bond them to the ship. Make sure they can handle heat and friction if we have to set down on a world."

"An oxygen world?"

"Any kind," answered Cole. "We don't always have a choice."

"I'll get right on it, sir," said Sokolov. "Do you want me to show it to you before I make a bunch of them up for Slick?"

"What do I know about designs?" said Cole. "Show them to Lieutenant Mboya. She's got the most orderly mind on the ship."

"Yes, sir."

Sokolov went to work on his computer, and Braxite turned to Cole. "Would I be correct in assuming that we plan to pose as a cargo ship to attract pirates?"

"A cargo ship in distress," said Cole. "If we were just a cargo ship en route to a destination, they couldn't be sure they could catch us, so they'd probably shoot to disable us—and at those kind of distances and speeds, who knows? What they think of as a disabling shot could be off by two seconds of a degree and blow us all to hell. Much better to give them a ship that's already disabled."

"We can't be the first ship to think of this, sir," said Braxite. "I'll bet the Navy does it all the time out on the borders between the Republic and the Frontier."

"I doubt it," said Cole. "The pirates have no reason to board a Navy ship. They'd blow it to bits from a safe distance."

"Then a cargo company that's tired of being hit—"

"Look," said Cole, fighting back his annoyance. "The Inner Frontier covers something like a quarter of the galaxy. We've been here, traveling at light speeds, for more than twenty Standard days, and so far we've seen three ships. I don't know where all the pirates are. Four Eyes doesn't know. Now, unless *you* know, it makes more sense to entice them to come to us than the other way around."

"I apologize, sir," said Braxite. "I didn't mean to be argumentative."

"There's nothing wrong with questioning orders that don't seem to make sense," replied Cole. "Unless we're being shot at, at which time I'd really appreciate some blind obedience." He paused. "I'm getting hungry. Tell Mr. Odom to meet me in the mess hall."

"Yes, sir."

Cole left the bridge, walked over to the airlift, rode it down a level to the mess hall, walked past three tables that were in use, and took an empty one in the back. A moment later Mustapha Odom, the ship's chief engineer, and the only crew member allowed to work with the nuclear pile, entered, spotted Cole, and joined him.

"You wanted to see me, sir?"

"Yes," said Cole, ordering a sandwich and a cup of coffee from the menu that suddenly appeared in midair. It vanished when his order was complete and he found himself facing Odom again. "At some point, tomorrow or in the next few days, we'll want to convince another ship that we're disabled. We have to assume they're not stupid, that their sensors are going to go over every millimeter of the *Teddy R* before they try to board us. We're going to need to keep the life-support systems working. If the light drive is dead, is that possible or does it look too suspicious?"

"No problem. We've got an emergency power reserve for life support and for the infirmary, too. I think just about every ship does."

"I don't want to just float in space waiting to be approached. That smells too much like a trap. If the light drive is dead, can we travel at sublight speeds?"

"You'd be traveling at light speeds even with no drive," answered Odom. "The only time we really need it is to accelerate or brake. Once you're at the speed you want, there's no gravity or friction to slow you down."

"That won't do," said Cole. "If they wait too long, we'll be able to reach a planet. Hell, if we're faster than they are, they might never be able to catch us even if we've theoretically blown the light drive. I need them to think we're a sitting duck, there for the taking, totally helpless."

"Let me think about that, sir," said Odom. "What else?"

"If our weapons are functional, is there any way to fool an enemy's sensors into thinking they're not?"

"None."

"Wait a minute," said Cole. "I'm not thinking clearly."

"Sir?"

"If we turn off all power to the weapons systems, they'll read as if they're dead, won't they?"

"Yes," said Odom, smiling. "But they won't *be* dead. You can activate them on a second's notice."

"Yeah, that should work," said Cole. "Hopefully we won't need them, but you never know. Now, if the life-support systems are on, can the communications systems be functional?"

"Internally? Absolutely."

"How about the subspace radio?"

"Right now it's powered by the nuclear pile, but if that stops working, I'd have to rig it to run off the emergency system." He paused. "Are you sure you'll need it?"

"How are we going to broadcast an SOS without it?" asked Cole.

"Okay, I'll take care of it."

"Any way we can hide the fact that our small arms are functioning?"

"Not with our burners and screechers, sir," answered Odom, referring to laser and sonic pistols. "They run off battery packs, and nothing that happens to the ship's pile would affect them. Pulse guns, perhaps. Have you got any projectile pistols on board, the kind that shoot bullets?"

"I sure as hell doubt it."

"Too bad. How about knives?"

"They're not standard military equipment," said Cole. "I suppose we can rob the mess hall—but I'd hate to put a kitchen knife up against a burner."

"Like I said, let me think about it. Maybe I can come up with something."

"I'm open to suggestions," said Cole. "Just remember: We have to assume that our prey isn't stupid, so we can't pretend we've all got some new alien disease or anything like that. It's got to be something that not only makes sense, but happens often enough that they don't become so suspicious they just decide to walk away from it."

"All right," said Odom. "Give me a couple of hours to think about it."

"Where'll you be?" asked Cole.

"Right here."

"Don't you need access to your computer?"

"Why?" asked Odom. "I know everything it knows. Besides, you're asking me to improvise, and computers aren't very good at that."

I just hope we're a little better at it than computers, thought Cole as he left the mess hall.

Cole lay back on his bunk, reading a book on the screen that hovered just in front of him and trying to ignore the miscoloration on the ceiling. Suddenly the text vanished and Sharon Blacksmith's face appeared.

"What is it?" he asked.

"You've been talking to everyone else all day," she said. "I thought you might care to let the Chief of Security know what your plans are."

"Since you've doubtless been observing and recording me, you already know," said Cole. "So what's your real reason?"

"I'm bored."

"Cherish the feeling," said Cole. "Once the action starts, you'll probably remember your moments of boredom with great fondness."

"I know," she said with a sigh. "But this isn't like the war with the Teroni. No one's going to fire on us just for being the *Teddy R.* Once you start playing dead in space, it could take days, maybe weeks, before anyone approaches us."

"It'll take less than a day," he assured her. "If the pirates don't come, some well-meaning do-gooder will try to rescue us."

"That doesn't make me any less bored."

"If this isn't the preface to a sexual proposition, I can give you something to do."

"What?"

"We'll need a boarding party of half a dozen, so I want you to start picking out some names. Once we attract a ship and subdue *their* boarding party, we still have to board them and come away with something valuable enough to make it worth the effort. However many they send onto the *Teddy R*, they'll leave more aboard the ship. It won't be any cakewalk, subduing them and appropriating whatever they've got."

"Has it ever occurred to you that they might not have anything valuable on board?" asked Sharon. "I mean, if they've recently plundered a ship or a colony, wouldn't it make sense that they'd have dropped the goods off with their fence before going back out?"

"It's a possibility."

"And if it happens?"

"Then we'll steal information from the crew, which can be more valuable than anything else." He smiled at her. "I assume that the Chief of Security knows a little something about extracting it?"

"The Chief of Security has access to about half a dozen drugs that will elicit any information we need."

"Good," said Cole. "Because I've been thinking that the best way to fill out our own crew is with pirates we capture, and at least this way I'll know whether to believe their pledges of fealty."

"You're assuming that we're going to survive and capture some of the enemy," she noted.

"There wouldn't be much sense in making plans and attending to details if I expected to lose," answered Cole. "Getting back to that boarding party, I'll need four names, and I definitely want Eric Pampas on the team."

"The Wild Bull? Good choice. But that's only five. I thought you wanted six."

"I'm the sixth."

"You can't leave the ship!" said Sharon adamantly. "You're the Captain."

"So what?"

"It's against regulations."

"I wasn't aware that pirate ships *had* regulations," said Cole dryly.

"Damn it, Wilson! You're our leader. Every crew member walked out on the Republic solely to serve with you. We can't have you getting killed on our first encounter."

"I don't plan to get killed."

"Have you ever known anyone who did?" she shot back. "Wilson, you didn't win all those medals because of your brawn. Let me put together a boarding party composed of Bull Pampas and Luthor Chadwick and that Mollute, what's his name, Jaxtaboxl . . ."

"I call him Jack-in-the-Box," interrupted Cole. "Jack for short."

"I don't care what you call him!" she said. "Let me add three more like that to the list, and you stay in command of the ship where you belong."

"A Captain is supposed to lead his crew, not follow them."

"A Captain is suppose to delegate authority and run his ship," said Sharon. "Damn it, Wilson—you know I'm right!"

"I'll think about it."

"What would you have said if Fujiama or Podok had left the *Teddy R?*" she asked, referring to the last two Captains.

"If Podok had gone, I'd have said good riddance," replied Cole. "And if you'll recall, Fujiama *did* leave the ship."

"And promptly got killed," she reminded him.

"I'm not Fujiama."

"Wilson, you lead a boarding party and you can find a new bedmate."

"What the hell," he said. "Rachel's chomping at the bit, and except for being ten years younger than you and twice as pretty—"

"And three times as dumb!" snapped Sharon.

"That's not always a disadvantage in bed."

"Take a good long look at her and engrave it in your memory," said Sharon. "Because if you lay a finger on her, I'm going to claw your eyes out."

"I'm certainly glad to see we're maintaining the simple, uncommitted relationship we agreed upon," said Cole with a smile.

"You're not leaving the ship," she repeated.

"May I go back to reading my book now?"

"Fuck you, Wilson Cole!" she snapped and broke the connection.

"I guess that means yes," he said to himself.

The problem was, he knew she was right. He was a little shorter than average, a little older than average, and would never have survived his first year in the service if he'd had to count on his physical abilities instead of his brain. And much as he resented it, that brain told him that his place was on the *Teddy R*, not boarding an enemy ship that could be hiding fifty armed men or be rigged to explode.

The problem was that he trusted himself more than he trusted anyone else. He didn't believe in senseless bloodshed, even if it was all being spilled on the other side. He'd recently freed the planet Rapunzel without firing a shot. He'd taken command of the *Teddy R* not to kill more of the enemy, but to avoid killing five million Men who were in the middle of things through no fault of their own. He didn't doubt for a second that Bull Pampas and Jack-in-the-Box and the others could handle an attack in close quarters far better than he could—but he was convinced that no one aboard the ship could *prevent* such an attack better than himself.

He was still considering his options when Mustapha Odom contacted him.

"I hope I'm not disturbing you, sir," said the engineer.

"No," replied Cole. "I've been waiting to hear from you. What have you come up with?"

"There are a number of ways to do it, but I think the best way is to disable our external stabilizer."

"Would you care to put that in terms I can understand?" asked Cole.

"The external stabilizer is what prevents the ship from rolling or spinning if one thruster becomes inoperative. If I disable it, as well as shutting down the power plant, we could spin gently in a circle without going anywhere, or we might enter into an endless series of—how can I describe it?—somersaults in space." Odom smiled. "*That* should convince any observers that we're helpless."

"Why will that be more convincing that just shutting down the light drive?"

"They know that anyone can shut down a power plant and then start it up again if the situation gets too dangerous," answered Odom. "But if you try to go to light speeds while the ship is spinning or some-saulting in space, you'll break it into pieces."

"How will it affect the crew inside the ship?" asked Cole. "Will we have to strap ourselves in?"

Odom shook his head. "Not if we spin in a circle rather than head over heels. Part of any ship's emergency life-support system is the artificial gravity."

"Right," said Cole. "Can't have internal organs and body parts floating away during emergency surgery." He paused. "So you're assuring me that no one will float away, or lose their lunches?"

"That's right, sir."

"How long will it take to set it up?" asked Cole.

"Once you reach the spot you want and we brake to sublight speeds it'll take from one to ten minutes to come to a complete stop in space, depending on how fast we were going, and then just a few seconds to start a very gentle spinning."

"If I were a pirate ship approaching the *Teddy R*," said Cole, "I'd want to know how it managed to start spinning if its power was dead."

"Allah was not a neat craftsman, sir. The universe is filled with His leftovers. Any solar debris could set us spinning. It couldn't be something as big as a meteor or an asteroid; that would crush us or break us apart. But I assume we're not going to be doing this inside any star system, so we're not going to come across any meteors or asteroids anyway."

"All right. As soon as we decide upon the area we want, I'll have you contact Christine Mboya and explain what kind of debris we're looking for, and she can have Pilot position the ship so we're surrounded by it. This debris isn't going to stop another ship from approaching, is it?"

"Not as long as they've got power, sir," answered Odom promptly.

"And if they didn't, they couldn't approach anyway," concluded Cole. "Thank you very much, Mr. Odom. You've been most helpful."

Cole broke the connection, decided he wasn't interested in reading after all, got to his feet, walked out into the corridor, tried as always not to wince at the dilapidated condition of the ship's interior, and took the airlift to the bridge. Forrice was there, along with Domak, a warrior-caste Polonoi female, and Christine Mboya.

"Don't say it," muttered Cole as Christine jumped to her feet and announced: "Captain on the bridge!"

Forrice didn't bother to salute, but Domak and Christine did. They knew better than to wait for Cole to return their salutes, and both sat back down at their stations.

Cole walked over to Christine, glancing at all the incomprehensible formulae on her various screens. "Any progress?" he asked.

"I think so, sir," she replied. "The closest of the major trade routes seems to be between Binder X and Far London, which is at the edge of the Republic, just two parsecs from the Inner Frontier. We could position ourself between them in less than a day at maximum speed, maybe sooner if Wxakgini can pinpoint a hyperspacial tunnel."

"Keep looking," said Cole. "That's too damned close to the Republic. We may have removed our insignia, but if they spot an unidentified class-JZ starship, a type that hasn't been manufactured in close to a century, they're going to guess who it is and come after us full force."

"I beg to differ, sir," said Christine. "The Teroni Fleet recently launched a major attack in the Terrazane Sector, and my guess is that every available ship from this section has been transferred there. They may have left a few ships behind to protect the local planets against a surprise attack, but they're not going to desert their posts just to chase after a ship that may or may not be the *Theodore Roosevelt*."

"I didn't know about the Terrazane attack," admitted Cole.

"There's no reason why you should have, sir," she replied with a smile. "You were in jail, awaiting your court-martial, when the attack came."

"All right, that's where we'll set things up. Once you've picked out an area, have Mustapha Odom speak to Pilot and explain exactly what kind of conditions we're looking for."

"Yes, sir."

"So we're all set?" asked Forrice.

"Pretty much so," answered Cole. "I've got Sharon working on the boarding party."

"You, me, and who else?" asked the Molarian.

"The Captain and the First Officer don't both leave the ship at the same time," said Cole. "That's the stupidest thing you've said in months."

"All right—me and who else?"

"Why you instead of me?"

"To start with, I'm stronger, faster, and younger than you, and I can see better in the dark. Besides, the Captain can't leave the ship in enemy territory."

"Since when has the Inner Frontier been enemy territory?" asked Cole.

"Since we became pirates," answered Forrice promptly. "You've got to stay with the ship."

"*Et tu, Brutus?*" said Cole.

"I don't understand the language or the reference," said Forrice. Suddenly he smiled. "But I can intuit the meaning."

"Sir?" said Christine.

"Yes?" asked Cole, glad to have the conversation interrupted.

"I'd like to volunteer for the boarding party."

"Absolutely not," said Cole. "I need you aboard the ship."

"But—"

"If Four Eyes is going to go, I need someone I can trust right here." He paused and stared at her, then nodded his head as if he'd made up his mind about something. "You're my new Second Officer."

Her eyes widened. "Me?"

"Would you rather I *didn't* trust you?"

"No, sir."

"Then it's settled. Choose your eight-hour shift—red, white, or blue. I'll try to arrange to sleep while you're in charge."

"You'll need a Third Officer while I'm off the ship," said Forrice.

"I'm working on it," answered Cole. "That's enough promotions for one trip to the bridge."

"You really meant it, sir?" asked Christine, still surprised.

"Why not?" answered Cole. "You certainly know the ship better than Four Eyes or I do."

"I'll try to prove worthy of it, sir," she continued.

"No speeches," said Cole. "You've already proven worthy of it or you wouldn't have been given it. Now the sooner you decide where we're going to play dead, the sooner Mr. Odom can tell Pilot where to park us."

"Yes, sir," she said, saluting again, then turning her attention back to her computers.

He lingered a few minutes, decided there was nothing else for him to do on the bridge, and returned to his cabin, where he found Sharon waiting for him.

"I guess you're not such a bastard after all," she said.

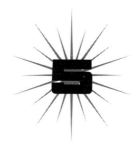

"Sir?" said Christine Mboya's voice.

Cole came awake instantly. "What is it?"

"I think I've found the right spot. There's all kinds of minor debris there, just the sort of thing Mr. Odom tells me could set us spinning if the power failed." Pause. "Sir, I think something's wrong with the communication system. I can hear you but I can't see you."

"Give me a minute to fix it," said Cole.

He nudged Sharon awake, put a finger to her lips before she could speak, and gestured toward the bathroom. She immediately got out of the bed and walked out of camera range, carrying her uniform into the bathroom with her. Cole quickly got dressed, then activated his holo camera and ordered it to transmit his image as well as his speech.

"About how long will it take to reach our chosen destination?" he asked.

"Wxakgini says we'll be there in two more hours, sir," replied Christine.

"Two?" repeated Cole. "I thought we were a day away."

"He found a wormhole that took about eighteen hours off the journey, sir."

"Okay," said Cole. "If Four Eyes is around, tell him to take a nap. There's no sense all of us being up at the same time. I'll relieve you in about ninety minutes, and then I want you to go to your cabin and spend the next eight hours sleeping."

"I don't know if I can, sir," said Christine. "I think I'll be too tense."

"Find a way," he said firmly. "If the ship we want to attract arrives in nineteen hours instead of nine, I want to know that whoever's in charge of the *Teddy R* will be fresh and well rested."

"In charge?" Christine's eyes widened. "I've never done anything like this before, sir."

"Neither have I," answered Cole. "You'd be surprised how little schooling the Navy gives its senior officers in the art of piracy."

"I mean—"

"I know what you mean," he cut her off. "You're my choice. Live with it."

He broke the connection as Sharon, now in uniform, emerged from the bathroom.

"Time to pick that boarding party," Cole told her.

"I was listening. Two hours?"

"Two hours to get there. It could be ten or twenty before we have company."

"I'll have your party selected in an hour."

"It shouldn't take that long. We've decided on three of them already, and there's no way I can keep Four Eyes off it, so I only need two more."

"How about Slick?" she asked. "You seem to think highly of him. Or is he an it?"

"I don't think gender applies to Tolobites," said Cole. "And don't ask him."

"Oh?"

"I've got better uses for him."

"All right," replied Sharon. "I'll come up with two more and let you know."

"It's your call, of course—but if I were you, I'd consider Domak. Warrior-caste Polonoi of either sex can be pretty hard to kill."

Sharon shook her head. "She's too good at running the ship's systems. If Christine is going to be off duty when you're on the bridge, you might need her."

"Fine. Like I said, it's up to you. Just complete the party in an hour."

"It'll look better if I contact them from Security," she said, walking to the door. "I'll see you later. Remember to make your bed; it's a mess."

"Try not to be so cloyingly romantic and clinging," said Cole sardonically. "I enjoyed it too, but you don't see me carrying on about it."

"I think I'll lock you in a room with Rachel Marcos for a couple of days," said Sharon. "What little remains when she gets finished with you figures to be much more tractable."

She walked out into the corridor and the door sprang shut behind her.

Cole began going over the details of the plan in his mind, feeling vaguely uneasy. There were so *few* details, he had to be overlooking something, but he couldn't see what. Find an empty spot, not far off a major trade route, a spot the *Teddy R* might reasonably be thought to have wound up at after a total shutdown of the power plant. He had the exterior cameras check the ship's insignia; it all proclaimed that this was a ship of the Samarkand Cargo Lines. Christine had created an SOS message to his specifications, and the ship would broadcast it on more than two million frequencies simultaneously. It would reach close to forty light-years in every direction. He would have his own boarding party hidden near the main hatch, but he wouldn't send them over until he'd subdued the pirates' boarding party. Whoever was manning the sensors on the bridge would read the atmosphere aboard the pirate ship, as well as the gravity; the *Teddy R*'s boarding party would have space suits handy in case the conditions aboard the pirate ship were inimical to carbon-based oxygen-breathing life. There were three starfaring races that had no eyes, that used some as-yet-undefined senses to maneuver, but none of them were supposed to be on the Inner

Frontier. Still, it couldn't hurt to make sure Forrice and the rest of the party were equipped with night-vision lenses to enable them to see the interior of the pirate ship.

There was just one last thing to do before he went to the bridge. He activated his communicator and contacted Slick.

"Yes, sir?" said the Tolobite's image.

"Drop whatever you're doing and meet me in the Gunnery Section right away," said Cole.

He broke the connection even before Slick could answer, then contacted Pampas, gave him the same instructions, left his cabin, walked to an airlift, went down a level, and made his way to the Gunnery Section, where he found the Tolobite waiting for him. Pampas arrived a moment later.

"Bull," said Cole to Pampas, "you used to be Chief Gunnery Officer. I need your expertise."

"It sounded better than Sergeant, sir," replied Pampas with a smile.

"We're *all* officers since we became pirates," said Cole. "Anyway, you know this section better than anyone else, so as of this moment you're the Temporary Chief Communications Officer."

"What do you want me to do, sir."

"I don't care if you do it yourself or supervise it," said Cole. "First, I want you to rig the communication system here so that there's a constant visual of the bridge. One-way. I want Slick to be able to see the bridge, but I don't want anyone on the bridge to see the Gunnery Section."

"That's easy enough."

"There's more," said Cole. "I also want Slick to be able to see the main hatch. When the pirates board the ship, I want him to know it."

"One-way again, sir?"

Cole nodded his assent. "Right."

"Since the weapons will be aimed from the bridge, we don't need all the viewscreens that are tied in to them." Pampas indicated one that was attached to a pulse cannon. "We'll have the hatch showing on this one. Is that all, sir?"

"Not quite," said Cole. "I also want you to make up a dozen explosive devices that can be detonated from wherever Slick happens to be, inside the ship or outside it."

"How powerful?"

"Not powerful enough to ruin the structural integrity of a ship's hull, but strong enough to take out a weapons system."

"It would have to be an external weapon, sir," said Pampas.

"That's right."

"The pirates' weapons?"

"Can you think of any other weapons we might want to disable today?"

Pampas smiled. "No, sir. And by the way, thank you for putting me on the boarding party."

"I just hope you're as good at disabling pirates as you are at disabling your fellow crew members," said Cole. Before Pampas could protest, Cole held up a hand. "That was said in admiring tones, Bull. After all, you did it on my orders."

"Yes, sir," said Pampas uneasily.

"Okay, you'd better get to work. Enlist any help you might need, but try to get it done in two hours." Cole turned to Slick. "You've figured out most of it, I presume?"

"You want me to attach the explosives to any external weapons on the pirate ship," said the Tolobite.

"And all but one of their shuttlecraft," said Cole. "That's assuming they have any shuttles, and that they're attached on the ship's exterior."

"Why all the screens, sir?" asked Slick.

"Because it's always possible that an ambulance ship, or simply a ship full of decent beings, will be the first to reach us. I don't want you to leave the *Teddy R* until your observations convince you that these really *are* pirates. If they shoot anyone when they enter the hatch, you'll know immediately. If they wait until they reach the bridge and try to take over the ship, you'll know then. But once you know, I want you to go out through the shuttle port, not the main hatch, and start attaching all the explosives."

"When do I detonate them, sir?"

"I want you safely back in the ship first," said Cole.

"I'll be perfectly safe out there," replied Slick. "There are no shock waves in space."

"I know—but there will be a lot of flying weapon fragments. Unless your symbiote is impervious to them, it could get chopped up pretty badly, and I have to assume once it's dead or even punctured, you can't survive in space any longer than I can."

"You're quite right, sir," said Slick. "We hadn't thought of that."

"We?" repeated Cole.

"Myself and my Gorib, sir."

"It understood what I said?" asked Cole. "As far as I can tell, it's just an epidermis. I didn't know it had any sensory receptors."

"We are telepathically connected. It doesn't need sensory inputs when it can use mine."

"You know, I've never really asked you about it. Do you and your Gorib ever argue?"

"We are symbiotes, sir," answered Slick, as if that explained everything.

"Well, as I said, I want you back inside the ship so neither you nor your Gorib can be harmed by the explosions. Once you're back, wait for my signal."

"Yes, sir. Will there be anything else, sir?"

"No," said Cole. Then, "Yes."

"Sir?"

"Has your Gorib got a name?"

"You couldn't pronounce it, sir."

"Are you sure?"

"You can't pronounce my name, sir, and we share it. If you wish to refer to my Gorib, call it Slick."

"I call *you* Slick."

"We are symbiotes."

Cole got the feeling that every line of inquiry about the Gorib would end with that same answer, so he left Pampas and Slick and went up to the mess hall. All but two tables were empty, and he sat down in a corner and ordered coffee and a sandwich. One of the other diners, tall, slender, young, with close-cropped blond hair, stood up and walked over, carrying his drink and what was left of a rather plain dessert.

"Do you mind if I join you, sir?" asked Luthor Chadwick.

"The man who broke me out of the brig can join me any time he wants," replied Cole.

"The whole ship broke you out, sir."

"But you were the prison guard with the code to the locks. What can I do for you, Mr. Chadwick?"

"I just want to thank you for the opportunity, sir," said the blond man.

"The opportunity to be a member of an outlaw ship that's wanted by the Republic and the Teroni Federation?" said Cole with a smile. "You're an easy man to please."

"No, sir," said Chadwick seriously. "I meant the opportunity to be part of the boarding party."

"It's no great honor. You'll be the first to get killed if this doesn't work out."

"I've been feeling like I'm not earning my pay," began Chadwick.

"You're not *getting* any pay," interrupted Cole.

"I mean my keep, sir," Chadwick corrected himself. "We're carrying a crew of thirty-three, and there simply isn't much for an Assistant Chief of Security to do, especially with Colonel Blacksmith around. She is so efficient and has things so much under control that I've felt totally useless, sir, and I'm just glad that I'm finally being given something to do."

"You may feel differently about it when the shooting starts," said Cole.

"I doubt it, sir."

"Just be careful, Mr. Chadwick," said Cole. "We're traveling with less than half the normal contingent of crew members. Nothing on any pirate ship is worth as much as any of your lives. If it looks bad, if you smell a trap, if you have any reason to think we've bit off more than we can chew, I strongly suggest that the boarding party gets the hell off the pirate ship and lives to fight another day."

Chadwick smiled. "That's just what Commander Forrice told me not half an hour ago, sir."

"Just goes to show that even a hardheaded, stubborn, sarcastic Molarian can learn," said Cole.

"You two have been together a long time, haven't you?" asked Chadwick.

"On and off," said Cole. "We've known each other for years. He's probably as good a friend as I've ever had. I don't begin to understand eighty percent of the aliens I meet, including some on this ship, but Four Eyes feels like a brother. Hell, all Molarians do; in ways they're more human than Men are."

"I've noticed that, sir," said Chadwick. "I never heard any other being laugh—just Men and Molarians."

"Let's hope all the *Teddy R*'s Men and Molarians are still laughing tomorrow," said Cole.

"They will be. After all, you're Wilson Cole."

"If I thought that was the real reason for the crew's confidence, even you would find me unbearable," said Cole. He finished his sandwich and drained his coffee container. "I'm off to the bridge. I'd recommend that you try to get some rest. It could be a few hours, or even a couple of days, before anyone shows up."

"Yes, sir," said Chadwick, standing up and saluting. "And thank you again, sir."

The young man turned and left the mess hall, and somehow Cole knew that, far from sleeping, the blond man was going to get more excited and tense by the minute. Finally Cole stood up, walked to the nearest airlift, and went up to the bridge.

"How soon?" he asked Christine Mboya.

"Maybe ten minutes," she said. "Wxakgini tells me we've been braking to sublight speeds for about two minutes now."

"I barely felt it," said Cole.

"That is precisely what you can expect to feel, as long as I'm the pilot of this vessel," said Wxakgini from his pod high above them.

"That's what I like in a pilot," said Cole. "Modesty." He turned to Christine. "You're relieved. Go get some sleep."

"But my shift isn't over yet," she protested.

"You're relieved anyway." He turned on the intercom. "Ensign Marcos to the bridge." He turned to Domak. "Are you good for another six or seven hours, Lieutenant, or do you need some sleep or nutrition?"

"I am fully capable of remaining at my post for the next seven hours," replied the Polonoi.

"I'm sure you are—but in all probability nothing's going to happen right away. Would you *like* some rest?"

"Like?" repeated Domak with a frown, as if she didn't comprehend the word.

"Forget I asked," said Cole. "Stay at your post." Suddenly he raised his voice. "Is Security monitoring the bridge?"

"You don't have to yell," said Sharon's image, which appeared instantly before him.

"How's that boarding team?" he asked as Rachel Marcos came onto the bridge. "All chosen?"

"All chosen."

"How many races?"

Domak, Christine, and Rachel all turned and stared at him curiously.

"Three," replied Sharon. "Four Men, Forrice, and Jack-in-the-Box."

"Lose one of the men and get me another member of another race."

"I picked the best crew members for the job," replied Sharon.

"I don't doubt it, and I'm not being a bigot," said Cole. "But we don't know what race will be on the ship we're hoping to attract. Probably it'll be Men, just because there are more Men than anything else on the Inner Frontier—but if it's some other race, let's try to increase the chance of their finding a fellow member in our boarding party. It may encourage them to talk rather than shoot."

"I doubt it," said Sharon.

"To tell you the truth, I doubt it too," agreed Cole. "But it couldn't hurt, and there's a very slight chance that it might help."

"Okay," she said. "You can have Lieutenant Sokolov back if you need him."

"Not right now. Tell him he's replacing Lieutenant Domak in six hours. In the meantime, if he's awake, send him down to the Gunnery Section and have him help Pampas. I want Bull leading our boarding party. In fact, if Sokolov knows how to finish the job, have him relieve

Bull instead of just helping him. The same with Braxite. If he's not doing anything vital, send him down to Gunnery to help."

"Right," said Sharon, breaking the connection.

"Rachel, get over to the computer station," said Cole. "Christine, get the hell off the bridge and go to bed."

Rachel Marcos seated herself in front of the computers, and Christine Mboya sighed, grimaced, and otherwise made her unhappiness at being relieved clear, then walked to the airlift and went to her quarters.

"Sharon, is Slick tied in to the bridge and the hatch yet?" asked Cole, raising his voice.

"You don't have to shout," said Sharon's image, appearing once again. "We monitor the bridge every second even on days when we don't expect all hell to break loose. And in answer to your question, yes, Slick can watch everything that happens on the bridge and at the hatch."

"At some point he's going to leave the ship," said Cole. "Once he gets back, I want him to be able to hear me wherever he is."

"No problem."

"You're sure?"

"I'm sure."

"Okay, you can vanish again."

Sharon's image disappeared.

A few minutes later Wxakgini announced that the ship had come to a stop.

"Start it spinning," said Cole. He turned to Rachel. "Start sending out that SOS Christine created—the one that says our power died, our external stabilizer has been damaged, and we're helpless. And patch me through to Odom."

Mustapha Odom's image instantly appeared.

"All right, Mr. Odom," announced Cole. "We're stopped and we're spinning. I think it's time to turn off the drive and put the ship on emergency life-support power."

"It'll take about three minutes to shut the power down," said Odom.

"How long does it take to power up again, if we need it in a hurry?" asked Cole.

"Maybe a minute, but remember—you can't be spinning when we start moving."

"I know. Shut it down now, Mr. Odom."

With the emergency life-support power on, there was no noticeable change inside the *Theodore Roosevelt*. If Cole hadn't gotten dizzy watching one of the viewscreens, he'd have sworn that they were still speeding across the Frontier.

"How long do you think it'll be, sir?" asked Rachel Marcos.

Cole shrugged. "More than an hour, less than a Standard day."

"I wonder what they'll be like?" she mused.

"Greedy."

"So are we," said Domak. "There is no difference."

"There's one," said Cole.

"What is that, sir?"

"If we saw a ship spinning helplessly in space," answered Cole, "a ship that was broadcasting an SOS, we'd help it. They're coming to rob it."

"Then we're not very efficient pirates," concluded Domak, her fierce face displaying no expression.

"We're new at the game," replied Cole easily. "We're still learning." He paused, then continued more seriously: "But if we ever reach the point where we'd attack and plunder a ship that had put out an SOS, then we're no better than the ships we're planning to loot. And on that day, the *Teddy R* can find itself a new captain."

Domak fell silent, Rachel continued monitoring her computers,

Wxakgini remained blissfully remote from everything except the navigational computer that was wired into his brain, and after a few minutes Cole decided to go to the tiny officers' lounge and relax. He called up a musical entertainment, and had watched about half of it when the singers and dancers suddenly disappeared, to be replaced by Sharon Blacksmith's holograph.

"Would the Captain condescend to move his ass back up to the bridge?" she said.

"What's up?" asked Cole.

"We're about to have company."

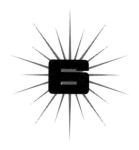

Cole's first words as he walked onto the bridge were: "What kind of ship is it?"

"Class LJD, sir," replied Rachel.

"Armaments?"

"The LJD is a luxury space yacht, sir. It isn't built with any weaponry, but they've jury-rigged two pulse cannons, one on each side of her nose."

"Can they rotate?"

"I'm sure they can spray their fire," answered Rachel. "But if you mean, can they do a one-eighty and fire behind the ship, I can't tell."

"And there's just two cannons?" asked Cole. "You're sure of that?"

"Yes, sir."

"A luxury yacht? Well, they like their comfort, I'll give them that," said Cole. "If it was me, I'd have bought a heavily armed and armored military ship from a defeated power like the Sett and adapted it for my crew's needs." He turned to Domak. "Any indication what kind of crew it's carrying?"

"The sensors pick up fourteen life-forms," answered the Polonoi. "But I can't tell yet— Wait! They are oxygen breathers."

"Men?"

She shrugged. "Bipeds. I won't know their race until they get a little closer."

"Are their cannons armed?"

"Yes, sir."

Suddenly Christine Mboya appeared on the bridge. "I saw that they've arrived, sir. I request permission to take my station."

"You don't have a station," said Cole. "You're the Second Officer, remember?"

"I request permission to take my former station," she amended.

Cole stood stock-still for a few seconds, making up his mind. Then he nodded his assent. "Rachel, you're relieved."

"But sir—" protested Rachel.

"I haven't got time to be diplomatic," said Cole. "Christine's the best we've got at what she does, and we're putting our lives at risk. You can still make yourself useful. Slick is going to be moving some things down to the shuttle bay. Give him a hand." Rachel looked as if she was about to cry, which was the last thing he needed at this moment. "It's not busywork," he assured her. "You drop anything and the pirates won't *have* to blow us out of the ether. We'll do it for them."

Rachel saluted and left the bridge, and Cole turned his attention back to Domak. "Do we know what they are yet?"

Domak shook her head. "Soon."

"Christine, can those cannons rotate or can they only shoot ahead of the ship?"

"I can't tell from the configuration, sir," answered Christine, "but all logic says they can. A pirate ship is more likely to fire at pursuers than prey; after all, it can't loot what it's totally destroyed."

"Makes sense." *Yes*, he thought, *at a time like this, you're the one I need at this station.*

"Sir?" said Slick's voice, and his image appeared in front of Cole. "If we're using explosives on the weapons, what difference does it make if they can fire behind the ship or not?"

"Not to cause you undue consternation," replied Cole, "but while we'll be doing our best to distract them and hide your presence, there's always a chance they might spot you and blow you and your Gorib to hell and gone. Under those circumstances, I would have to assume they're watching for replacements, and I'd just be wasting anyone else I sent out to complete the job."

"Thank you, sir," said Slick, looking not the least bit distressed. "I was just curious."

"Try to contain your curiosity," said Cole. "We're going to be very busy here for the next few minutes."

No sooner had he spoken than Christine signaled him that a message was coming in from the approaching ship.

"Put it on visual," ordered Cole, "and let's pray that it's not an ambulance out to save us."

The holograph of a human form appeared, a tall, dark-haired bearded man. He wore what looked like a surplus military uniform with the sleeves cut off. A little pornographic tattoo on his left arm was in constant motion, more laughable than erotic. He carried a burner, a screecher, and a pulse gun, none with holsters, all bonded onto his belt.

"Attention, cargo ship," he said. "My name is Montegue Windsail, and I am the commander of the *Achilles*. We picked up your distress signal and came immediately. What is the nature of your problem?"

"This is ship number eighty-one of the Samarkand line," answered Cole. "I am Captain Jordan Baker," he continued, using the name of his court-martial defense attorney on the assumption that his own name might be instantly recognized. "Our light drive has gone dead, and at least one of our external stabilizers has malfunctioned. We're on emergency power right now, but I can't stop the spinning. Thank you for coming to our rescue."

Montegue Windsail allowed himself the luxury of a smile. "Well, now, rescuing you wasn't exactly what I had in mind. I was thinking of something more along the line of a trade."

"A trade?"

"Those are a nice quartet of laser cannons you have, Captain Baker. You give them to me, and I'll transport your crew to the nearest colony world."

"This is extortion!"

"This is business," replied Windsail calmly. "And if you don't like my terms, you can wait here and hope a better offer comes along."

"Maybe we'll just show you how well our laser cannons work," said Cole.

"That seems fair," said Windsail, smiling again. "You aim at us while you're spinning in space, and we'll aim our cannons at you, and let's see who's the more accurate."

"Wait!" said Cole, hoping he sounded desperate enough. "I need a minute to consider your offer."

"Take two minutes, Captain Baker," said Windsail. "But after two minutes either you agree to let us come aboard or we open fire. There's no third way."

The *Achilles* broke the connection.

"Did you see him?" asked Cole, struggling not to laugh. "The man looks like a cartoon character pretending to be a pirate. That tattoo—and those hand weapons! I wonder if he knows just how ludicrous he looks?"

"What are we going to do, sir?" asked Christine.

"Part of it depends on whether their boarding party approaches us in a shuttlecraft, or whether they link the *Achilles* with the *Teddy R*," answered Cole. "Let me know when ninety seconds have passed, and then reestablish the connection with them."

"Do you want us to subdue them when they come aboard?" asked Forrice's image.

"No," said Cole. "You just stand by near the hatch, keep out of sight of their boarding party, and be ready to storm the *Achilles* when the time comes."

"Wilson," said Forrice, "I've got an armed party right here. If we don't confront them, there's nothing to stop them between the hatch and the bridge."

"Why don't you let me worry about that?" responded Cole.

"Okay . . . but I hope you know what you're doing."

"If our sensors know where they are on board their ship, it's only reasonable to assume their sensors can do the same thing," said Cole. "If they see you clustered by the hatch or on the bridge, they won't come aboard."

Christine signaled him that he had ten seconds left. He broke the connection with Forrice, then nodded to her, and suddenly he was facing Montegue Windsail again.

"Well?" said the pirate.

"Before I agree, I want your promise that you won't harm my crew," said Cole.

"We're only interested in your cannons and your cargo," answered Windsail. "And speaking of cargo, just what are you carrying?"

"Nothing," said Cole. "We're deadheading back to Far London."

"You had better be telling the truth, Captain Baker," said Windsail. "If not, I will consider it an abrogation of our agreement."

"Wait," said Cole, looking defeated.

"Yes?"

"We're carrying one hundred sixty-three pieces of alien artwork to the Odysseus Art Gallery on Far London."

"Thank you, Captain Baker. You may lose your cargo, but you have saved your crew's lives. We'll rendezvous with you in approximately three minutes. I will lead a boarding party to your bridge, where you will order your crew, in my presence, to turn over your cargo to us and not to hinder us in any way while we are appropriating your laser cannons. Is that understood?"

Cole glared at him.

"Is that understood?" repeated Windsail ominously.

"It's understood," said Cole.

"Good. I'll see you in a few minutes."

Windsail broke the connection.

"Get me Odom!" said Cole urgently.

The engineer's image appeared a few seconds later.

"Mr. Odom, I want you to kill all the power to one of the airlifts on my signal."

"You mean you want to kill the gravity?" asked Odom.

"The gravity, the oxygen, everything."

"No problem. Which airlift?"

"Whichever one the pirates take to get from the hatch to the bridge."

"The fall could kill them before the lack of air does," offered Odom.

"Well, that's the chance you take when you decide to become a pirate." He paused briefly. "It occurs to me that we may need someone to go with them, so they don't smell a trap. That means Slick, since that Gorib of his can keep him going without air for a few hours. Can we rig something he can grab hold of while everything else is plunging down? Once they hit bottom you can turn the gravity back on, as long as it's still airless."

"I can't rig anything they won't be able to spot," said Odom.

"I'm willing to risk it, sir," said Slick, his image appearing across the bridge from Odom's. "If I'm ready, if I'm prepared, I can probably land atop them and break the fall."

"I can't take the chance, Slick," answered Cole. "I need you for later. You're the one crewman who can't be incapacitated."

"Sir," said Sokolov, his image appearing beside Slick's. "I've been down here working with Slick, so I've heard what's been said. I'd like to take a shot at it."

"Are you feeling especially suicidal today, Mr. Sokolov?" asked Cole. "The reason I thought of Slick is that he can live without air for a few hours. Unless you've been holding out on us, you can't."

"No, sir," answered Sokolov. "But I can act so damned eager to misdirect them that I'll bet I can get them to order me off the airlift."

"What you're betting is your life," said Cole. "Are you sure you want to do that? We can arrange a pretty hot reception for them on the bridge if we have to, but I've only got about a minute and a half to prepare it."

"Let me try it, sir. They're going to have their weapons drawn when they reach the bridge. You'd be risking too many casualties."

"Even if you survive the fall, there won't be any air," said Cole. "We may not get you out of there in time."

"This is war, sir," said Sokolov. "It's not the one I signed up for, but the principle is the same. They're the enemy, and I'm ready to do whatever has to be done to win."

"Okay, I'm out of time," said Cole decisively. "Meet them at the airlock and let's hope you're as obnoxious an actor as you think you are."

The *Achilles* reached the *Theodore Roosevelt* half a minute later. An extension reached out from its hatch, bonded to the *Theodore Roosevelt* over *its* hatch, and the two ships were locked together, spinning slowly. Even Cole had to admit that it was a hell of a nice job of maneuvering.

A moment later Montegue Windsail, looking every bit like a refugee from a bad holo entertainment, boarded the *Theodore Roosevelt*, followed by seven men, all humans.

"Greetings, Captain Windsail," said Cole, his holograph appearing at the end of the short corridor. "The man who is stationed at the hatch to guide you is Vladimir Sokolov. He will take you to the airlift that leads directly to the bridge."

"Why is he armed?" demanded Windsail. "We have an agreement. No harm will come to your crew if you honor your end of it."

"Pirates killed my brother and my wife," growled Sokolov. "I don't trust any of you bastards."

"Perhaps they were killed because they would not relinquish their weapons," suggested Windsail. "I think it might be best if you relinquished yours."

"Not a chance," said Sokolov. "My orders are to take you to the airlift. Let's go." He indicated the direction.

"After you," said Windsail.

"I don't turn my back on pirates," said Sokolov. "Just get on the airlift, and keep your hands where I can see them."

"That's the airlift?" asked Windsail, indicating the shaft.

"That's right."

"Then I think we can dispense with your services."

"My orders are to go with you," said Sokolov coldly. "Captain Baker said to take you up to the bridge, and that's what I'm doing."

Don't overplay it, thought Cole. *He's already told you to stay out of the airlift. Let it drop.*

But Sokolov had read his audience correctly. "I'm in charge now," said Windsail. "And I say you're staying behind. I don't need an armed enemy standing behind me on the bridge."

"Fuck you!" said Sokolov heatedly. "I don't take orders from pirates!"

"Vladimir," interjected Cole, "do what Captain Windsail says."

"But sir—"

"You heard me," said Cole.

"Yes, sir," muttered Sokolov, glaring hatefully at the pirates.

"Thank you, Captain," said Windsail, as he led his crew of seven onto the airlift. It rose half a level; then Cole said *"Now!"* and the eight pirates plummeted down four levels. Their cries became inaudible gurgles as the air vanished from the shaft.

"Not the brightest bears in the woods," said Cole. "Christine, share Domak's sensors and see if one of you can spot how many men are still on the *Achilles* and where they're located. *Slick!*" he said, raising his voice. "Time to get to work."

Forrice's image floated in front of Cole.

"Are we ready to board the *Achilles* now?" asked the Molarian.

"Soon," answered Cole. "We're just finding out where all the bad guys are. By now their sensors will have shown them that their captain and his team are dead."

"Then we'd better move fast," said Forrice. "They may decide to cut and run."

"It won't do them any good," said Cole. "The two ships are bonded together."

"Sir?" said Christine.

"Yes?"

"There are six of them on board. They seem to have gathered in the control room."

"You mean the bridge?"

"Pleasure yachts don't have bridges. I guess a control room's as close as they can get."

"You heard it, Four Eyes. They're in the control room. Christine, put a floor plan of the *Achilles* on every private and public screen on the ship. Four Eyes, Luthor, Jack-in-the-Box, the rest of you—study it so you know where everything is when you get there."

"It's too small for them to hide in," said Forrice. "Either they surrender or we kill them."

"Let's give them a chance to think about it," said Cole. "Christine, patch me through to the *Achilles*, audio and video, all frequencies."

"You're on," said Christine a moment later.

"Crew members of the *Achilles*, this is Wilson Cole, the Captain of the *Theodore Roosevelt*, the vessel that Captain Windsail thought was a distressed cargo ship. You six are the only remaining crew of the *Achilles* still alive. We will soon be sending a boarding party onto your ship." He paused. "You have three choices: you can pledge your allegiance to us and join us as members in good standing of the *Theodore Roosevelt*, a former Republic warship which is now"—he searched for the right words—"an independent contractor. You can surrender and choose not to join us, in which case your weapons will be confiscated and you will be set down on the nearest colony planet with an oxygen atmosphere and acceptable gravity. Or you can refuse to join us or surrender, in which case you will suffer the consequences. I'm going to give you five minutes to make up your minds. This channel will remain open."

The bridge became silent. Then, some three minutes into the countdown, Slick's image appeared.

"I'm done, sir."

"Are you back aboard the ship?" asked Cole.

"Yes, sir," answered the Tolobite. "I'm on my way to the Gunnery Section."

"Blow them right now."

A brief pause. "Done, sir."

"Crew of the *Achilles*," said Cole, "if it will help you to reach a decision, I can now inform you that your laser cannons have been disabled."

Two more minutes passed, and the *Achilles* offered no response. Cole made a slashing motion across his neck, and Christine killed the connection.

"Now?" asked Forrice.

"Something's wrong," said Cole. "They've got six men and nothing more than hand weapons against a military ship that for all they know is carrying a full crew. Let's let 'em sweat for another few minutes."

"What do you think is going on, sir?" asked Christine.

"I don't know," answered Cole. "We're not at war. They can't be willing to blow up their ship in a fit of patriotism or pique. Whatever loot they're sitting on, it's not worth dying for. I'm missing something, and I'm not sending my people over there until I figure out what it is."

"Sir?" said Christine, staring at her sensors and frowning. "Something very strange is happening."

"What?" demanded Cole, suddenly alert.

"Now there are only three men on the bridge. The rest seem to be heading down toward the belly of the ship."

"*Shit!*" exclaimed Cole. "Now I know! Four Eyes, get your party over to the *Achilles* on the double! I don't think you'll meet much resistance in the control room, but that's not your destination. Get down to the shuttle level as fast as you can! That's where you'll find them!"

"We're on our way," said the Molarian, spinning his tripodal body through the hatch like some alien dervish.

"That's what I was missing," said Cole to Christine. "I had Slick not only blow the cannons, but also all but one shuttlecraft. I figured we'd stick any survivors on it and set it to land on a colony world—but they've already figured out what I should never have forgotten: that they've got an operative shuttle. My guess is that they're loading their loot onto it right now. They might leave one or two misdirected idiots behind to make a lot of noise and try to slow us down."

"But they know we'll be able to destroy them at more than a light-year's distance," said Christine. "It doesn't make any sense."

"It makes a *lot* of sense," answered Cole. "They're counting on the fact that we're not going to destroy the shuttle when it's got their treasure aboard it, and they're hoping they can get to a friendly planet before we can catch them."

"*Are* there any friendly planets out here?" she asked.

"I told them who we are, remember? You total up the rewards the Republic is offering for me, for Sharon, for Four Eyes, and for the *Teddy R*, and just about every damned planet on the Frontier will give aid and comfort to anyone who can lure us there."

"That right," she admitted. "I'd forgotten."

"Sir," said Domak, staring at a screen, "at least one of our party is down. Just from the positioning, it looks like there's a pitched battle in the control room. One of the non-humans, I can't tell from the readings if it's Forrice or Jaxtaboxl, has reached the shuttle bay. . . . Now a human has joined him."

"It's my fault!" said Cole, furious with himself. "We've got shuttles to spare. I should never have told Slick to leave that one alone!"

"The battle in the control room seems to have ended. Two *Achilles* crewmen and two of ours are dead or disabled."

"And we still haven't got a doctor on this fucking ship!" grated Cole. "It's a damned good thing I'm not still in the Navy or they'd be taking another command away from me!"

"Well, I'll be damned!" blurted Christine, still glued to her monitors. "Good for you, Forrice!"

"What happened?" said Cole.

"One of them, Forrice or Jaxtaboxl, blew the mechanism that opens the shuttle bay. Now it can't leave the ship!"

"That should do it," said Cole, relieved. "There's no escape. They'll surrender, and then we can try to save the ones who aren't already dead."

Suddenly Forrice's image appeared above Christine's bank of computers. There was the purple fluid that passed for his blood running down his arm, and his neck had been singed by a burner. He was crouched down behind the disabled shuttlecraft, pulse gun in hand.

"Are you there?" he asked urgently. "Is this getting through to you? I've got to speak to Cole!"

"I'm here," said Cole. "What is it, Four Eyes? It looks like the shooting's over."

"Yes and no," said the Molarian, grimacing in pain as he shifted his position.

"Explain."

"We have what I would call a situation," said Forrice.

"I'm on my way," said Cole, walking toward the airlift.

"I thought the Captain and the First Officer never left the ship at the same time in enemy territory," grated Forrice.

"We're in neutral territory," answered Cole. "And as long as the *Achilles* is bonded to us, I consider it an extension of the *Teddy R.*"

"That's my Wilson," said Forrice.

"I'll see you in about a minute."

"Wilson, one more thing," said the Molarian.

"What?"

"Don't rush blindly in."

Cole approached the yacht's control room cautiously, burner in hand, but it wasn't necessary. Two of the pirate ship's crew lay dead on the floor. So did one of the *Theodore Roosevelt*'s three Bedalians. Luthor Chadwick was propped up against a bulkhead, blood running out of his ears, his eyes barely able to focus.

"I've got to go to the shuttle bay," said Cole. "We'll get help for you as soon as we can."

"I can't hear you, sir," rasped Chadwick.

"I said I've got to go to the shuttle bay!" said Cole, raising his voice.

Luthor pointed to his ears. "I took a heavy blast from a screecher, sir," he said. "I can see your lips move, but I can't hear anything. I think the rest of our team is down in the shuttle bay."

Cole nodded, and headed off toward the bay. There were no sounds of combat as he neared it, but as he approached Forrice he saw a sudden flash of motion and dropped to the ground as an energy pulse burned itself into a bulkhead where his head had been.

"What the hell's going on?" he asked, crawling toward Forrice over the fallen bodies of two of his crewmen.

"You're not going to believe it, sir," said Pampas, who was crouched behind a disabled shuttlecraft.

"Let's have it," said Cole. "These guys have no means of escape, they're outnumbered, we've killed most of their crew including their captain, and we've offered them positions on the *Teddy R* or safe passage to a colony planet. Why are they still fighting?"

"The man the late Captain Windsail left in charge of the ship told them we were slave traders," said Forrice. "It was actually pretty effective propaganda to stiffen their resolve. They think if we capture them we're going to sell them."

"Bullshit!" said Cole.

"Pampas told you you wouldn't believe it," said Forrice with the Molarian equivalent of a smile.

"*Is* there any slavery on the Inner Frontier?" asked Cole. "Why would they believe him? I thought the last of it had been wiped out centuries ago."

"Probably there is, sir," said Pampas. "There is no actual law to speak of on the Frontier, just some planetary governments and some bounty hunters. I'd be surprised if at least half a dozen worlds aren't trafficking in slaves."

"And the *Teddy R* is big enough to carry a cargo of slaves," noted Forrice.

"This is ridiculous," said Cole. "It's time to end it."

"They're pretty well protected, sir," said Pampas.

"I didn't say I was going to shoot them," answered Cole. "I said I was going to end it." He paused for a moment, lost in thought, then looked at the Molarian. "Four Eyes, what was your mother's name?"

Forrice looked at Cole as if he had gone mad.

"Come on," said Cole. "I haven't got all day."

"Well, roughly translated, it would be—"

"No translation. Tell me the Molarian name."

"Chorinszloblen."

"Fine." He raised his voice. "Crewmen of the *Achilles*, this is Wilson Cole, Captain of the *Theodore Roosevelt*. Can you hear me?"

"I'm not coming out!" yelled a voice.

"*I'm*"? thought Cole. *So there's only one of you left.* Aloud he said, "I want you to listen carefully, because I'm only going to say this once. We are not a slave ship. We do not traffic in sentient beings. My original offer still stands. If you surrender, you can join my crew as an equal member and today's action will not be held against you, or I can set you down on a colony planet. In either case, you will not be harmed. But I'm all through waiting, and I won't spend any more lives. I have with me a cannister of chorinszloblen, a powerful nerve gas. My crew members all have protection against it. It won't kill you, but it will incapacitate you, and it will almost certainly burn out most of your neural circuits. You can surrender now or you can become a vegetable; it's your choice. You've fought a brave fight, but it's over. You're all out of time."

Cole stopped speaking. After thirty seconds a pulse gun and a burner were tossed out into the open. Then, very slowly, a young man arose, hands behind his head, and walked across the bay.

"I'm your prisoner," he said.

"He's just a kid!" said Pampas, staring at him.

"Even kids can kill," said Cole. "Four Eyes, make sure he's unarmed. Bull, keep an eye on him."

Forrice quickly examined the prisoner. "He's clean," announced the Molarian.

"Okay. Bull, check out his companions."

"They're all dead," said the young man bitterly.

"That makes you the sole surviving member of the *Achilles*," said Cole. He turned to Pampas. "Bull, Luthor Chadwick is in a bad way up in the control room. I want you and Jack-in-the-Box to bring him back to the *Teddy R* and see if anyone can stop the bleeding. And dope him up until we can get him to a doctor."

"Colonel Blacksmith has confiscated all the drugs, sir," said Pampas.

"She'll release some for this. Just let her take a look at him."

"Right, sir," said Pampas as he and Jaxtaboxl went off to the control room.

Cole turned his attention back to the prisoner. "What's your name, son?"

"I don't have to tell you," said the young man defiantly.

"No, you don't," agreed Cole. "But it means until we set you off on a planet you're going to have to answer to 'Son' or 'Hey you.'"

"You're really going to set me free?" said the prisoner.

"I told you we would."

"But Captain Windsail said—"

"Captain Windsail lied," interrupted Cole.

The young man stared at him. "Maybe he did, maybe he didn't, but you killed every other crew member from my ship."

"Your ship tried to plunder *my* ship," noted Cole. "Let's not forget that little fact. Now suppose you save us some time and tell me where your cargo is. The sooner we appropriate it, the sooner we can set you loose."

"That wasn't part of the deal," said the young man.

"The battle's over," said Cole. "Why do you insist on being difficult?"

"If you use that chemical, that chori— . . . chori-whatever-it-is, on me, you'll burn out my memory," said the young man pugnaciously, trying to hide his nervousness. "Then you'll never find it."

"I would never dream of using chorinszloblen on you," answered Cole. "I don't think my First Officer would approve." Forrice uttered a pair of hoots that passed for Molarian laughter. "We'll find your treasure with or without your help. I know it and you know it, so why not just tell me what and where it is?"

"How do I know you won't kill me after you get your hands on it?"

"This is a goddamned yacht, not a dreadnaught," said Cole irritably. "How the hell many places can it be? If I was going to kill you, I'd do it right now, for putting us through the trouble of finding it."

"All right," said the young man. "We're carrying about four hundred uncut diamonds from Blantyre IV, and there's some jewelry that Captain Windsail stole the last time he was on Binder X."

"Where is it?"

"Captain Windsail never told us, but I'm pretty sure it's in the galley."

"Why?"

"He'd never keep it in his cabin. That's the first place anyone would look."

"Why the galley?" persisted Cole.

"That's the one place none of us have searched," was the answer. "We were all afraid of cutting off a hand reaching back behind all those food synthesizing machines."

"All right, we'll search the galley first. If you're right, you can have a handful of diamonds as a grubstake when we set you down."

The young man stared at him curiously. "You'd really do that?"

"I just said so," replied Cole.

"Esteban Morales."

"I beg your pardon?"

"That's my name—Esteban Morales." He paused. "Is your offer still open?"

"Which one?"

"To join your crew," said Morales. "I could prove very useful to you."

"I'm listening."

"I know all the places the *Achilles* went—all the worlds that gave us safe haven, all the people Captain Windsail dealt with."

"You're hired, Mr. Morales," said Cole. He reached for the communicator that was bonded to his shoulder and touched it. "Christine, the shooting's all done. Have Briggs round up a party of six or seven and come on over."

"Will he be removing the bodies, sir?" asked Christine Mboya.

"He'll remove *our* crew's bodies," replied Cole. "Send over some airsleds and body bags. I'll read over them when they get back to the ship. And tell Briggs to start hunting for treasure in the galley. He's looking for uncut diamonds, maybe four hundred of them, and some jewelry, no description."

"Four hundred *diamonds*?" she said. "That's not a bad day's work."

"Also, we have a new crew member, human male, name Esteban Morales. Assign him a room and have Sharon make sure the computer registers his voiceprint, thumbprint, and retinagram when he gets there so he can lock and unlock the damned thing."

"Got it."

"Then hunt up the nearest world with a medical facility, put Sokolov in charge of a shuttle, and have him transport Chadwick there."

"Should he wait?" asked Christine.

"We'll all be back in the *Teddy R* long before he gets there, so have him contact me once he hears what they have to say."

"Yes, sir. Will there be anything else?"

"Not that I can think of. Just get Briggs and his party here in a hurry. The *Achilles* probably wasn't the only pirate ship to hear that SOS, and we're a sitting duck while we're bonded to it."

He broke the communication and turned to Morales. "Let's check out your companions."

"They're all dead."

"Probably, but it never hurts to make sure. If any of them are even mildly alive, we'll stick them on that shuttle that's taking my man to a hospital."

"You're a strange kind of pirate, sir."

"I'll take that as a compliment," said Cole, walking over and examining the bodies lying on the floor of the shuttle bay. All three were dead. Then, accompanied by Morales, he returned to the control room. The two crewmen were dead; so was Ensign Anders from his own ship.

Malcolm Briggs showed up a moment later, leading five members of the *Teddy R.*

"Mr. Briggs, this is Mr. Morales, our newest crew member. Mr. Morales, show them where the galley is," said Cole. "Mr. Braxite, start putting our fallen comrades in body bags." Morales led them to the *Achilles'* galley, then returned alone to the control room.

After five minutes had passed Christine Mboya contacted Cole and told him that the shuttle had been dispatched to the single hospital on Sophocles, a farming world nine light-years distant. And ten minutes after that Briggs uttered a shout of triumph, and Cole knew they'd found the diamonds and the jewelry.

"That's it," said Cole. "Let's get the treasure and our dead back to the *Teddy R.*"

"Don't you want to see the diamonds?" asked Morales.

"There's plenty of time to admire our plunder after we cut the *Achilles* loose," said Cole. "And you've got some work to do."

"I do?"

Cole nodded. "I'll want the names and locations of the worlds where we won't be harassed if we land. And I especially need the name of Windsail's fence."

"His fence, sir?"

"These diamonds cost us two lives and put a third in the hospital," said Cole. "We'd damned well better get a price that makes that sacrifice worthwhile."

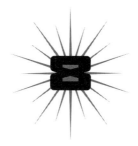

"We have a count on the diamonds, Captain," said Christine Mboya.

"And?"

"Four hundred and sixteen, all uncut. Most of them are pretty big; it's almost as if they threw the small ones back until they grew up." She paused. "There's also a ruby ring, matching earrings, a gold-and-diamond necklace, a gold tiara with about seventy-five gems set into it, a gold bracelet with a set of unknown stones on it, and a ring with a diamond that's bigger than any of the uncut ones."

"Well, it's a start," said Cole. "I suppose we'd have done better if we'd robbed a spaceliner, or even one of the bigger jewelers back in the Republic, but this way there was no collateral damage to innocent civilians, and we didn't kill anyone who wasn't trying to kill us."

"It may turn out that the most valuable thing we came away with was Mr. Morales," she said. "Rachel Marcos is handling his interrogation, and he's been speaking for two hours. Colonel Blacksmith has captured everything on her computer. Once she sorts it out, I'll feed all the data on friendly worlds and profitable commercial routes into the navigational computer."

"Rachel Marcos?" he repeated, surprised. "I know we're only carrying a skeleton crew of thirty-two—well, twenty-nine now—but she's about twenty-fifth in rank."

Christine smiled. "Men like to talk to her, or haven't you noticed?"

"I know men like to pounce on her," replied Cole dryly. "I wasn't aware of the talking."

"She's well protected," Christine assured him. "We've got Mr. Pampas with her."

"Yeah, that should do the trick," said Cole. "Providing he doesn't pounce first."

"He won't," said Sharon Blacksmith's voice. "I'm watching them like a hawk."

"There haven't been any hawks in two thousand years," said Cole.

"All right," amended Sharon. "I'm watching them like the best Security Chief in the business. And we've only got a crew of twenty-eight since this morning. Three dead, Luthor in the hospital."

"I want him to get the best medical help they've got," said Cole. "He's the man who unlocked my cell when his job was guarding me. In the meantime," he continued, "we've added Esteban Morales to the crew. That makes twenty-nine, in a ship that was designed to carry sixty-four."

"Esteban Morales has barely started shaving," said Sharon. "Once he tells you everything he knows about the pirating business, what else can he do?"

"We'll find out," answered Cole. "Hell, what could any of us do when we were that young? If he needs training, we'll train him."

"Maybe we'll lock him in a room with Rachel and see who hollers 'Uncle' first."

"Maybe we'll sic him on the Chief of Security when the Captain doesn't want to be bothered," replied Cole with a smile.

"He's only eighteen," said Sharon. "He could be an old man before that happy day arrives."

"I shouldn't be listening to this," said Christine.

"You're Second Officer," replied Cole. "No one ever promised that the job would all be killing bad guys and spending their money. You just have to learn to put up with the difficult stuff too."

She seemed about to make a serious reply, obviously thought better of it, and went back to studying her computers.

"Just a minute," said Sharon. There was a moment of silence. "Christine, find out the official name for a world named Riverwind, stick it in the navigational computer, and tell Wxakgini that's our destination."

"That's where Windsail's fence is?" asked Cole.

"Yes," said Sharon. "According to Mr. Morales, this guy is not just Windsail's fence; he's the biggest fence on the whole damned Inner Frontier."

"Has he got a name?"

"Given his business, he's probably got twenty of them, but Mr. Morales says they know him as the Eel."

"Aw, come on," said Cole. "No one calls himself the Eel."

"Just a minute," said Sharon. "Right, that's just what Rachel and Bull pointed out. Clarification: *Windsail* called him the Eel, but only to his crew, never to the man's face. His name, at least the one Morales knows him by, is David Copperfield. Try not to laugh."

"What's so funny about that?" asked Christine as Cole tried unsuccessfully to repress a broad smile.

"He's a fictional character."

"I'm not aware of him."

"It's from a book that was written more than a thousand years before the Galactic Era," answered Cole. "Could be worse. At least we're dealing with someone who reads."

"I read, sir!" said Christine heatedly.

"Let me amend that," said Cole. "At least we're dealing with someone who reads classics from when Man was still Earthbound—and there aren't that many of us left. Better?"

"I had no right to object to what you said originally, sir," said Christine.

"We're not in the Navy anymore, and we haven't written any regulations for pirates yet."

"What about 'Pirates Are Not Innocent'?" asked Sharon's voice.

"That applies to all pirates *except* us," answered Cole. "And it's a statement of policy, not a regulation."

"Sir?" said Christine suddenly.

"What is it?"

"The computer says there are *two* worlds named Riverwind," she said, frowning. "They're both Earth-type planets."

"Of course," said Cole. "What alien would give a Terran name to a world? All right, put Mr. Morales's debriefing on audio and visual."

Suddenly images appeared of Morales, Rachel, and Pampas, all seated at a small table.

"Sorry to interrupt," said Cole, "but we need some clarification. There are two planets called Riverwind. Can you help us out, Mr. Morales?"

"This one had polar ice caps," answered Morales. "I remember seeing that whenever we'd approach it."

"Christine?" said Cole.

She checked her computers, then shook her head. "They both have polar caps, sir."

"What else can you tell us about it, Mr. Morales?" asked Cole. "Do you know the name of the star system?"

"No," said Morales. He lowered his head in thought, then looked up suddenly. "I remember that it had four moons. Does that help?"

"It ought to," said Cole. He turned to Christine again. "Does it help?"

"Yes, sir," she said. "The other Riverwind has one moon. The one we're interested in is Beta Gambanelli II."

"Okay, Rachel and Bull. He's all yours again." Cole nodded to Christine, who broke the connection. "Beta Gambanelli," he mused. "There was an officer in the Pioneer Corps named Gambanelli some centuries ago. I can't remember what the hell he did, but there was a statue of him on Spica II. I wonder if this is the same one?"

"I can find out, sir."

"It doesn't matter. Just get those coordinates locked in, and tell Pilot to get us there."

"At top speed, sir?"

"Compute the fuel and use your judgment. Then contact whatever hospital Chadwick's at and find out how long before he recovers and how soon they can release him."

"He was in a bad way, sir," said Christine. "They may have to give him a new set of eardrums—either artificial or cloned from what's left of his own."

"Sounds expensive," said Cole.

"He was injured in the line of duty," said Christine. "Surely the *Teddy R* will pay for it."

"Lieutenant, the *Teddy R* is the most wanted ship in the whole damned galaxy," responded Cole. "Of course we'll pay for Chadwick's treatment, but not directly. It's not cost-productive for the Republic to hunt aimlessly all across the Inner Frontier for us, but if they know where we are, you can bet they'll send a battleship or two after us."

"I hadn't thought of that, sir," admitted Christine. Then: "Do you want me to see if I can find out who David Copperfield really is after I give Wxakgini the coordinates?"

"Why bother?" responded Cole. "We don't care who he was ten or twenty years ago. Out here he's David Copperfield, and that's who we have to deal with." He began walking toward the airlift. "If anyone wants me, I'll be in the mess hall, grabbing a cup of coffee."

"We could have your coffee sent to the bridge, sir," offered Christine.

He shook his head. "No. I was just hanging around up here. It's, let me see, 1400 hours. That means we're still on white shift, and you're in charge for two more hours. I'll be up to relieve you when blue shift starts."

He took the airlift down to the mess hall, saw Forrice sitting there drinking a bubbling green concoction, and joined him.

"How's it going?" asked Cole.

"I set the *Achilles* to self-destruct in another ten minutes. We're light-years away from it now, so we won't even get to see the explosion. But it should satisfy any do-gooders who come out here in answer to our SOS. They'll see the rubble floating there, just about where the message originated, and my guess is they won't stay to examine it and make sure it's the *Samarkand* or whatever you said we were." He paused. "They'll never suspect that we'd destroy a ship we could have sold, just to throw them off our trail—but to make doubly sure, I sent Slick out to remove all identifying names, numbers, and insignia from the *Achilles* before we left."

"Good," said Cole. "Sometimes I think you're the only totally competent officer on this ship. Besides me, that is."

A small message appeared in the air in front of him:

I hope you enjoy sleeping alone for the next 7,183 years.

"Okay, Forrice and you are the only competent officers."

Too late. That's going to cost you 900 uncut diamonds. I'll take today's haul as a down payment. After you cut, polish, and mount them.

"If there's one thing I hate," said Cole, "it's an uppity Security Chief."

That's not what you said in bed last night—or shall I quote you?

"Please don't," said Forrice. "I just ate."

"Enough humor, Sharon," said Cole seriously. "I've got business to discuss. Listen or don't, but no more interruptions." There was no answering message, and he turned back to Forrice. "You took care of the *Achilles'* bodies the way I told you to?"

Forrice nodded his massive head. "We put them all in the shuttle and aimed it at the middle of the nearest star. It should be burning up right about now."

"You checked to make sure no one could reach it before it burned up?"

"Of course."

"Good. All we did was defend ourselves from a criminal attack, but no one will ever believe it," said Cole. "Now let's get down to cases," he continued. "What are four hundred uncut diamonds worth?"

"You're asking me?" said the Molarian. "How would I be expected to know?"

"You're not," said Cole.

"But?" said Forrice. "I can feel a 'but' there."

"But you're expected to find out."

"How?"

"I take it back. There's one less competent officer on the *Teddy R* than I originally thought." He paused. "Go to the container that's holding the diamonds. Pick one out that seems average for the bunch—not the biggest, not the smallest, not the brightest, not the dullest. Contact a couple of legitimate jewelers. Tell them it's a family heirloom and you just inherited it. You want to insure it, but you've no idea how much to insure it for."

"What about the jewelry?"

Cole shook his head. "I have a feeling that a golden tiara with all those precious stones will be too easy for any jeweler to identify."

"Are you sure?" asked Forrice. "It's a big galaxy."

"No, I'm not sure," said Cole. "Now let me ask you one: Do you think it's worth taking the chance?"

"No," admitted Forrice. "Probably not. All right—just the diamond. Then what?"

"I know it's going to strain your poor Molarian brain," said Cole sardonically, "but then you multiply its value by four hundred and sixteen."

"I meant, do we then land and have at least one more jeweler examine it in person to make sure of the value?"

"I don't see any point to it. What if one jeweler says that the diamond's worth fifty thousand credits and one says sixty-five thousand? All we need is a ballpark figure, because the only appraisal that really matters is David Copperfield's."

"If he's all that matters, why bother having them appraised at all?" asked Forrice.

"Because if he makes an offer I don't like, I need to know if he's wrong or I am," answered Cole.

"Well," said Forrice, "I guess I'd better go choose a diamond and get started. Where did you put them?"

"The science lab. No one ever goes there since Sharon removed all the paraphernalia they used to synthesize drugs."

Forrice got up from the table. "This shouldn't take too long. I'll let you know as soon as I've got some answers."

Cole leaned back on his chair, sipped his coffee, and considered the events of the last few hours—what the *Achilles* had done, what it hadn't done, what it should have done. The distress-call ploy wasn't going to work very often. It was far more likely that the *Teddy R* would be the attacking ship. He was prepared for that; after all, every member of the crew except for Morales had been in the military until a few weeks ago, and he had confidence that they would perform competently in military situations. But at some point, probably the point at which they boarded an enemy ship solely to plunder it, they stopped being military units and became pirates, with different goals and very likely different reactions. And since he had no intention of dying, at least not as quickly and easily as Windsail and his crew had, he had to consider every option and anticipate every possibility.

He had no idea how long he'd sat, motionless, but suddenly he was aware that his coffee had become very cold. He set it down, ordered a menu, waited until it materialized in front of him, then reached forward and touched the "coffee" icon. It arrived almost instantly, but before he could pick up the cup, Forrice entered the mess hall and swirled over to him with his oddly graceful spinning three-legged gait.

"Well?" asked Cole as the Molarian sat down on the opposite side of the table.

"I've spoken to five jewelers. Each one says that he has to see it before he'll write up an estimate for the insurance, but three of them offered guesses as to its value, ranging from twenty-seven thousand credits to forty-five. There was one, a very nice Mollutei female, who offered to cut it for free if I would indemnify her against any loss of value if she, I don't know, sneezed or blinked or did something while cutting the diamond that caused it to shatter or somehow lose its value. I'm not very clear on what can destroy a diamond, but I thanked her and told her I'd consider it. She was the one who put it at twenty-seven thousand." He paused. "The bottom line is that if thirty-seven or thirty-eight thousand is the average price, we're sitting on diamonds with a market value of better than fifteen million credits, probably more if we'll take Maria Theresa dollars or Far London pounds."

"Fifteen million?" repeated Cole. "*That'll* buy an eardrum or two."

"Have you heard back from the hospital about Chadwick?" asked the Molarian.

"Not yet. He's only been there a few hours. He's going to need a lot of work—but the nice thing about illegal transactions is that they're done with cash, so we can pay the medics and they won't be able to trace it."

"Even if they do, all they'll know is that it came from the *Samarkand*, and you can have Slick change the name in about half a Standard day."

"True," admitted Cole. "But I'd rather be very safe than merely safe."

"Can't argue with that," said Forrice. "Is there anything else we have to discuss?"

"Not that I can think of."

"Well, I've had a hard day of bloodletting and plundering," said the Molarian, getting to his feet, "so I think I'll go to bed and get a little sleep before I have to show up for red shift."

He left the mess hall, and Cole, restless, got up and returned to the bridge.

"Captain on the bridge!" shouted Christine, snapping to attention, as did Malcolm Briggs and Domak.

Cole gave them a lazy salute and they sat back down.

"Sir," said Christine, "we are on course to Riverwind, and should be braking to sublight speeds in about three hours."

"Too bad," commented Cole.

"Sir?"

"That'll be a couple of hours into blue shift. Four Eyes will be sleeping, and you've been up for almost a full Standard day. That means I can't go down to see David Copperfield right away, because we don't as yet have a Third Officer to take over command. I'll just wait until Four Eyes is awake and see if I can lure him onto the bridge a little early."

"I can remain at this post, sir," offered Christine promptly.

"Weren't you on your way to bed when we made contact with the *Achilles*?" Cole reminded her. "And I know you've been on the bridge ever since. We can wait an extra eight hours to unload the diamonds."

"I'll be all right, sir. You won't be long, and we're not under any threat here. Why wait?"

He stared at her for a long moment, considering her offer. Finally he shrugged. "What the hell. If you drink coffee, go load up on it now. If not, stop by the infirmary and grab something to help keep you awake. We'll see how you're doing when we finally reach Riverwind. This should go smoothly enough."

Which only proved that he wasn't much of a prognisticator.

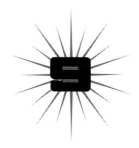

When it was viewed from orbit, there seemed to be no logical reason that Riverwind should have been given its name. It had an ocean that covered about four-fifths of its surface, and a pair of island continents. There were polar ice caps, and hundreds of tiny islands dotting the ocean, but the only two rivers that were clearly discernible ran directly north to south, one on each continent, without any hint of winding.

"I don't want to land the ship," Cole announced. "I don't mind their knowing that we're a former Navy ship, but I don't want to give them any added opportunity to identify which ship we are. I know that Slick changed all the insignia, but there are other means of identification."

"Which shuttle will you be taking, sir?" asked Briggs.

"The only one I've ever been in is the *Kermit*"—the ship's three shuttles were the *Kermit*, the *Archie*, and the *Alice*, all named for Theodore Roosevelt's children; a fourth, the *Quentin*, had been lost in battle months earlier—"so that's the one I'll take. I assume Slick got rid of the insignia?"

"Yes, sir, I'm told that he did," said Briggs. "Will you be going alone?"

"No. I don't think that would make the proper impression. Have Bull Pampas, Esteban Morales, and Domak meet me at the *Kermit* in five minutes."

"Only those three, sir?"

"I have a feeling that if there's any trouble, we'd be outnumbered even if I took the whole crew, and if there's not, three's enough. *Somebody's* got to stay up here and fly the *Teddy R*."

"Braxite has volunteered to come with you too, sir," said Christine.

"No."

"I'm sure he's going to ask me why not."

"It's known that Four Eyes and I are the highest-ranking officers on the *Teddy R.* If anyone down there suspects who I am, having a Molarian along will probably clinch it." He held up a hand. "Before you say it, I know they won't care if they're dealing with Wilson Cole or not. They're probably all in favor of mutineers and fugitives. But they're criminals, and doubtless would be quite willing to extort money and favors for keeping the *Teddy R*'s secret from the Republic." He turned to Briggs. "Pampas, Morales, and Domak. Five minutes."

"I've fed the landing coordinates into the *Kermit*, and given it false registration data," said Christine. "It won't hold up to close scrutiny, but I don't imagine David Copperfield could stay in business here if they started giving close scrutiny to his visitors."

"I agree. Once we touch down, I'll rent some transportation and have Morales direct me to Copperfield's."

"Don't you want to let him know you're coming?" asked Briggs.

"No," said Cole. "*You're* going to let him know."

"Me, sir?" said Briggs, surprised.

"If I don't hear any conditions, I don't have to obey them. When we're within a minute of touching down, contact him, tell him our radio is on the blink, and you're making the call for me."

"Would you rather I wait until you're on the ground, sir?"

Cole shook his head. "If he's the kind of guy who says do it his way or he shoots, I'd like to know that *before* we leave the ship and lose contact with you." He began walking to the airlock. "Oh, and have Bull bring the booty. I was thinking of having Sharon come up with a sensorproof case for it, but then I figured, hell, if they examined everything that came through the spaceport, Copperfield would be out of business, so I think we're safe carrying it as it is, and I'd rather not waste the extra time."

He reached the airlock, and a moment later joined Domak in the shuttle bay. Pampas, carrying a sturdy case, arrived in less than a minute, and finally Morales showed up.

"Sorry it took me so long," he said. "I knew I was meeting you at the *Kermit*, but no one told me where or what the *Kermit* was."

"Just as well you didn't get here first," replied Cole. "It's not the *Kermit* anymore, though that's the way we still think of it. It's the *Flower of Samarkand* now. Let's all get aboard it. Domak, you're the best pilot among the four of us. Take us down to the spaceport. It's programmed into the shuttle's navigational computer, so you can do most of it on automatic. I'll handle any messages from the spaceport or anywhere else."

"Yes, sir," said Domak, saluting and entering the shuttle. The three Men followed her and took their places as she ordered the bay door to open, activated the engine, and the shuttle shot out from the belly of the ship.

"Tell me a little about David Copperfield," said Cole to Morales as they neared the stratosphere.

"I've never actually met him, sir," answered Morales. "None of us did."

"Then you don't know how to get to his headquarters, or warehouse, or wherever the hell it is that he does his business?" asked Cole.

"Yes I do, sir," said Morales. "But Captain Windsail knew him long before he set up shop on Riverwind. They were old friends, and we always waited outside Mr. Copperfield's home for him. In fact, I've never actually seen Mr. Copperfield."

"What kind of protection does he have?"

"I never saw any," said Morales. "But I was told not to step outside the vehicle, that there were ten or twelve guns trained on it."

"Well, that's comforting," remarked Cole.

"What's comforting about the fact that he has twelve gunmen covering the vehicle?" asked Domak.

"If he's got twelve outside, he's got at least that many inside, where the goods are. I find it comforting that he can keep twenty-four people employed. It implies that he knows his business and how to sell what he buys, and that in turn implies that he should be willing to buy what we've got."

"That's an interesting chain of reasoning," said Domak noncommittally.

The radio came to life. "This is the Eastern Continent Spaceport. Your ship has identified itself and requested permission to land. Are you here for business or pleasure?"

"Business," answered Cole.

"Nature of business?"

"Am I required by law to answer that question?"

"Only if you require a visa for more than twenty-four hours," said the voice.

"We don't. I think eight-hour visas for myself and my associates should suffice."

"Your ship has transmitted their IDs. Your visas will be waiting for you upon your arrival."

"Thank you," said Cole, breaking the connection.

"That was almost too easy, sir," said Pampas.

"The biggest fence on the Frontier *has* to make it this easy," answered Cole. "Otherwise people will take their business elsewhere. Other pirates don't want close scrutiny any more than we do, though for different reasons. Or maybe the same reasons, now that I think about it."

Briggs's image suddenly appeared against a bulkhead.

"I've contacted them, sir, and they're expecting you. The only restriction they mentioned is that you must leave any weapons at the spaceport or in the vehicle that transports you there."

"Thanks, Mr. Briggs. We'll leave them here in the ship. Compute our ETA and transmit it to Copperfield."

Briggs saluted, and then his image vanished.

"Why didn't we get a visual from the spaceport, I wonder?" said Pampas.

"That's easy enough. If we can see them, they can see us—and a lot of Copperfield's visitors doubtless prefer not to be seen or identified. Our crimes, such as they are, were against the Republic, which might actually make us very popular with certain elements on the Inner Frontier; but their crimes were committed right here, and people might be more inclined to betray them to bounty hunters or whoever else is enforcing the law out here."

They touched down in another five minutes, and soon were approaching a trio of Customs and Immigration kiosks. There were short lines at each, mostly composed of Men, but they were being processed very quickly.

"You'd better give that case to me now," Cole told Pampas.

"It's pretty heavy, sir."

"That's okay. If they ask any questions, I want to answer them myself. I'll give it back to you once we've cleared Customs."

Pampas handed over the case, and Cole walked up to the Customs robot, which was actually a part of the kiosk.

"Name?" asked the robot.

Cole shoved his passport disk across the counter. "It's all there," he said. "My companions and I have applied for eight-hour visas. Please add them to our passports and let us through."

The robot's eyes extended on long metal stalks and an intense beam of light shot out of them as it read Cole's passport disk. The color of the light changed very slightly as it added the visa.

"This visa will disappear from your passport in exactly eight hours. If you are still on Riverwind at that time, you must report back to Customs and Immigration, Mr.—"

"Thank you," said Cole, interrupting the robot before it could say his name aloud.

"What is in the case you are carrying?"

"Check your regulations and see if someone who is here on an eight-hour visa is required to answer that question."

"No, sir, you are not required to answer it unless you will be here one full day or more."

"And you know I will not be here one full day, because I only have an eight-hour visa," said Cole.

"That is correct, sir," said the robot. "You are free to enter the public areas of the spaceport."

He passed through Customs, idly wondering how the hell Copperfield ever got the regulations changed. He waited until his crew also cleared, returned the case to Pampas, and began walking toward the door.

"That was your real passport, wasn't it, sir?" asked Pampas.

"Yes."

"Shouldn't you have used a phony?"

Cole shook his head. "Sharon couldn't fix one that could pass muster in the short period of time we had after dispatching the *Achilles*. Besides, this is the Inner Frontier, not the Republic. I'm not wanted here, so there's no reason for the robot to report my presence to any authority. I just didn't want it saying my name aloud in front of any bystanders, who might want to sell it, and our location, to interested parties."

They reached the exit. Cole was about to ask where he could hire some transport, but before he could seek out an information kiosk, a large, burly man who dwarfed even Pampas approached them.

"Mr. Smith?" he said, stopping in front of Cole. "Mr. Copperfield sends his felicitations, and requests that you follow me."

"Fine," said Cole. As they began walking, he turned to the man. "How did you know my name was Smith?"

"I call all visitors Mr. Smith," he said.

"I approve," said Cole. "And have you a name?"

"Mr. Jones," replied the man. He stopped in front of a large, luxurious aircar. "Please get in."

The four of them joined Copperfield's representative. A robot, which was also a component of the vehicle, began driving and the aircar skimmed along, perhaps a foot above the ground. It didn't go far, less than a mile, and they were still inside the city limits when it stopped and all the doors irised to let them out.

It wasn't the warehouse Cole had anticipated, or the grubby underworld hideout. They found themselves in front of an elegant mansion, built to resemble a country home from a bygone England that still possessed a vast, world-encircling empire. Two footmen in livery—but with burners clearly visible in shoulder holsters—stood at either side of the front entrance.

"Is this the same place?" whispered Cole.

"Yeah," said Morales. "But I never even got this far. The Captain had his own aircar, and we weren't allowed to leave it."

"Please come in, sir," said one of the footmen as the other opened the large wooden door.

Cole and his party entered, and found that the inside of the house fulfilled the exterior's promise. The furnishings were of a piece, all reproductions from the nineteenth century A.D., some three thousand years ago. They were ushered down a long corridor, past drawing rooms and libraries, and while Cole couldn't spot anyone he got the uneasy feeling that his every step was being observed. At last they came to a chamber that was hidden from them by a magnificent set of double doors.

The footman who had opened the doors and then brought up the rear of their little procession now moved up to the double doors.

"Only Mr. Smith is allowed beyond this point," he announced. "The rest of you are welcome to relax in the first lounge we passed. This gentleman"—a new footman bowed—"will show you to it, or you can return to the aircar and wait for Mr. Smith there." He walked over to Pampas. "I'll take this burden from you, sir. You can trust me to be exceedingly gentle with it."

Pampas and Domak looked questioningly at Cole, who nodded his assent. "Do as the gentleman says. I'll rejoin you shortly."

Pampas and Morales followed the footman to the lounge, while Morales retraced his steps and went back outside to the vehicle.

"If you will follow me, sir," said Mr. Jones, opening one of the doors.

Cole walked into a large library, filled with more books than he had ever seen in his life, most of them bound in leather, all resting on dark hardwood bookshelves. There was a matching hardwood desk in the middle of the room, and leather chairs in comfortable groupings. Behind the desk sat a creature of vaguely human proportions, from a race Cole had never before encountered. He wore the clothing of a Victorian dandy, but his eyes were set at the sides of his elongated head, his large triangular ears were capable of independent movement, his mouth was absolutely circular and had no lips at all, his neck was long and incredibly flexible, his torso was broad and half again as long as a man's, and his legs, short, stubby, and broad, had an extra joint in them. Cole couldn't tell anything about his feet, because they were inside a pair of highly polished leather shoes.

"Greetings and felicitations!" he said with no trace of an accent. "Allow me to introduce myself. I am David Copperfield. And to whom do I have the honor of speaking?"

"Call me Steerforth," replied Cole.

The alien called Copperfield threw his head back and laughed. "So you're a reader too! I can tell we're going to become great friends as well as business partners. And between us, perhaps we can get Mr. Jones to change his name to Barkus—that is, if he's willin'." He laughed again at his own joke, then suddenly became serious. "So what treasures have you brought me, Steerforth?"

Mr. Jones carried the case over to the desk and opened it. Copperfield reached in—Cole saw that his hands were seven-fingered—and pulled out a handful of uncut diamonds.

"Very nice," he said softly. "Very nice indeed." Suddenly his left eye seemed to double in size and bulge out, as he held a diamond up to it. "Excellent!" he said, putting the diamond back into the case as his eye resumed its original shape. "And how many have you brought me, my friend Steerforth."

"Four hundred and sixteen," said Cole. "I assume you'll want to count them."

"You cut me to the quick!" said Copperfield in mock hurt tones. "I thought we were friends. Of course I trust you." He paused. "But they *are* diamonds. Yes, I'll have them counted, just as a matter of form. Mr. Jones will do it before you leave. A gentleman like myself doesn't sully himself with such mundane tasks." He leaned over the case. "What else is in the bag?"

"Jewelry," said Cole. "Mostly gold, with a lot of inlaid stones. Some rubies, too."

"I love gold!" enthused Copperfield, pulling out the tiara. "Ah, but this is exquisite! I'll wager there's not another like it in all the galaxy!"

"How *much* will you wager?" asked Cole.

"I beg your pardon?"

"You've seen the quality of my goods," said Cole. "What kind of offer are you prepared to make?"

"Why, the best of any resale specialist—I abhor the word 'fence,' don't you?—the best of any resale specialist on the Inner Frontier."

"That's encouraging," said Cole. "Name a figure and we can conclude our transaction or at least have a basis for negotiating."

"How very civilized of you," said Copperfield. "You, sir, are a man after my own heart. Let me see . . . four hundred sixteen diamonds . . . well, why haggle? I'll give you my top offer."

"Don't forget the jewelry."

"I'll make a separate offer for it. I assume it's all unique, so I'll have to examine each piece. But for the diamonds . . ." He closed his eyes for a moment, as if computing figures. "For the diamonds, my dear Steerforth, I will offer you six hundred and twenty-five thousand credits."

"*What?*" yelled Cole, so startling the alien that he almost lost his composure.

"Six hundred and twenty-five thousand credits," repeated Copperfield. "Trust me, that's the best offer you're going to get anywhere."

"Just a minute," said Cole. "How much do you think one of these diamonds is worth?"

"They're really quite exquisite, as I said," replied Copperfield. "I should think thirty thousand would not be an unfair estimate."

"We've had higher, we've had lower," continued Cole. "But let's say, okay, thirty thousand. When I multiply thirty thousand by four hundred—"

"It's four hundred sixteen," noted Copperfield.

"I'm making the math easy," answered Cole. "When I multiply thirty thousand by four hundred, I get a market value of twelve million."

"That is correct," said Copperfield. "Give or take. There may be a few truly exceptional stones, but there may be a few inferior ones."

"Now, I know you're not going to pay market value. I can't prove ownership, nor would you expect me to, and you have to make a profit too. But I was figuring any fence would offer between a quarter and a third of market value. You offered . . ."

"Five percent," said Copperfield promptly. "It's the best offer you're going to get anywhere. If you can find a better one, I'll match it."

"No wonder you're living in a mansion, if all you pay is five percent," said Cole angrily.

"That is a *generous* offer, my dear Steerforth," said Copperfield. "Would I be correct in assuming you're new to this business?"

Cole made no answer.

"I thought so. Please understand, Steerforth, not all my offers are at five percent. Show me provenance, show me certificates of authenticity, and I would happily offer thirty percent. But these diamonds come from the mining world of Blantyre IV. The blue-green tint at the heart of each of them makes it certain—and it happens that seven miners were killed on Blantyre when a pirate ship robbed their outpost and made off with approximately four hundred diamonds. That is common knowledge to every jeweler and collector on the Frontier and in the Republic, as well as to every law-enforcement bureau. I cannot sell these diamonds in quantity, and I shall probably have to sit on them for at least five years before I begin selling them at all.

"Or," he continued, "let us take the jewelry. I didn't have to look beyond the tiara. It was taken from the dead, shattered head of the diva Frederica Orloff when she was robbed and killed at a charity ball on Binder X. The insurance company has sent holographs of that tiara, and the ruby earrings, and all her other missing possessions, to every jeweler, every trader, every buyer, every collector, and every police department from the Rim to the Core. For the risk I would be taking by selling it, five percent is actually far too much to pay. I consider that I'm offering three percent to you and two percent to the memory of Charles Dickens." He suddenly smiled. "You really should be a little more careful who you kill. Had you merely stolen the diamonds and the jewelry, there would not be quite so many vengeful people looking for them."

Cole was silent for a long moment. "It sounds reasonable," he said at last. "I don't know if you're bullshitting or not, but it makes sense."

"Then have we got a deal?"

Cole shook his head. "No. I have a feeling you've known all along who I am—I've made no attempt to disguise my face, and my passport was probably transmitted here the instant I produced it at the space-port—and if so, then you know that I've got a crew to pay and feed, and a ship to power, munitions to keep in stock, and a *lot* of enemies to avoid. I can't do that on five percent of market value, now or in the future."

"I happen to know the gentleman you appropriated these from, though I have no idea how you did so or whether he is still alive, nor am I asking," said Copperfield. "But I must point out that he lived most handsomely on his percentage."

"His ship didn't cost a tenth of what mine costs to run, he had a far smaller crew, he didn't begin to have the armaments or the cost of their upkeep, he had less concern for human life—and he wasn't being pursued by two navies."

"Two?"

"The Teroni Federation is the enemy of *all* Men. The Republic is the enemy of *this* man."

"I am going to do a remarkable thing," said Copperfield after a moment. "I am going to let you take your goods and leave. I could stop you, you know. Even as we speak, more that twenty weapons are trained on you and your companions. But any man who knows enough to call himself Steerforth to my Copperfield deserves one free pass. Go in peace and friendship, and remember that my offer still stands: if you get a bona fide bid of more than five percent, I'll match it. But I tell you truthfully, you never will."

"The young man with me used to serve under Captain Windsail," said Cole. "He told me that Windsail liked you. I can understand why."

"I hope we shall meet again, my dear Steerforth," said Copperfield as Cole closed the box, locked it, picked it up, and headed to the double doors. "Mr. Jones, please escort Steerforth and his party back to the spaceport."

All the way back to the *Theodore Roosevelt* Cole considered his options, rejecting one after another. When he arrived he was still wondering how Blackbeard and Captain Kidd ever made ends meet.

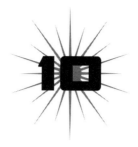

Cole was sitting in his rarely used office, speaking with Sharon Blacksmith, Christine Mboya, and Forrice.

"It's something I hadn't considered," he said. "In this era, with the whole damned galaxy interconnected, steal a necklace on the Inner Frontier and an hour later every dealer and every cop on the Rim, on the Spiral Arm, in the Quinellus Cluster, and in the Republic has already got a description and probably a holograph of it. Five percent probably *is* the best offer we're going to get."

"Can we survive on that?" asked Sharon.

"We don't have much of a choice," answered Cole. "It's not as if the Navy will welcome us back with open arms. Hell, they're more likely to welcome us back with open prison cells, and that's only if they're feeling friendlier toward us than they were when we left."

"There must be other alternatives," said Christine.

"Like what?" shot back Cole. "We're not in the cruise-ship business." He sighed deeply. "There's *got* to be a way to make a decent return on those diamonds. I mean, hell, all our lives we've watched dramas and read thrillers about jewel thieves. It can't be as hard as it seems."

"It's starting to appear that the only easy part was acquiring our illicit goods in the first place," complained Forrice.

"Captain Windsail wasn't starving," noted Sharon. "How did *he* pay his crew and fuel his ship?"

"Once we figure that out, we'll know what to do," said Cole irritably. "It's the damned technology, like I said. You steal something today, and everyone's got all the data on it by tomorrow morning."

"How?" asked Sharon. "I don't have any holographs of my necklace or bracelet. How would I get them once the jewelry was gone?"

"Not to be insulting, but your necklace and bracelet aren't worth stealing," said Cole.

"Get back to the question," said Forrice. "How *do* they get the information so quickly and thoroughly?"

"If the stuff's any good, I suppose the insurance company passes it on," said Cole.

"What if it's not insured?" persisted the Molarian.

"If it's any good, it will be," said Cole.

"So you think it's the insurance companies that spread all the information?"

"Wouldn't you?" asked Sharon. "They're on the hook for it if it's not returned."

"I suppose so," said Forrice. "Well, that's another dead end."

"No, it's not," replied Cole suddenly.

"What are you talking about?" asked Sharon.

"I've got the solution. At least, I think I do."

"Can we help?" asked Christine.

"Yeah, let's try a little Socratic dialogue here," said Cole.

"Whatever that may be," retorted Forrice.

"Let's hypothesize that I just inherited a very valuable necklace, made of pearls from the freshwater ocean on Bareimus VII. I say it's worth fifty thousand credits. You say it's worth forty-two thousand. Sharon says it's worth forty-five thousand. Who's right?"

"How should I know?" asked Forrice.

"You shouldn't," agreed Cole. "So how do we find out?"

"We hold an auction, and the sales price is what it's worth," answered the Molarian.

"That presents a problem," said Cole. "It was bought when the economy was booming, and now we're in a deep recession. Besides, we don't want to sell it for peanuts. We want to know what it's worth, and then either sell it or hang on to the necklace until we *can* get a decent price for it."

"All right," said Forrice, annoyed that Cole kept putting up new obstacles, even if they were just imaginary ones. "Take it to a jeweler and get it appraised."

"I'll do better than that," said Cole. "I'll take it to three jewelers. One says fifty, one says forty-five, one says forty-two. Now what? How do I get the real value for the necklace?"

"You go to an insurance company, and whichever appraisal they choose is the right one."

"And if they disagree with all three and bring in their own appraiser, then what?"

"Then that's the official value of the necklace."

"Why?" asked Cole.

"Because that's the amount they'll pay out if it's stolen," answered the Molarian.

"Very good," said Cole with a smile.

"I don't even know what I'm saying," complained Forrice irritably.

"You will, and soon," promised Cole. "Now once this necklace is stolen, its description and holograph go out to five million worlds, right?"

"Right."

"Why?" asked Cole. "It's not the insurance company's necklace. It's mine."

"But they're on the hook for it's full value," said Forrice, "so they're every bit as anxious to see it recovered as you are. Maybe more so."

"One last question," said Cole. "You're the thief who stole the necklace. Who would you rather deal with—a fence who might pay you four or five percent of its appraised value because it's hot property and he might have to sit on it for years, and even then he's risking jail time every time he tries to sell it, or an insurance company that's got to pay its full value if it's not recovered?"

"I see!" said Forrice with an expression of dawning comprehension on his face. "That's it!"

"And that's what we're going to do," said Cole. "Even estimating lower than anyone else has suggested, those diamonds have a value in excess of ten million credits. As for the jewelry, who knows? But *we'll* know when we find out who insured it and for how much."

"You can't just walk up to these companies and say, 'I stole your diamonds or your tiara or whatever, and I want what they're worth or I won't give them back to you,'" said Forrice.

"Of course not," answered Cole. "There's no reason for them to deal with us under those circumstances, when there's no profit to be made. But let's get back to my hypothetical necklace again. You're the insurance company. I walk into your office, and I hand you my own holograph of the necklace with some way to date it so you know I took the holo after it was stolen. I don't ask for the full value. Hell, you'd call the police and lock me away. No, I explain to you that my profession is retrieving lost articles. I explain that I heard about the necklace and was fortunate enough to retrieve it. I'll return it to your company in exchange for a reward amounting to one-third of its market value, and since I don't like the way you're staring at me, I also want a pledge from you, in writing, that you won't prosecute me or discuss our transaction with any authorities."

"Damn, that's good!" said Forrice.

"Let's get back to the diamonds, and let's say they're worth twelve million credits. You pay me four million, you get them back and return them to their legal owner, and the crisis is over. On the other hand, if you turn me in to the police or refuse to deal with me, you may feel morally superior, but do you feel superior enough to pay out another eight million credits? And if you think you may someday be able to blackmail me on your own or the company's behalf, I'll agree to—in fact, I'll insist upon—a one-question test while tied in to a Neverlie Machine, and that one question will be: Are you the one who stole these diamonds from Blantyre IV? And of course I will say I didn't, and the Neverlie Machine will confirm it, because I stole them from the pirates who stole them from Blantyre IV."

"And if they ask more?"

"I'm not so foolish as to have the necklace on my person while they're negotiating with me. If they stick to my terms and our mutually agreed-upon resolution, I'll deliver it to them within twenty-four hours. If they don't, they've lost the full insurance value on the necklace, and I guarantee they're not going to let that happen. They're not lawmen out for justice. They're a business that's concerned with profit and loss. What do you think they'll do?"

"I think you've solved it, Wilson," said Sharon. "If we're going to survive out here, that's clearly what our version of piracy has to be."

"Less romantic and more profitable, I agree," said Cole. He turned to Forrice. "As soon as this meeting breaks up, I want you to find out who insured the diamonds, how much they were insured for, and where the company's nearest branch office is. Sharon—do the same with the jewelry. In the meantime I want Christine to compute exactly what it costs to run the *Teddy R* for a Standard day, a week, and a month—fuel, food, hydroponics garden, repair, ammunition, everything. Then we'll be able to figure out if we're in profit or loss—and if we're in profit, I suppose we'll need to hand out dividends."

"You make it sound awfully colorless and businesslike," said Forrice.

"Let's hope that's exactly what it becomes," said Cole.

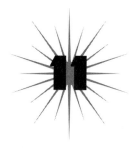

Cole contacted the hospital and learned that they had given Chadwick prosthetic eardrums. Right at the moment they were working *too* well; he was complaining about the volume, and the fact that he could over-hear conversations taking place ten and twelve rooms away. Cole decided that wasn't such a bad weapon to have in his arsenal, and asked if there was some way they could allow Chadwick himself to adjust the volume as he wished. The answer was negative. They told him that they'd have the volume right in another few hours, and he made arrangements for the shuttle to bring Chadwick back to the *Teddy R* as soon as the doctors finished with him.

"Four Eyes, this is Cole," he said, adjusting his communicator.

"I know who it is," replied the Molarian. "Your ugly image is staring at me from three feet away."

"Actually, it's staring well beyond you," said Cole. "I just ate."

"Are we through insulting each other," asked Forrice, "or do we trade a few more before you tell me why you're bothering me during red shift?"

"How are we coming on finding out who insured the diamonds and the jewelry?"

"The diamonds were insured by the Pilargo Company."

"Republic or Frontier?" asked Cole.

"Republic," answered the Molarian. "They're headquartered on Deluros VIII."

"Shit! Wouldn't you know it?" Cole paused for a moment. "What's their closest branch? Have they got any offices on the Inner Frontier?"

"I thought you might ask," said Forrice, "so I checked. They don't have anything on the Frontier. Their closest branch is on Benjamin II, but it's awfully small. I don't think they'd have the kind of money we're looking for. My guess is we'll have to go to New Madrid."

"New Madrid?" repeated Cole. "That's a good four hundred light-years into the Republic!"

"Next time we're going to screw an insurance company, I'll be sure to tell them to relocate to Keepsake or Binder X," said the Molarian.

"Did you find out how much the diamonds were insured for?"

"That's a little problematical," answered Forrice. "They have a blanket policy covering all their shipments from Blantyre IV at ninety percent of market value. They don't insure each batch separately."

"Okay, we can work from there," said Cole. "How about the jewelry?"

"Still working on it. It's harder to find, since they belonged to an individual rather than a publicly traded or Republic-owned company. I imagine we'll know within a Standard day or two. Christine is much better at this kind of detail work than I am. Once she takes charge during white shift, it ought to go a little faster."

"All right," said Cole. "Now tell Morales I want to meet him in the mess hall."

"I think he's there already."

"Tell him to stay there. I'll join him in just a minute or two."

Cole broke the connection, walked to the bathroom, splashed some cold water on his face, left his cabin, and took the airlift up to the mess hall. Esteban Morales was sitting alone at a small table, staring at him.

"Good morning," said Cole. "Or afternoon. Or evening. Whatever your schedule is."

"Hello, sir," said Morales. "Mr. Forrice told me you wanted to see me?"

"Four Eyes is a lot of things good and bad," said Cole with a smile, "but I'm pretty sure 'Mister' isn't one of them."

"I'm sorry, sir."

"I was just commenting, not correcting." He stared at Morales for a moment. "I'm betting you're too young to have ever served in the military. Am I right?"

"Yes." Then, "Excuse me. I meant yes, sir."

"You're still not in the military," said Cole. "Forget about the sir."

"Yes, sir," said Morales. "I mean, yes."

"I've got a job for you," continued Cole. "It's simple enough, but it just so happens that you're the only person aboard the ship who can do it."

"Oh?" said Morales, unable to hide his excitement. "What is it?"

"I want you to rent a small ship. One-man or two-man, no bigger."

"Rent a ship?" repeated Morales, disappointed. "Anyone can do that."

"Yeah, but you're the only one who can do it in the Republic without getting arrested."

"I don't understand, sir." Morales fidgeted awkwardly. "I mean, I don't understand."

"If you're more comfortable calling me sir, go ahead and do it," said Cole. "I just wanted you to know that you don't have to." He ordered a sandwich from the floating menu, then returned his attention to Morales. "Every other member of the crew is either a mutineer, or helped break a mutineer out of the brig, stole the *Teddy R*, and fled to the Inner Frontier. If anyone else on the ship tries to do anything requiring identification, they'll set off alarms from here all the way to Deluros."

"I don't have any money, sir," replied Morales. "I joined the *Achilles* when I was fifteen, and Captain Windsail didn't pay us very often or very well."

"That's not a problem," answered Cole. "We'll give you enough money to rent it for a day or two. But you're the only one whose ID won't be connected with the *Teddy R*."

"I'm happy to do it, sir," said Morales. "But we have our own starship and three functioning shuttles. Why do you need to rent a ship?"

"We've done what we can to erase all traces of the ship's and shuttles' registration, but they're close to a century old, and there can't be that many military vessels of this age still in service. Most people don't know it or think about it, but the Navy doesn't sell old ships to private parties; it salvages what it can and then scraps them. So if I land in the shuttle, or orbit the world we're going to in the *Teddy R*, there's always the possibility that someone will be bright enough to report it to the authorities, and the world I'm going to is four hundred light-years into the Republic; if there's a Navy ship anywhere in the area, we probably can't outrace it to the Frontier, and we sure as hell can't outgun it. And even if we reach the Frontier ahead of it, it doesn't have to stop when it's in hot pursuit—especially against the one ship that the Republic wants even more than they want the enemy."

"I'll rent a two-man ship and come with you, sir," said Morales.

"I'm going alone. It's a one-man job."

"If you're disabled in any way, you'll need someone to pilot the ship."

"If I'm disabled, I'm not going to be able to get back to the ship."

"Sure you will," said Morales. "You're Wilson Cole. We heard all about you, even on the Frontier."

"You never heard that I made a getaway after being torn up by pulse and laser blasts," said Cole.

"Just the same, I think I should come, sir," continued Morales. "What if the spaceport insists that the pilot be the man who rented the ship?"

"All right, Mr. Morales, that's a valid point," admitted Cole. "You'll come along. But you won't leave the ship once we touch down."

"How soon do you need me to rent the ship, sir?" asked Morales.

"As soon as possible. The *Teddy R* can only enter so many more atmospheres before it burns up or falls apart, so take the shuttle."

"I could leave it as collateral," suggested Morales.

Cole shook his head. "I don't want to give anyone a full day to identify it. I'll assign a crew member to take you down and drop you off. The shuttle will stay on the planet until you signal it that you've got the ship."

"Then should I follow it back up to the *Teddy R?*"

"Take a good look at it," said Cole. "If it looks like transferring from here to there will be easy, follow the shuttle up. If not—and most of these one- and two-man jobs were never designed to transfer people or anything else between ships—then tell whoever's piloting the shuttle to bring me back down and I'll get onto the ship at the spaceport."

"So should I leave right now?" asked Morales.

"Check with Four Eyes, or if it's close to white shift, with Christine Mboya, have whoever's in command spot the next inhabited planet along our route and radio ahead to make sure you *can* rent a ship, and then take it from there." He raised his voice. "You paying attention to all this, Colonel Blacksmith?"

Sharon's image suddenly appeared. "Yes."

"Pick a crew member—not Christine, and not yourself—to go down with Mr. Morales when he's ready to procure a ship."

"How's he going to pay for it?"

"How much does a ship cost to rent?"

Sharon laughed. "You've been in the service too long, Wilson."

"What does that mean?"

"It means I'll bet you've never rented a ship, or even an aircar."

"You'd win," said Cole. "What am I missing?"

"They're going to want a refundable deposit. They may only charge you a thousand credits or so for a day, but they're not about to trust a total stranger with a three-hundred-thousand-credit spaceship without a substantial deposit."

"We haven't got that much money on the *Teddy R*. That's what we're renting a ship *for*, so we can go get it." He lowered his head in thought for a moment. "Okay, here's what we'll do. I'll give Mr. Morales half a dozen diamonds. That should be a sufficient deposit. And I'll send Bull Pampas and Braxite and maybe the tall woman who's never in the science lab when I need her—what's her name?— Idena Mueller. Might as well give her something to do."

"What, for instance?" asked Sharon.

"I should have thought that would be obvious," answered Cole. "If they won't accept the diamonds, we're going to steal the ship."

"And take it to a planet that'll be on the lookout for it?" demanded Sharon.

"We'll have Bull, Braxite, and Mueller stay there and explain, gently but firmly, that the ship will be returned within one Standard day and, as long as the people connected with the rental agency are reasonable and behave themselves, they'll be paid their fee plus a bonus."

"And if they're not?"

"Then the fee will go to their survivors and we'll keep the bonus."

"You'd really kill them?"

"Hell, no," said Cole. "But I won't tell them if you won't. And you have to admit that Bull and Braxite are pretty impressive-looking specimens of their respective races."

"Then why send Idena Mueller at all?"

"There might be twenty employees. You might have a female customer in the ladies' room when they make their threats, a customer who can contact the cops. That's not to say that Sokolov or some other man can't do the job, but why upset people more than we have to?"

"That from a guy who's going to threaten to kill them," said Sharon in amused tones.

"I know from many long and vigorous nights spent together that subtlety isn't your strong point," said Cole, "but there's a difference between killing them and threatening to kill them."

"Were you being subtle last night before or after you—?"

"Don't say it," he interrupted. "You'll shock our newest crew member. Just contact the three I mentioned and have them standing by."

Her image vanished and he turned back to Morales. "Okay, come with me to the science lab."

"The science lab?"

"Yeah. That's where I've stashed the diamonds."

"Is there any particular reason why?"

"Yeah. In all the time I've been aboard the *Teddy R*, I have never seen anyone willingly go there. At least, once I made sure they couldn't stash their drug supplies there."

"They took drugs?"

"Once upon a time," said Cole. Suddenly his face hardened, and there was something cold, almost frightening, about his eyes. "Not anymore."

For the first time Morales saw some hint of what made this very pleasant man the most decorated officer in the Fleet—and even why the Fleet would declare him its greatest enemy.

"I'm sorry, sir," said Morales as the two-man ship sped toward New Madrid.

"It wasn't your fault," replied Cole. "No honest man was ever going to take those diamonds as a deposit." He shrugged. "It was just our bad luck—and his—that we ran up against an honest man."

"And his?" repeated Morales. "Are you going to kill him when we get back?"

"No, of course not," said Cole. "But if he'd been a reasonable man, not made a fuss, and promised to keep his mouth shut, I'd have left him a diamond or two. We're going to need to rent ships again; it would have been nice to find someone we could trust. Now that we know he's going to turn over descriptions and any holodisks he's got of the four of you to the authorities, I figure he's blown a very handsome tip. Which reminds me," he added, "when we return the ship and pick up Bull and the others, let's go over every inch of that place and see if we can find and destroy any images he's got of us."

"He doesn't have any of you, sir."

"I've got half a trillion Men out for my scalp, and almost as many Teronis," responded Cole. "One more enemy doesn't really make a hell of a lot of difference." He looked at the controls. "How much longer?"

"At this multiple of light, maybe six more hours," announced Morales. "If I can find the wormhole Wxakgini told me exists just outside the Romeo system, maybe forty minutes."

"Look for it. I hate shuttle food."

Cole got up and began walking toward the back of the shuttle.

"Is something wrong, sir?" asked Morales.

"No sense both of us being bored," replied Cole. "I'm going to take a nap. Wake me when we get there."

Morales tried to find the wormhole, but he lacked Wxakgini's skills, and it was six hours later that he woke Cole and announced that they were in orbit around New Madrid, had been cleared to land, and would be touching down in about five minutes.

Cole stood up, stretched, and sent a message to the New Madrid branch of the Pilargo Company, asking for an appointment with whomever was in charge of the office. He refused to answer any questions, and merely said that it was a matter of major importance. When the reception robot was reluctant to make an appointment, he asked for the name and address of the largest rival insurance company on the planet. *That* got a human response, and by the time the ship had landed his meeting was confirmed.

"Are you going to take the diamonds with you?" asked Morales, looking at the small case.

"And have them taken away at gunpoint?" replied Cole with a smile. "Not a chance. We'll leave them right here."

"In the ship?"

"I'd love to put them in a locker at the spaceport and just trade the combination for the cash, but they'd be crazy to make the deal before they knew the combination was valid—and once they knew it, we're back to the same scenario: they take the diamonds, hold a gun on me, and call the cops. At least this way we can make sure no one's armed before we let them aboard, and I get back to the ship in one piece."

"Do you think they'll go for it?"

"To save a few million credits? Absolutely. They'll make sure they can identify the ship, and I'm sure you had to give its registration number when you got permission to land, but since it's not our ship and we're never going to see it again after tomorrow, we don't really care about that."

"How long should I wait, sir?" asked Morales. "In case something goes wrong?"

"Well, let's see. I gather that once I clear Customs I should get to their office within five minutes. Give me two hours to negotiate. They're going to bluster and threaten and scream bloody murder before they give in. We'll give them another hour, tops, to get the money from their bank." He paused, considering everything that could delay him. "If I'm not back in four Standard hours, I'll try to contact you and give you the order to take off."

"You'll *try?*"

"If they decide to grill me, shall we say, *forcefully*, they'll probably remove my communicator." *And half my skin.* He picked it off his belt, where it had been bonded, and laid it down. "Come to think of it, I'm better off without it. I don't want anyone to be able to home in on the signal, or send you a false message. After all, I'm just the negotiator; the treasure's right here on the ship. Just remember: wait four hours, and if I'm not back, take off."

"If I do, I'll be back tomorrow with the *Teddy R.*"

"That's a command decision," replied Cole, "and if I'm not there, Four Eyes will be the one to make it. Let's assume that these are all hypotheticals and that I'm going to be back in an hour or two loaded down with money."

Cole walked to the hatch, climbed down to the ground, and walked to Customs and Immigration. He used an ID that he'd picked up before disposing of the *Achilles'* crew members, and Sharon had altered it to match his voiceprint, thumbprint, and retinagram. It wouldn't pass muster on Deluros VIII or any of the more populated worlds of the Republic, but he was pretty sure he could get away with it out here, so close to the Inner Frontier. He knew that within a day or two—hopefully even longer—some computer somewhere would latch onto the fact that Sales Representative Roger Cowin and mutineer Wilson Cole had the same retinagram and looked an awful lot alike, but he felt he was safe for the next few hours, which was all he cared about.

He caught public transportation to take him into the nearby city, then asked a glowing street sign how to find the Pilargo Company, waited while it printed out a holomap with audio instructions, and soon entered the insurance company's premises.

There was a shining silver robot sitting at the reception desk.

"May I help you?" it asked in lilting feminine tones.

"My name is Roger Cowin," said Cole. "I have an appointment with a Mr. Taniguchi."

"I will inform him that you are here." The robot was motionless for some twenty seconds. "He will see you now. His office is at the end of the corridor on your left."

"Thank you," said Cole, but the robot gave no indication that it had heard him. He walked down the corridor, came to the last office, and waited for the door to iris and let him pass through. He found himself confronting a heavyset man with thinning black hair and a goatee that was too neatly trimmed, that looked more like paint or makeup than hair.

"Mr. Cowin?" said the man, rising and extending his hand.

"That's right," said Cole, taking and shaking it.

"And I am Hector Taniguchi."

"I'm pleased to meet you."

"Our computer says that we have never had any dealings with you before, Mr. Cowin. You claim to be a sales representative, though you did not identify your company. I am wondering why you feel you have to speak to me personally, rather than our purchasing director."

"I think what I'm selling may be a little out of his bailiwick," said Cole.

"Oh?" said Taniguchi, trying unsuccessfully to hide his interest.

"Yes. But first I wonder if you have a Neverlie Machine on the premises?"

Taniguchi frowned. "Most major companies have one. It's not as sophisticated as the ones the police have, of course, but it's functional."

"Good. Before we begin, I'd like you to ask me two questions while the machine is monitoring my answers. Once you're convinced that I'm telling the truth, we can proceed with our business."

"You make this sound quite intriguing, Mr. Cowin," said Taniguchi. "*Have* we any business to transact?"

"Oh, yes," Cole assured him. "We very definitely have business to transact."

Taniguchi summoned a subordinate and had Cole hooked up to the machine two minutes later.

"What now, Mr. Cowin?"

Cole took a small cube out of his pocket and handed it to Taniguchi. "Have your man leave us alone. Then put this in your computer. It contains two questions. I will answer only those and no others while I'm tied to the machine. If you ask me any other while the machine is monitoring me, I will walk out of this office and you will never see me again."

"Will that be such a terrible thing?" asked Taniguchi.

"Lose your assistant, ask the questions, and then you can decide."

Taniguchi nodded to his subordinate, who silently left the room. Then he inserted the cube and read the questions, frowning as he did so.

"Mr. Cowin," said Tanaguchi, "have you ever been to Blantyre IV?"

"No, I have not," said Cole.

"Did you steal four hundred and sixteen uncut diamonds from Blantyre IV, or kill anyone who worked for the mining company there?"

"No, I did not," said Cole. He paused. "What does the machine say?"

"That you're telling the truth."

"Okay. Unhook me."

"I'd like to know if—"

"If you finish that question while I'm still tied to the machine, I'm leaving," said Cole. *I hope that sounds convincing. You're probably the only guy alive who'll pay me more than five percent. I'd never walk out, but hopefully you won't figure that out too soon.*

Taniguchi disconnected Cole from the machine and deactivated it. "All right, Mr. Cowin—so you didn't kill any miners or steal any diamonds. There are doubtless trillions of men who can make that same statement."

Cole pulled another cube out of his pocket. "But they don't have your four hundred diamonds, and I do. Put that in your computer, and have any expert in this complex examine it."

Taniguchi called in another man, handed him the cube, and said, "Find out where these are from."

The man left with the cube, and Taniguchi sat down again, facing Cole.

"How did you come by them?" he asked.

"I'm a treasure hunter," said Cole. "My profession is retrieving lost articles."

"These weren't lost," replied Taniguchi. "They were stolen, and a number of men were murdered in the process."

"That's not my concern," answered Cole. "You know I didn't steal them or kill your miners." *You at least know I didn't steal them on Blantyre; let's hope you don't notice the subtle difference.*

"Where are they now?"

"In a safe place."

The door irised and the man with the cube stepped through.

"Well?" asked Taniguchi.

"Definitely from Blantyre IV," said the man.

"Is there any possibility that you could be mistaken?"

The man shook his head. "The computer says no other diamond has that exact color at the center of it."

"Thank you," said Taniguchi, dismissing him. "Well, Mr. Cowin," he said when he and Cole were alone, "what is your proposition?"

"My information is that everything on Blantyre IV, or everything shipped *from* Blantyre IV, is insured for ninety percent of market value. Now, I think market value on these diamonds—there are six missing; all the rest are there—should be about thirteen million credits, but I'm willing to be shown that I'm wrong." Suddenly he smiled. "I may even have undervalued them."

"That's more than double what they're worth," said Taniguchi.

"If you're going to lie that blatantly, I'll just put my own value on them and stick with it," said Cole.

"If you think I'm going to pay you thirteen million credits . . ." began Taniguchi heatedly.

"Of course not. I'm a businessman, not a thief. I just want a finder's fee."

"All right. Name a price."

"I'm going to ask you one more time before I do," said Cole. "How much are these things worth on the open market?"

"We would have to examine each stone separately to determine its value."

"Since you've yet to see a stone, how do you know the amount you have to pay on the insurance claim?"

"I'm not at liberty to discuss our methods with you, sir," said Taniguchi.

"Fine," said Cole. "Then I will arbitrarily declare their value to be twelve million credits. They're insured for ninety percent. Even if you hedge and finagle and talk them down to ten million market value, you're still going to be out nine million credits. Do you agree?"

Taniguchi merely glared at him.

"Well, you don't disagree, so clearly we're making progress. Mr. Taniguchi, I am prepared to save the Pilargo Company six million credits. If you will pay me three million in cash, I will turn over the diamonds to you before I leave the planet, which I will do this afternoon with or without reaching an agreement with you."

"Three million?" snapped Taniguchi. "That's outrageous!"

"No, sir," said Cole. "That's business."

"We won't pay it."

"That's your privilege," said Cole, getting up and walking slowly toward the door.

"*Wait!*" said Taniguchi.

Cole turned and stared at him.

"Two million," said Taniguchi.

Cole resisted an urge to smile. *You blinked. Now it's all over but the shouting.*

"This isn't a negotiation," answered Cole. "I asked you to give me a value before, and you refused. Now my price is three million. You can pay it and save your company six million credits, or you can refuse to pay it, in which case I will walk out of your office right now, and you will never see me again. You will have to pay nine million credits, and probably more, to settle the claim, and your head office will be informed that you were given the opportunity to pay a finder's fee for the diamonds and refused."

Taniguchi was silent for a long moment, then spoke: "Three million, you say?"

"That's right. In cash."

"It will take half an hour to get it."

"That's fine. In the meantime, I'll want a written and holographed pledge from the Pilargo Company not to harass or prosecute me for any reason whatsoever."

"You never mentioned that."

"I'm mentioning it now," said Cole. "Look, you know I didn't rob the mine or kill the miners. If the police hook me up to another Neverlie Machine, it'll say the same thing. Do you really want to look like a fool for the home office?"

Taniguchi considered what Cole said, and finally nodded his assent. "I agree to your conditions. Now where are the diamonds?"

"I'll give them to you when I get my hands on the money."

"Why should I believe you?"

"Why should I lie? I assume that you'll have weapons trained on me from the second I get the money until the second you get your diamonds. I'm mercenary and avaracious, not suicidal."

"Wait in the reception area," said Taniguchi. "I'll let you know when the money arrives."

"Fine," said Cole, walking the rest of the way to the door, which sensed his approach and let him pass through.

Taniguchi delivered the money some twenty-four minutes later, and Cole led a procession of executives and armed security guards to the spaceport. He allowed Taniguchi and one security man aboard the ship after making sure their weapons had been removed, had Morales turn over the diamonds, and took off before anyone from Pilargo could contact the spaceport authorities and detain them.

"By God, this is going to be easy!" said Cole as they hit light speeds.

"I was worried, sir," said Morales. "I know it sounded good when you talked about it, but you were still walking in cold and demanding millions of credits."

"They didn't have any choice."

"You sure don't run the pirate business the way Captain Windsail did, sir," said Morales. "I'm glad I joined the *Teddy R.*"

"Your Captain Windsail never understood that the reward has to be commensurate with the effort," said Cole. "He'd risk his crew's lives, he'd risk his ship, and then his profit margin barely paid for his fuel and his ammunition. Dumb way to run any business—especially the pirate business."

"I know," said Morales. "But when I was alone in the ship waiting for you, I kept worrying that something had gone wrong."

"If you plan it properly, not much can go wrong," answered Cole confidently.

He was right in principle, but he was about to find out just how wrong he could be in practice.

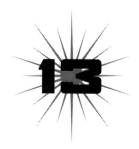

"Three million!" exclaimed Sharon Blacksmith as she, Cole, and Forrice stood together in the science lab. "I've never seen as much as ten thousand in a single lump before!" She ran her hands over the neat stacks of thousand-credit notes. "Isn't it beautiful!"

"And you had no trouble at all?" put in Forrice.

"No more than expected," said Cole. "He screamed, he threatened, he held his breath until he turned blue—and then he gave in and saved his company six million credits. Probably more. I like my original estimate of thirteen million better than ten."

"Why didn't you stick to it, then?" asked Forrice.

"Get me an ID that can stand up to close scrutiny and I will," said Cole. "My guess is that by now the Navy knows I was on New Madrid."

"What we really need is a mole who can get into the Master Computer on Deluros VIII," said Sharon. "Someone who can put someone else's prints and retinagram together with your name, and yours with some other identity."

"Why don't you wish for a million credits while you're at it?" said Cole.

"Why bother?" she replied with a smile. "You've already given me three million."

"Believe it or not, that's not all for you," said Cole. "We've got a ship to run and a crew to pay."

"No one's bitching," said Sharon. "Yet."

"We don't have anything to spend it on anyway," added Forrice. "We're going to need shore leave pretty soon."

"Talk to Morales and find out what shores are hospitable to us," replied Cole. "We're going to need to refresh the nuclear pile one of these days. We might as well do it on a friendly world."

"I'll go talk to him now," said the Molarian.

"Talk to him whenever you want, but we're dumping the jewelry first," said Cole.

"Three million credits isn't enough?" demanded Forrice. "We have to have more before we can drink stimulants and hunt up lady Molarians in season?"

"With the money we get for the jewelry I want to buy a small ship," replied Cole. "The closest we came to real trouble was renting the one I used. They're going to scrutinize us a lot more closely when we're renting a ship that's worth hundreds of thousands than when I show up on a planet with nothing in my hands."

"You know, I just hate it when you make sense," muttered the Molarian.

"While I'm thinking about it," continued Cole, "has Christine found out who insured the jewelry yet?"

"I haven't asked her," said Sharon.

"Nor have I," said Forrice. "It didn't seem vital when you were hundreds of light-years away dumping the diamonds."

"Well, find out for me while I go grab some lunch," said Cole. "Have we got any further business here?"

"None," said Forrice, heading for the airlift.

"That's a beautiful pile of money," said Sharon admiringly. "I hate to leave it."

"As the Chief of Security, you're in charge of it," noted Cole. "I expect it to remain intact."

"You're not even going to pay me for sexual services rendered?"

"What the hell—fair is fair," said Cole. "Take ten credits and don't bother me again."

"Wait'll the next time you're taking a shower and Security informs your room that it's now being occupied by a methane breather."

"Okay, fifteen."

She laughed and began locking the money away. Then Christine Mboya's image appeared in front of him.

"I've found the insurer, sir," she reported. "It's a division of the Amalgamated Trust Company."

"Where is it located?"

"Phalaris II, sir."

"Never heard of it."

"It's headquartered in the Albion Cluster, sir."

"Hell, that's a third of the galaxy from here," he complained. "If they're an arm of Amalgamated, they should be all the hell over the Republic, maybe even on the Inner Frontier. See if you can hunt up something closer."

"Working . . ." said Christine, obviously studying her computer. "There's a very small office on Binder X, but as far as I can tell they just sell, they don't handle claims. I think your best bet is the branch on McAllister IV, sir."

"A Republic world?"

She nodded. "Yes, sir."

"Figures," he said. "How far away is it?"

"From our current position?" said Christine. "About three hundred and ten light-years."

"All right," said Cole. "That's where we'll sell them back their jewelry. Find me a populated Frontier world where we can rent a ship."

"Will you be sending Mr. Morales again, sir?"

"No. Even if he had a new ID, they've got his prints and holograph on record. If he walks in, it'll set off every alarm on the planet. Let me think about that while you're hunting up an appropriate world."

He broke the connection.

"You know," said Sharon, who had finished securing the cash, "as long as the money for the jewelry is earmarked for a ship, why not buy it now out of these funds and pay yourself back when you unload the jewelry? It might cause a lot less problems than renting another ship."

"That's not a bad idea," Cole admitted. "I knew there was some reason I let you stick around after you put your clothes on."

"Then let me give you another one," she said. "If you can bear to part with about a hundred thousand credits, I can probably pick up whatever we need to give everyone passports and identities that'll pass muster even in the Republic."

"Since when does printing and coding equipment cost that much?"

"It doesn't. I can get the equipment for well under fifty thousand credits."

"What's the rest for?"

"The forger."

"Can't you do it yourself?"

"I'm good, but I'm not *that* good. If we want to beat the Republic's security, we need a real pro."

"Are you on good terms with many expert forgers, Colonel?" he asked sardonically.

"No," answered Sharon. "But when word gets out that I'm willing to spend that kind of money on one, I'll have to fight them off with a stick."

"How long do you think it'll take?"

"To find someone who can forge ID disks and passports?" she replied. "They're on every populated world on the Frontier. The trick is to find a good one."

"I mean, how long will it take him to do the job?"

"There are forgers who can give you an ID that'll pass every test my

Security department can devise, and they can produce it in three hours or less. We're carrying a complement of about thirty. We'll have to get one for Morales, now that he's blown the one he used to rent that ship, but on the other hand Wxakgini might spend the next ten years in his little plastic cocoon, tied in to the navigational computer, so he certainly doesn't need one." She paused, as if counting up the hours. "I'd say a dozen Standard days should do it."

"I'm not going to hang around some planet for twelve days while we get new IDs made for the whole crew," said Cole. "We'll give him half the money up front, I'll wait long enough to get an ID for myself and maybe a couple of others, and then we'll come back with the rest of the money after he's had time to do the job."

"I don't imagine that any forger will object to that," said Sharon. "After all, he'll have the retinagrams, voiceprints, fingerprints, and holos of everyone he's making them for."

"But if he's on the Inner Frontier, who's he going to turn them in to?" said Cole with a smile.

"Bounty hunters," she replied seriously. "They're just about the only law the Frontier's got. Some of them are really good at their jobs."

"How do you know all this stuff?"

"When I'm dressed, I'm the Chief of Security, remember?"

"Okay," he said. "I'll leave it to you and Christine to choose a planet. Once I get my new ID, I'll buy a ship and go transact our business on McAllister while the rest of the IDs are being made."

"Sounds reasonable," said Sharon.

"Fine. Then I'm finally off to grab some lunch," he said, walking to the door of the lab. "I'll catch up with you later."

"Now that you're worth three million credits, bring money."

Cole bought a ship on Hermes II, and stuck around long enough to get a better ID. The *Teddy R* remained in orbit while Sharon arranged for IDs for the rest of the crew, and Cole took off in the new ship, alone this time, for McAllister IV.

Once there he landed at the planet's only spaceport, cleared Customs, and went to an information kiosk, where he was given instructions for getting to the Amalgamated Trust Company.

It was a large building for a thinly populated planet. Then he remembered that insurance was just a small piece of the action that Amalgamated Trust had carved out for itself, and that McAllister was probably the banking center for a dozen nearby agricultural planets and twice that many mining worlds.

He entered the building and looked around. Clearly the main floor was strictly a bank. Most of the tellers were human, but there were a few Lodinites, Atrians, and even a Mollute. As one neared the Inner Frontier and got farther from Deluros VIII and the other major worlds of the Republic, the credit was in much less demand. There was a very busy exchange booth that flashed an ever-changing rate, to four decimal places, for the credit, the Maria Theresa dollar, the Far London pound, the New Stalin ruble, and half a dozen other currencies that were likely to show up at this end of the Republic.

Finally Cole walked up to a human guard.

"Excuse me," he said. "I'm looking for the insurance company."

"There are three of them in this building," answered the guard. "Do you know which one you want?"

"Amalgamated."

The guard nodded. "Yeah, that's the biggest of them. They've got the whole fifth floor. Take the airlift that's off to your left, not the one across the lobby."

"Thanks," said Cole.

"When you get there," continued the guard, "if you don't know the name of the person you want to see, at least tell the receptionist whether you're here to buy some insurance or make a claim."

Cole thanked him again, and headed off before the guard could offer any more self-evident advice. He ascended to the fifth floor, stepped out onto a glistening resilient floor, and walked directly to the well-marked reception area.

"Good morning and welcome to the Amalgamated Trust Insurance Company," said a furry Lodinite, speaking into a T-pack and waiting for the translation to come out in a dull monotone. "How may I help you?"

"Who's in charge of your claims division?" asked Cole.

"If you have a claim to file, I can give you the proper form to fill out," said the receptionist. "What type of property was insured?"

"I don't want a form," said Cole. "I just want to know who the head man is."

"Head man?" repeated the Lodinite, offering its equivalent of a frown. "All men have heads. All men within my experience, anyway."

"Who is in charge of the claims division?" Cole asked again with growing irritation.

"I must not have made myself clear," said the Lodinite. "First you must fill out a claim form. Then I will send you to see the next available agent."

"If you don't direct me to the man in charge, I will go to one of the other insurance companies in the building," said Cole. "But first I'll need your employee number and the exact spelling of your name for the letter of complaint I intend to write, so Amalgamated will know who to blame for losing all of my corporation's business."

The Lodinite stared at him silently. If it was nervous or frightened or angry, Cole was unable to tell from its expression. Finally it spoke: "I will tell Mr. Austen that you are here to see him."

"Thank you."

"But I will not tell you my name or how to spell it," it added. Cole imagined that the pre-translated tone was petulant.

"That is no longer necessary."

"I must see your identification," said the Lodinite.

"No."

"But—"

"You don't have to see it," said Cole. "I've already passed through security at the spaceport and again when I entered the bank on the main floor, so you know it's valid. All you need is my name, which is Luis Delveccio."

Another long silent stare. Finally the Lodinite spoke softly into a communicator, then looked back at Cole. "Mr. Austen will see you now."

"Thank you."

"He is a very busy man," added the Lodinite. "This had better be important."

"It's important to me, and the customer is always right," replied Cole. "Where is his office?"

"I will take you there," said the Lodinite, getting to its feet and waddling off without another word.

Cole followed it down a corridor, where it turned right and went all the way to the next corner, stopping at a large office. It ordered the door to vanish, announced that Mr. Delveccio was here, waited for Cole to enter, then stepped back into the corridor and ordered the door to reappear.

Austen was a young man, dressed and groomed to perfection, but looking just a bit haggard, as if he'd dealt with either too many serious claims or too much office politics. He stood up, walked around his polished desk, shook Cole's hand, and asked him to take a seat as he returned to his own chair.

"It's very rare that I meet personally with one of our clients, Mr. Delveccio," said Austen. "But you clearly have convinced our receptionist that no one else here can handle your particular problem. May I inquire as to its nature?"

"Let me begin by saying that I'm not a client," said Cole.

Austen frowned. "Then you want to speak to someone in Sales, not Claims."

"Why don't you hear me out?" suggested Cole. "I assure you I'm speaking to the man I need to speak to."

"All right, Mr. Delveccio," said Austen, staring at him curiously. "How can I help you?"

"You can't," said Cole. "But I think I can help you."

Austen arched an eyebrow. "Oh?"

"My profession can loosely be defined as treasure hunter," said Cole. "I recently came into possession of some items your company has insured—very valuable items. I'll be happy to show you a number of holos so you can positively identify them."

"For which you want . . . ?"

"We'll negotiate later. First I want you to have someone bring a Neverlie Machine here."

"That won't be necessary," said Austen.

"I think it will."

"Mr. Delveccio, I meet so-called fortune hunters every week. You're going to swear that you didn't steal the items in question, and for whatever reason the Neverlie Machine will confirm your testimony, quite possibly because of the way you word the question. We can save some time if I stipulate up front that I am prepared to accept your word."

"Are you also willing to sign a statement that Amalgamated will not pursue any legal action against me or cooperate in any police prosecution involving these items?" asked Cole.

"If we agree to terms, I will sign such a statement," said Austen. "Now, Mr. Delveccio, what have you got?"

Cole pulled a cube out of his pocket and laid it on the desk. Austen picked it up and inserted it in a computer that was hidden in one of his desk drawers, and an instant later the surface of the desk was covered by holographic images of the tiara and the other jewelry.

"Do you recognize it?" asked Cole.

Austen nodded his head. "They belong to Frederica Orloff, the widow of the Governor of Anderson II. Magnificent, aren't they?"

"I'd say they're worth six million credits, easy," suggested Cole.

"No," said Austen. "They are worth seven million four hundred thousand credits."

"Whatever you say."

"I say that, Mr. Delveccio, because that is the amount we paid on the Orloff claim," replied Austen. "You are in possession of stolen jewelry. They are worth nothing to Amalgamated, as we've already paid off the claim."

"Then I guess I'll take my leave of you and sell them elsewhere," said Cole, suddenly wary.

"You're not going anywhere," said Austen. "I don't know how you came by the jewelry, whether you stole it from Mrs. Orloff yourself or whether you stole it from the man who did, but you're a thief, and it's my duty to detain you until the police arrive." He smiled. "Of course, if you were to turn over the jewelry to me, I might be so blinded by its magnificence that I couldn't see you escape . . ."

"And then, without telling Amalgamated that this meeting ever took place, you'd get a partner to sell it to Mrs. Orloff for maybe half of what you already paid her?" suggested Cole. "Now that I know who it belonged to, I can do that myself."

"Only if you can leave the building," noted Austen, "and I can hit the alarm on my computer before you can reach me."

He's probably not bluffing—so my first order of business is to get out of the building in one piece. If the police detain me for even an hour, they're going to find out who I really am.

"All right," said Cole. "You seem to have the advantage. Let's deal."

"There's no dealing involved," said Austen. "Your take me to the jewelry—I assume you're bright enough not to have it on your person—and I let you leave McAllister without turning you over to the police."

"I deserve a little something for getting the jewelry and bringing it to you," persisted Cole. *You'll never agree, but it might scare you off if I don't behave in a normal manner, and a thief—even one who was just caught in the act—would normally ask for a piece of the action after having gone to all the trouble of obtaining the jewelry.*

"We'll discuss it—*after* I get my hands on the stuff."

Cole paused an appropriate length of time, as if considering, then shrugged. "All right. I guess I'm going to have to trust you."

"A wise decision," said Austen, opening a drawer and pulling out a small burner. He got to his feet and gestured toward the door. "Shall we go?"

Cole got up and walked to the door.

"Remember," said Austen, pressing the burner into Cole's back. "No sudden movements."

Cole walked back to the reception area, then stepped into the air-lift. Austen followed him.

"Keep your back to me."

Cole stood facing the wall of the airlift until they reached ground level, then walked out into the bank lobby and headed for the exit.

"Stop," said Austen. He spoke softly into a communicator. "I've ordered my aircar. It will be here in a minute and can take us to the spaceport—unless you've hidden the goods between here and there?"

"Get the car," said Cole.

"I keep getting the feeling that I've seen you before," remarked Austen as they walked outside and stood waiting for the aircar.

"This is my first time on McAllister."

"I know. I've only been here three months myself. But you seem very familiar."

The aircar pulled up and hovered a few inches about the ground. Cole got in first, and after they were both seated Austen ordered it to head to the spaceport.

"Is it here?" he asked. "On the planet, I mean?"

If I say yes, you'll kill me right now, because you'll know the only place it can be is on my ship.

"No," answered Cole.

"Where then?"

"Elsewhere."

"You know I'll kill you if I decide you're lying to me," said Austen.

"And you know you'll never see the jewelry if you kill me," replied Cole. "Just relax and you'll see it soon enough."

"Then it's somewhere in the solar system?"

"No comment."

"I'll take that as an affirmative," said Austen.

"Take it any way you want," said Cole. "But remember that there are fourteen planets and fifty-six moons in the system. You'll never find it without me."

They rode in silence for the next few minutes, and then the aircar came to a halt.

"We have reached the spaceport," announced the aircar.

"Take us to the area reserved for private ships," said Cole. "Aisle 17, Slot 32."

"I am not programmed to respond to your voice, sir," said the robot.

"Aisle 17, Slot 32," said Austen, and the vehicle immediately began approaching the location. "You're sure we've never met before?" he said, staring intently at Cole.

"Never." He looked out a window. "We're here."

"Return to my reserved space beneath the Amalgamated building when we exit, and once there go to standby mode."

"Yes, sir," replied the aircar.

They climbed out and approached Cole's ship.

"No sudden moves," warned Austen.

"Sudden moves aren't my style," replied Cole. He stood before the hatch and uttered a seven-digit number.

Nothing happened.

Frowning, he uttered the number again.

Still nothing.

"I just bought the damned thing," he said apologetically, "and I guess I haven't memorized the codes yet." He began reaching his hand into a side pocket.

"Hold it!" snapped Austen sharply. "What are you doing?"

"Getting the code log," answered Cole. "Unless you want to stand here all day."

"You stand still," said Austen. "I'll get it."

"I'm not armed."

"Maybe not with a burner or a screecher, but how the hell do I know what you have in that pocket? It could be a knife, it could be anything."

Austen reached a hand into Cole's pocket—and as he did so, Cole spun around and knocked the burner from his hand. It went flying through the air, landing on the concrete some twenty feet away and skidding for another ten feet.

Austen cursed and took a swing at Cole, who blocked it with a forearm and lashed out with a foot, catching Austen on the knee. There was a crunching sound and the young man collapsed, writhing in pain.

Cole walked over to where the burner lay and picked it up, then returned to Austen.

"This is your lucky day, Mr. Austen."

"Fuck you!" muttered Austen.

"Oh, you probably feel that you've lost a fortune, and maybe you have, but I'm letting you live, and that ought to be even more to you than filthy lucre."

"You wouldn't dare kill me!" snarled Austen. "There are security cameras all the hell around the spaceport. Within an hour every world in the Republic would be on the alert for you!"

"I thought the Republic had more important things to do," commented Cole dryly.

Suddenly Austen's eyes went wide at the mention of the Republic. "*Now* I know where I've seen you! Your holo's been on every newscast in the galaxy! You bet your ass the Republic has more important things to do than chasing down a jewel thief or a killer! They've got to hunt down Wilson Cole and kill him for the goddamned turncoat he is!"

"Brave words for an unarmed man with a shattered knee," commented Cole.

"Fuck you, traitor! Shoot and get it over with!"

"Don't tempt me," said Cole. He pointed the burner at a spot between Austen's eyes, and the younger man immediately fell silent. "You know," continued Cole, "I spent more than a decade as an officer

in the Republic's Navy. I won four Medals of Courage. I can't tell you
how many times I put my life on the line. It's when I realize I did all
that for people like you that I feel like the biggest sucker ever born."

"So now you fight for the Teroni Federation!" accused Austen.

"I have no more use for them than I have for the Republic,"
answered Cole. "Now I fight for me."

"That just makes you a common criminal."

"No," said Cole. Suddenly he smiled. "I prefer to think of myself
as an uncommon one. I'm so uncommon that I'm not even going to
shoot you down in cold blood. You're going to walk with a limp for
the rest of your life, and your superiors will be informed of what you
planned to do behind their backs. I think that's punishment enough."

He ordered the hatch to open.

"I'll tell the Navy, and they'll come after you!" vowed Austen.
"They'll never rest until you're dead!"

"There's a war going on," said Cole just before he closed the hatch
behind him. "They've got better things to do than chase after one man."

He said it with bravado, and it sounded logical—but deep down
in his gut, he knew it wasn't true.

Cole knew he had to get rid of his ship before rejoining the *Teddy R.* There were no signs of pursuit, but the registration was a matter of record, and he was sure Austen would have reported his presence to the authorities even before he was carted off to the hospital.

He set the ship's scrambler on a prearranged code and then made contact with the *Teddy R.*

"Where are you, sir?" asked Rachel Marcos, who was running the communications system when the connection was made.

"I'd prefer not to say, just to be on the safe side."

Rachel frowned. "Are you all right, sir?"

"So far so good. But I've got to dump this ship and either find another one or contact you later and tell you where to pick me up."

"If you're in danger—" she began.

"I'm not in any immediate danger," said Cole. "Capture my transmission and pass it on to Four Eyes, Christine, and Sharon."

"Yes, sir. How long before we hear from you again?"

"I don't know. Probably no more than a day or two. I want to go deeper into the Frontier to make sure I'm not being followed. Then I'll see about replacing this ship."

"At least you have the money from the jewelry to pay for it," said Rachel.

"We'll talk about that when I rejoin the *Teddy R.* I'm going to break off the communication now. If this transmission's being monitored, I don't want anyone to trace it to your end, and Christine tells me that it takes about two minutes. I've been in contact for ninety seconds."

He broke the connection, then had his navigational computer throw up a three-dimensional map of the sector in which he found himself. There were ninety-three inhabited worlds within five hundred light-years, fifty-one of them human colonies, agricultural and mining worlds, and various outposts. He recognized only a few names—Ophir, a gold-mining world; Bluegrass, an agricultural world specializing in enormous mutated cattle; and Alpha Jameson II, known more commonly as Bombast, valued for its uranium deposits and famed for its erratic and frequent volcanic eruptions. Finally he hit upon Basilisk, a small world that seemed to have only a single tradertown, one of those ramshackle ports that appealed to independent miners, adventurers, and misfits. Most tradertowns boasted a few hotels (though in bygone days bed-and-breakfasts would better describe them), survey and assay offices, whorehouses that were rarely populated exclusively by females or even humans, a few bars, a few drug dens, and a casino or two. Cole never understood the attraction of the tradertowns, but then he never understood what would make a man want to farm or mine a desolate world a trillion miles from the comforts of civilization. He was an officer in the Republic's Navy by choice, and a pirate on the Inner Frontier merely by happenstance.

He saw no reason to remain awake during the voyage, so he directed the computer to take him to Basilisk, and to wake him when the ship entered orbit around the planet or received a transmission from Basilisk's spaceport.

"One more thing," he said as he leaned back and his command chair morphed into a small bed. "There's a chance that we're being followed. If we are, they're being damned clever about it. No one's going to be directly on our tail, but keep an eye out and let me know if you spot anything funny."

"I have no eye, and therefore cannot keep one out," answered the computer. "And I have no sense of humor, so I cannot possibly identify anything funny."

"That being the case," said Cole, "just let me know if we're being followed."

He leaned back, clasped his fingers behind his head, and was asleep within a matter of seconds.

"Sir," said the computer's mechanical voice.

"What is it?" asked Cole. "Am I supposed to sign off before I take my nap?"

"We are entering orbit around Basilisk," announced the ship.

"You're kidding!"

"I am incapable of any form of humor," the computer explained.

"It feels like I just closed my eyes a second ago," said Cole. "How long was I asleep?"

"Five hours, seventeen minutes, and four seconds, sir, based on your pulse, heartbeat, blood pressure, and respiration."

"Has anyone from the planet asked for your registration, my ID, our flight plan, anything?"

"No, sir."

"They've got to know we're here." Suddenly a satisfied smile crossed Cole's face. "That means I chose the right world. It's so small we're not going to need permission to land, and they won't ask for your registration or my passport. There'll be no Customs, no Immigration, no temporary visas, nothing." He paused. "Okay, from the information that was programmed into you, there seems to be just one tradertown. Find out where all the ships and shuttles are clustered and land there."

The ship entered the atmosphere and touched down a few minutes later. Cole climbed out, ordered the hatch to close and lock, and walked just under a mile to the largest of the three bars. There were a number of tables spread across the front half of the room; toward the back were the various gambling games. Men mingled with aliens, some dressed in brilliant finery, others wearing outfits that looked like they hadn't been washed in years. The newly rich and the newly poor rubbed shoulders at the tables and at the long polished bar.

Cole surveyed his surroundings, then walked over to the bar, shouldering his way through the crowd clustered there. A robot, all head, arms, torso, and wheels, slid down the length of it until it stopped opposite him.

"What can I serve you?" it asked.

"A beer."

"What brand, sir?"

"What have you got?"

"We have fifty-three brands from forty-two different planets, sir."

"You choose one."

"I am not programmed to make value judgments, sir. I can produce a list of our beer brands if you wish."

"Forget it. Give me whatever's on tap."

"We have fourteen brands on tap."

"He'll take a Blue Star," said a feminine voice off to his left. "And he'll buy me one, too."

"Sir . . ." began the robot.

"Do what the lady says," ordered Cole.

He turned to see who he was buying the beer for, and almost had to physically stop himself from doing a double take. Standing there— and he was sure she hadn't been there when he walked in a minute or two ago—was a woman with flaming red hair, proportioned like a model but standing an inch or two above six and a half feet. She wore an outfit of glistening metallic fabric that clung to her body, and a pair of thigh-high boots with the handle of a weapon peeking out of the top of each. She wore long gloves, and Cole could see the outlines of daggers through each one. He couldn't decide at first glance if she was a prostitute or an assassin, or maybe just a refugee from a masquerade; she seemed dressed for any of them.

"Thanks," said the woman as the robot delivered her beer.

"Happy to oblige," said Cole, taking a swallow from his glass.

"Blue Star's good drinking stuff," she said. "I know the guy who makes it. Well, I *knew* him," she amended. "But his family's carrying on and doing okay with it."

Cole picked up his glass. "It's getting a little noisy here. Care to join me at a table?"

"Sure," she said, following him to a small table about halfway between the entrance and the bar.

"Have you got a name?" he asked when they were seated.

"Lots of 'em," she replied. "This week it's Dominick."

"Dominick?" he repeated. "I never met a woman named Dominick before."

"You probably never will again," she replied. "He was my seventh lover. Or was it my eighth? No, seventh. So this week I'm memorializing his name. Fourth time around for it. Once or twice more and I'll know that I'll never forget him."

"So you really want me to call you Dominick?"

"This week, anyway," she said. "Last week I was the Queen of Sheba. And what do I call you?"

"Delveccio."

She shook her head. "No, that's no good."

"I beg your pardon?"

"That name's blown. Choose another one, Wilson Cole." She stared at him. "And keep your hands off your weapons. If I wanted to expose you, I could have done it at the bar when everyone could hear me."

"What makes you think I'm this Cole person?" he asked.

"Because you went and busted up some guy on McAllister, and he went public with who you are. Your holo is on every newscast in the Republic, on both Frontiers, and in the Arm." She smiled. "The Navy thinks you've been a naughty boy."

Cole looked around the bar. No one seemed to be paying him any attention.

"Don't worry, Commander Cole," said Dominick. "You're safe for the time being."

"Captain Cole," he corrected her. "And what makes you think I'm safe? If you could spot me, so can someone else."

"At least two others have," she replied. "Maybe three. But you're not in any immediate danger."

"Why not?" he asked.

"Because you're with me."

"You're that formidable?"

"I suppose you could ask the men who didn't think so, but they're mostly dead, or recovering in hospitals."

He stared at her. "I can believe it. You remind me of a Valkyrie."

"What's a Valkyrie?" she asked.

He told her.

"That's my new name," she announced happily. "Call me Val for short."

"It's none of my business, but why do you change names so often?"

"My real name drew a little more attention that I could handle, especially the last few years," replied Val. "Besides, I'm on a mission, and it's better that the people I'm after don't know where I am."

"It's not a mission for the Republic," noted Cole. "Not if you aren't interested in turning me in."

"It's for the *Pegasus*."

"The *Pegasus*?"

"My ship!" she said, her face a sudden mask of fury. "I was the greatest pirate on the Frontier until I lost it!"

"Well, I'll be damned!" said Cole with a smile.

"What's so funny?" she demanded.

"I used to read about pirate queens in adventure novels when I was a kid, and I'd see them in the holos, but I never thought I'd run into a real live one. Come to think of it, they all dressed like you."

"Yeah, well I'm a pirate queen without a ship," said Val. "When I get it back, someone besides me is going to rue the day they took it away from me."

"How did it happen?"

"We were attacked by the Hammerhead Shark."

"I beg your pardon?"

"He's an alien," she explained. "He's got scaly skin, and eyes sticking out to the sides like the hammerheads of old Earth's oceans."

"He's a pirate too?"

She nodded. "The worst. I fought like a woman possessed. I must have killed twenty of the bastards, but finally their numbers overwhelmed me. They set me down on Nirvain II and flew off with my ship."

"And your crew?"

"Those that survived had to swear fealty to the Shark," she said bitterly.

"Fascinating story," said Cole. He paused. "It'd make a great holo—but you wouldn't think much of me if I believed it. Why don't you tell me what really happened?"

"I was sleeping off a drunk right here on Basilisk and my fucking crew sold me out!" she bellowed.

"That one I believe."

"I'll kill every last one of the bastards when I catch up with them!"

"I believe that too."

"How about you?" she asked, calming down almost instantly. "What's the most wanted man in the galaxy doing on a grubby little world like this?"

"Making sure I haven't been followed before I rejoin my ship."

"Your ship?" she repeated. "You're not still in the Navy, are you? This hasn't all been some kind of ruse to get you close to the Teronis?"

"No, it's no ruse."

She smiled. "Then you're a pirate too. How else could you feed your crew and power your ship?"

"We're kind of apprentice pirates," he replied. "It's more complicated than it looks."

"I'll bet you were the ones who sacked the *Achilles*!" she said suddenly. "I knew there was a new player in the game, but until twenty seconds ago I didn't know who."

"Yeah, that was us. Getting their treasure was a nice, simple military operation." He grimaced. "Unloading it has proven a little more difficult."

"That's because Windsail was a fool," said Val contemptuously. "If you're going to be a pirate, you'd better learn the trade. You go around murdering Republic miners and trying to make a profit selling hot jewelry and you're begging for trouble."

"So I'm finding out—about the jewelry, anyway," said Cole. "What *does* the competent pirate steal these days?"

"Anything that you can sell directly on the Inner Frontier, without going through a middleman."

"For instance?"

"Grain shipments. Shipments of ball bearings and machine tools. Things that colony worlds need, things like frozen livestock embryos. When you think about it, who really needs a diamond necklace?"

"Makes sense," he admitted. "I guess I watched too many pirate shows when I was a kid." A sudden smile. "I've been a victim of false doctrine."

"You should have just asked someone on your crew."

"Except for a teenaged kid who doesn't really know the score, my crew came with me from the Republic," answered Cole. "We haven't had time to recruit anyone out here. In fact, except for the crew of the *Achilles*, all of whom wanted to kill us, I haven't met any pirates." He paused and stared at her. "Until now."

"Why are you looking at me like that?" she asked suspiciously.

"I'm about to make you a proposition."

"Sexual or business?"

"Business."

"All right, I'm listening."

"You need a ship. I need an education. Why don't you join the crew of the *Theodore Roosevelt* until we find out where the Shark has taken your ship? Once we hunt it down, we'll help you get it back in exchange for half of any loot he's stolen since taking it over. Anything that was in the ship before that is yours."

"Some pirate!" she snorted. "How will you know I'm not lying to you? Maybe I'll claim some stuff that the Shark stole."

"How do you know I'll let you take a damned thing?" countered Cole.

Val studied him for a moment, then laughed. "Cole, only an honest man would make such a dumb statement to me and expect to live. You've got yourself a deal!" She reached out and shook his hand vigorously. "When do we leave for your ship?"

"In another day or two, just to make sure no one is following me," he said. "I had to leave McAllister in a hurry."

She laughed. "Well, you wanted to be a pirate."

"No," he answered seriously. "I *didn't* want to be a pirate. It was forced on me—but as long as that seems to be my fate, I might as well try to be a competent one."

"I think I'm going to enjoy serving with you," she said. "Let's drink to it."

"You know the stock, you do the ordering."

She leaned forward and spoke into the table's communication port. "Two Cygnian cognacs. From the Northern Hemisphere. No later than 1940 G.E. Got it?"

"Understood," replied the computer.

"Make it fast," she added. "We're thirsty."

"If you're thirsty, drink water," said Cole. "For what this stuff costs, sip it slowly."

She was about to reply when two men, one burly, one tall and lean, approached the table.

"Go away," said Val.

"We want to talk to your friend, Dominick."

"Beat it," she said. "We gave at the office. And my name's Val."

"How the hell can anyone keep up with your names?" complained the tall man. "We just want to have a little chat with Mr. Cole here."

"Go away," said Val. "You're not even bounty hunters. You're just scum that thinks you can get drinking money by blackmailing this man."

"We plan on getting a little more than just drinking money," replied the tall man.

"You've got the wrong man," said Cole. "I don't know anyone called Cole."

"Our price for agreeing with you just went up," said the burly man.

"And your life expectancy just went down!" snapped Val. Suddenly she stood up between them. What happened next was a display of strength and skill the likes of which Cole had never seen in all his years in the service. Within seconds both men were on the floor, bleeding profusely and moaning in pain. Three of their friends charged the Valkyrie, who handled them as if they were awkward children rather than large, hardened men. Two went down in the first half minute. Then she grabbed the third before he could retreat, lifted him above her head, spun around a few times, and tossed him through the air. He landed with a bone-crunching *thud!* on an empty table, which broke beneath him. He fell to the ground, and lay motionless.

Cole got up, stepped over the five unconscious men, and headed to the door.

"Let's go," he said.

"Where?" asked Val.

"My ship."

"I thought you were waiting to make sure no one was following you."

"If I wait until those guys wake up, they won't have to follow me," said Cole. "They'll take one look and know exactly where I am."

"What about our drinks?" demanded Val.

"I'll buy you one on the next world we come to. Let's just get the hell out of here!"

"I can make sure they never get up," said Val. "No one will miss them."

"Save it for the Shark," said Cole. "We don't need twenty of their friends coming after us."

"They don't have any friends."

"Are you coming or not?" demanded Cole.

She shrugged. "What the hell. They're your problem anyway, not mine."

They walked the mile to Cole's ship, and he found that he had to work hard to keep up with her long strides. Once they'd taken off, he contacted the *Teddy R* to ascertain its position.

It was red shift and Forrice was in command. The Molarian looked at the image before him and said, "Who's that with you? A new girl-friend?"

"Four Eyes, say hello to the new Third Officer of the *Teddy R.*"

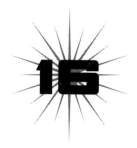

Cole sat in his cramped office aboard the *Teddy R*, facing Forrice, Christine Mboya, and Sharon Blacksmith.

"You're the Captain," Forrice was saying. "You can promote or demote anyone as the mood takes you, but we've got a lot of people who've risked their lives for you, who can never go back to their families, and they're going to resent making an outsider our Third Officer."

"She knows more about piracy than the rest of the crew put together," said Cole. "And she saved my life."

"Maybe it's slipped your memory," said the Molarian, "but there isn't a person aboard this ship who *hasn't* saved your life—or do you think you just walked out of the brig on Timos III on your own?"

"I know how I got out," said Cole. He paused and stared at Forrice. "Do you remember a month ago I told you that Slick was the most valuable member of the *Teddy R* because his symbiote enables him to function without air or physical protection in the cold of space, and on chlorine and methane worlds, for hours at a time?"

"Yes."

"Well, he's now the second-most-valuable member. This woman knows every friendly planet, every rival pirate, every place to unload the kind of cargo we're going to be stealing. She's a walking encyclopedia of piracy—and if that's not enough, she's commanded her own ship."

"And lost it," noted Sharon.

"I didn't say she was perfect," replied Cole. "I said she was valuable. She's got another virtue, too."

"What is it?" asked the Molarian.

"She can beat the shit out of you and any five crew members you pick to fight on your side."

"Just a minute," interjected Christine. "Before we go into raptures about her, let me make sure I understand the situation. She's not with us permanently. She's just here until we hunt down her ship and take it away from this Hammerhead Shark and his crew."

"Which also happens to be *her* crew," added Sharon.

"That's right."

"And then she leaves us and goes back to her own ship?" continued Christine.

"After we split up the Shark's loot," said Cole.

"What's to stop her from screwing up all our instruments and then turning her weapons on us?"

"I trust her not to."

"I don't mind you putting *your* life in her hands," said Forrice. "But I object to you doing the same with mine and the rest of the crew's."

"I appreciate your objections," said Cole. "But I've explained my reasons. She's our Third Officer. I'll stay in charge of blue shift until we finish debriefing her, but then I'm going to turn it over to her."

"And what will you do?" asked Christine.

"What I always do, but this time I won't have to do it in a constricted time frame." He looked from one to another. "Just remember: Every time I've ever taken any action aboard the *Teddy R* it's worked out to our advantage."

"That's why we can never go back to the Republic," said Forrice sardonically.

"That was *your* action," said Cole. "I didn't escape from the brig. I was broken out."

"I still don't like it," said Forrice.

"Neither do I," Sharon chimed in.

"Your objections are noted," said Cole. "And if this ever becomes a democracy, they may even be acted upon. But until that happy day, I'm the Captain and what I say goes." He paused. "Does anyone dispute that?"

Silence.

"All right. If I can sense all the hostility, I'm sure Val can too. I want someone to try to bond with her, become her friend, put her at her ease."

"I thought that was you," said Sharon bitterly.

"I've got a ship to run. It can't be Forrice or Christine, because they'll be commanding different shifts."

"Don't you look at me that way, Wilson Cole!" snapped Sharon.

"Can't you give it a try?"

"Bond with her?" repeated Sharon. "Hell, when I stand next to her, I'm staring into her navel! How do you bond with a lady Goliath?"

"You're the one who's going to be debriefing her," said Cole. "You'll be in her company a lot for the next few days. Just try to be more pleasant to her than you're being to me right now." He paused. "She's not my lover, and she's not looking to run the Security Department. She's just the possessor of a lot of valuable knowledge, and if we have any luck tracking down the Shark she's not going to be here too long, so I want to make her comfortable and talkative while we have the opportunity."

"Didn't she talk to you on the trip from Basilisk to the ship?" asked Sharon.

"Nonstop," said Cole. "I have improved my knowledge of cognac a thousandfold."

"And I'm supposed to become friends with that?" demanded Sharon.

"Just make an honest effort."

She grimaced. "All right, all right, I'll try."

"I'll try too, when I'm not on duty," said Christine.

Cole looked at Forrice.

"I'm still mad at you for pulling rank," said the Molarian. "I thought you called this meeting to ask for our opinions."

Cole shook his head. "I called this meeting to tell you my decision, not to argue for it."

"Well, I think it's a mistake."

"You're free to think so," said Cole. "In here," he added, as his voice took on a sharper edge. "One step outside that door, all disagreements end."

"I know the routine," replied Forrice sullenly. "But since we're still on this side of the door, I just want to say that I've never seen you this damned arrogant before."

"That's because you've never challenged my judgment before," said Cole. "We went into this pirate business cold. None of us knew anything about it except all the stuff we'd assimilated from bad books and worse holos. We lucked out and figured out how to dispose of the diamonds, but if that sonofabitch on McAllister had been a little more competent, I'd be in a Navy brig right now, strictly because of ignorance. And now we've got a phenomenal source of information on board. She's been a successful pirate for more than a decade. She's never had a ship shot out from under her, never been arrested, always been able to show a profit, stole things that didn't attract the Navy's attention. She knows where to pick up information. She knows the make and model of most of the major pirate ships on the Frontier. She knows the ships' captains and their methodologies. She knows where to hide when things get hot, from rivals as well as from the Navy. If we get into fighting at close quarters on a ship or a planet, she's worth two of Bull Pampas and six of anyone else. She's not military, and she's got more than her share of rough edges, and she sure as hell drinks too much—but we need her. And, just as important, I trust her." He paused and stared at each of the three officers in turn. "And as of now, the subject is closed."

"Hey, Cole!" said Val's voice, and her image appeared an instant later.

"That's not the way we open communications aboard the ship," said Cole. "But let it pass this time. What do you want?"

"I just saw the jewelry you were trying to unload on McAllister."

"And?"

"You're never going to dump it the way it is," she said. "It was famous even before you screwed up on McAllister. By now everyone knows that Wilson Cole is trying to get rid of it."

"You have a suggestion, no doubt?" asked Cole.

"Pull the diamonds and rubies and melt the tiara down. You can sell it as a block of gold."

"To a fence?" asked Sharon.

Val made a face. "I thought you guys learned your lesson with fences. Hell, there are dozens of commodities dealers who don't just buy and sell futures but handle actual gold, including a couple on the Inner Frontier."

"What about the jewels?"

"They're a lot harder to market. By now you know you can't make any money from a fence. I know a jeweler who'll take the rubies— they're harder to identify than the diamonds, because they haven't been laser marked, or at least these rubies haven't—but you'd be better off using them."

"Using them?" repeated Cole.

"As bribes. A diamond or a ruby in the right hand can buy some useful information—and the people you bribe can unload one stone a lot easier than you can unload a batch of them."

"Sounds good to me," said Cole. "Was there anything else?"

"Yeah," said Val. "Where do you keep your drinkin' stuff? You still owe me a Cygnian cognac."

"I don't think we have any on board," said Cole.

"Would you settle for an Alphard brandy?" asked Sharon.

"Sure as hell would!" said Val enthusiastically. "My room or yours—or maybe the mess hall?"

"Why don't we meet in the Security Department in ten minutes?" said Sharon. "We can start debriefing you in comfort."

"I'll be there," said Val, breaking the connection.

Sharon looked uneasy. "Well, you said to bond with her."

"She can probably drink you under the table," said Cole, "so let her do the drinking, and you do the questioning."

"You know," said Sharon as the door sensed her approach and irised to let her pass through, "she did make some sense, didn't she?"

"Why is she here?" asked Rachel Marcos, trying to hide her resentment.

"She's a pirate," replied Vladimir Sokolov. "The Captain thinks we can learn about piracy from her."

They were on the bridge with Forrice during red shift, waiting for Cole to choose their next destination.

"How good a pirate can she be?" persisted Rachel. "She lost her ship."

"How good an officer can the Captain be?" answered Sokolov, who was manning his computer station. "He was demoted twice and court-martialed once."

"You know why that happened," said Rachel.

"Yes, I do," answered Sokolov. "And until I know why the Valkyrie lost her ship, I'm inclined to rely on the Captain's judgment."

"I'm not the only one who has questions about her," said Rachel defensively.

"If you have questions, why not walk up to her and ask her?" suggested Sokolov.

"Have you *seen* her?" demanded Rachel. "She's not only a giant; she's a walking weapon shop!"

"I think she's sexy as hell," said Sokolov.

"You would," she said distastefully.

"That's enough," interjected Forrice. "Like it or not, she's our Third Officer."

"What do *you* think of it?" asked Rachel. "Why does she deserve it, instead of Lieutenant Briggs or Lieutenant Sokolov?"

"My opinion doesn't matter," said the Molarian. "The Captain has made his decision, and we can either accept it or leave the ship."

"Well, she may be the Third Officer, but except for the Captain she hasn't got a friend on the whole ship."

The exercise room was actually just an empty cabin that served as a bedroom for two alien crew members when the ship carried a full contingent. It was ten feet by twelve feet, and because it was created for races that were taller than Man, the ceiling was ten feet high, rather than the usual seven.

There wasn't much exercising possible in the cramped quarters, but Bull Pampas had appropriated some weights and barbells, and underwent a daily regimen of lifting.

It was during her third day on the ship, after she'd been thoroughly debriefed, that Val made her way down to the room toward the end of red shift. Bull had been there just long enough to work up a sweat. "What can I do for you, ma'am?" he asked when she entered. "Or is it sir?"

"Whatever makes you happy," answered Val. "I heard there were weights down here, and I thought I'd put in a little work."

"I'll get out of your way and come back when you're done, ma'am," said Pampas. He knelt down and began taking some of the weights off the bar.

"What are you doing?" asked Val.

"I'm a pretty experienced lifter," he said. "I'm making it a little lighter for you."

"I'm a pretty experienced lifter myself," she said. "Let me take a shot at what you've got right there."

"I don't want you to hurt yourself, ma'am," said Pampas.

"I hurt other people, not myself," she said, standing before the bar. She squatted down, put her hands on it, took a deep breath, and straightened up, lifting it above her head. "It's not that heavy," she said with a smile. "You got any more weights we can put on it?"

"How the hell did you do that, ma'am?" said Pampas admiringly. "I'm pretty strong and pretty experienced, but I worked like hell to clean and jerk that, and you lifted it like it was nothing."

"Maybe I can teach you a trick or two about lifting," she suggested.

"I'd sure be grateful, ma'am." He paused. "I hear that you're pretty good at taking care of yourself in a fight, too."

"I do okay."

"I'd be happy to work out with you," said Pampas, "though this room is awfully small."

"I'd like very much to work out with you, Mister . . . ?"

"Pampas, ma'am," he said. "Eric Pampas. But everyone calls me Bull."

"All right, Bull," she said. "And if you have any friends on the crew who want to keep in shape and maybe learn something about self-defense, invite them too."

"I sure will, ma'am."

"Call me Val."

Sokolov and Briggs were in the mess hall, each sipping a beer. The rest of the room was empty. Then Val entered, walked to a table, and seated herself. A menu immediately hovered in front of her, a few inches above the table.

"Give me a Blue Comet," she said.

"That is unknown to me," responded a mechanical voice. "Is this a human food?"

"It's a human drink."

"I do not find it in my data banks."

"Then pay attention," said Val. "Take two ounces of Antarean whiskey, one ounce of Nebodian liquor, one ounce of any citrus juice—and no soya substitutions. Add a pinch of bitters, and mix in one raw egg."

"I have no raw eggs."

"All right," she said. "An ounce of heavy cream."

"I have no heavy cream."

"Have you got any ice cream?"

"I have no ice cream."

"Some galley!" she snorted. "How about yogurt?"

"I have Delphinian yogurt."

"Okay, add an ounce of any fruit-flavored yogurt. Shake it for thirty seconds, put in a couple of ice cubes, and serve it."

"Working . . ."

"Excuse me," said Sokolov, "but we couldn't help overhearing. I've never come across a Blue Comet before."

"It was created on the Inner Frontier," answered Val.

"It sounds awful," said Briggs. "Like you're mixing too many things together."

"Computer," said Val, "make three Blue Comets."

"Working . . ."

"The only way to make up your mind is to try one," she said.

"That seems fair," agreed Briggs. "And when we're done, I'll have the galley make up some Denebian Slime Devils."

"I've had them," said Val without much enthusiasm.

"But not with Gray Vodka from Hesporite III."

"No," she admitted. "I've never had real Gray Vodka, just the stuff they make on Keepsake. Sounds interesting."

"Not as interesting as an Eridani Elephant," said Sokolov.

"An Eridani Elephant?" she repeated.

He began describing it as their Blue Comets arrived. "Ah, hell," he said. "It'll be easier to show you."

She took a swallow of her drink. "It's all right," she said, "but it really needs a raw egg."

"Does it have to be the egg of an avian?" asked Sokolov.

"I don't know," she admitted. "I never thought about it. Why?"

"Because we're as likely to touch down on a world where they sell reptile eggs, or something-else eggs, as avian eggs."

"Drink up, first," she said. "You may decide it's not worth the effort."

The two men downed their drinks.

"That's powerful stuff, ma'am," said Sokolov.

"But good," added Briggs.

"Still, it seems to be missing a little something," said Sokolov. "I think we'll definitely remember to pick up some eggs next chance we get."

The Denebian Slime Devils appeared a minute later, and the Eridani Elephants showed up just about the time they'd finished the Slime Devils.

"I'm sure glad you came aboard, ma'am," said Sokolov. "I can see where my free time is going to be a lot more interesting."

"And educational," slurred Briggs.

Twenty minutes later the two men declared eternal friendship with their new Third Officer. And five minutes after that, she stood up and left them snoring peacefully at their table.

"*Calioparie*," said Braxite.

"*Toprench*," said Domak.

"I'm telling you, *calioparie* is the most difficult and complicated game in the galaxy," said Braxite.

"Nonsense," replied Domak. "It's *Toprench*."

"You're both wrong," said Idena Mueller. "It's chess—the only game where the loser has no excuses."

"You've been in the Republic too long," said Val, who'd been listening from across the room.

"Oh?" said Idena. "And what does the pirate queen think it is?"

"You say that like an insult," replied Val. "I consider it a compliment. You ought to try being a pirate queen sometime. It's harder than it looks. And so is *bilsang*."

"What's *bilsang*?"

"A game that makes chess and *Toprench* look like kid's games," answered Val. "I've seen the ownership of whole planets change hands over a game of *bilsang*."

"What makes it so hard?" asked Braxite.

"Its simplicity," answered Val.

"That doesn't make any sense."

"That's because you don't know anything about it," said Val.

"Too bad you can't show us," said Domak sarcastically. "Now we'll never know if you were right."

"What makes you think I can't show you?"

"We don't have any *bilsang* games aboard the *Teddy R*," said Idena.

"It doesn't need a board, or cards, or a computer," answered Val. "Anyone can play it." She paused. "But not anyone can win it."

"How long does it take to play a game?" asked Domak.

"Anywhere from five minutes to three months."

"And you don't need anything special?"

"Just a brain," said Val. "You want me to teach you the basics?"

"How long will this take?" asked Idena. "I'm on duty in another half hour."

"Five minutes for the rules, a lifetime for the subtleties."

"What the hell, why not?" said Idena. "What do we need?"

"A flat surface, and twenty pieces. Coins will do. Or medals. Or anything that you can fit twenty of on a tabletop."

"All right," said Idena, reaching into her pocket. "I've got about ten coins."

"I'll contribute the rest," said Val. "Who knows? Maybe one of you will become good enough to challenge me."

The coins were placed on the table.

"What do we do now?" asked Domak.

Val explained the rules, and a few of the subtleties. Then Idena had to leave, but Braxite and Domak decided to play a game. They were still playing it, oblivious of all else, when Idena returned five hours later.

Within a week the whole ship was enmeshed in a *bilsang* tournament.

In two weeks she'd won over every member of the crew except Forrice and Rachel. When Rachel was finally convinced that the Valkyrie had no romantic interest in Cole, nor he in her, she relented and accepted her as a member of the crew.

Forrice was a harder case, but his opposition to her shattered one day when he and Val found themselves in the tiny officers' lounge during white shift. Nobody knows quite how it started, but when Cole entered the lounge he found them telling each other dirty Molarian jokes and laughing their heads off.

Everyone sympathized with her quest for her ship and her revenge against the Hammerhead Shark, but the general consensus was that it would be a shame if the *Teddy R* actually managed to find the *Pegasus*.

It was two Standard weeks to the day after the Valkyrie had joined the crew that the first word of the *Pegasus* reached the *Teddy R.*

It was during white shift, and Christine Mboya immediately summoned Cole and Val to the bridge, where Briggs and Jack-in-the-Box were manning the computer consoles.

"Sir," she said when Cole was standing before her, "I've just intercepted a call for help from Cyrano."

"What and where is Cyrano?" he asked. "And why did you summon Val?"

"Cyrano's a planet about ninety light-years from here, and the distress call mentioned the *Pegasus*."

"That bastard is endangering my ship!" Val bellowed furiously.

"What are you talking about?" asked Cole.

"Cyrano is Donovan Muscatel's headquarters," said Val. "He and the Shark are rivals, so the Shark decided to approach him in a ship he didn't recognize and then opened fire."

"So you figure it's over already?"

"I'm not saying Donovan is dead," answered Val. "I'm just saying that the *Pegasus* has blown his base to hell by now."

"Then why *isn't* he dead?"

"He's got four ships. They're never all in port at the same time, so there's a chance that he wasn't on Cyrano during the attack. But I guarantee by the time we get there all we're going to find is a hole in the ground."

"Pilot, take us there anyway, top speed," ordered Cole. Christine looked at him questioningly. "We've got to start somewhere," he explained. "If there are any survivors, they might be able to tell us where Muscatel's other ships are." He turned to Val. "The Shark would go after the other ships once he took care of the base, wouldn't he?"

"Once he starts, he can't allow any survivors or he'll be looking over his shoulder the rest of his life." Suddenly she slammed a fist against a bulkhead. "Damn his eyes!"

"What is it?"

"Donovan's got friends, and now they're all going to be after my ship!"

"Isn't that what *we're* doing?" asked Christine, looking confused.

"Yes," replied Cole. "But our purpose is to capture it and turn it over to Val after we appropriate some of its treasure for our trouble. You have to figure any friends of Muscatel are going to be out to destroy it and everyone who's in it."

"God have mercy on anyone who destroys the *Pegasus*," growled Val angrily, "because they're sure as hell not going to get any from me!"

"Save the threats for later," said Cole. "We've got other things to consider first. For example, if we approach the *Pegasus*, will the Shark talk first or shoot first?"

"Shoot."

"Even though he doesn't know you're aboard?"

"The Shark doesn't talk," said Val. "Ever. If you're approaching him, he'll assume you have a reason, and whatever the reason is, it's not going to be good news for the *Pegasus*. He'll shoot."

"The *Pegasus* is your ship," said Cole. "I want you to go down to Security and tell Sharon Blacksmith everything you know about it— its size, its weaponry, its defenses, its top speed, its weaknesses."

"I already did."

"Do it again."

"It's a waste of time."

"Perhaps, but there may be some little thing you missed the first time around. Sharon's monitoring this, so she'll be expecting you."

"No," said Val. "I told her everything I know about it."

"I'm getting tired of people questioning my judgment," said Cole. "I gave you an order. Disobey it and our pursuit of the *Pegasus* stops right now and I put you off on the first oxygen world we come to, inhabited or not."

She stared at him expressionlessly for a long moment. "This is your ship, so I'll do what you want," she said at last. "But don't you ever speak to me in that tone of voice on *my* ship."

She turned and walked to the airlift.

"You know," said Briggs, who was manning the sensors, "for just a minute there I thought she was going to take a swing at you."

"She could probably mop up the floor with me," acknowledged Cole. "But she wants her ship more than she wants anything else, so she'll do whatever's necessary to get it back. And if Sharon can get something useful out of her, maybe we can settle for disabling the *Pegasus* rather than destroying it."

Christine had been studying the various screens as they spoke. "She was right, sir," she announced. "The *Pegasus* has left the Cyrano system."

"Any idea where it's heading?"

She shook her head. "No, sir. Cyrano's not a planet with sophisticated technology, sir. Tracking a ship that's moving at light speeds through a Grade Three wormhole is beyond their ability."

"All right," said Cole. "I suppose we'll need a landing party to interview any survivors or eyewitnesses."

"I'd like to volunteer, sir," said Briggs.

"Fine. Report to the *Kermit* when we hit the outer reaches of the system."

"I'd like to volunteer too," offered Jack-in-the-Box.

"I appreciate it," answered Cole, "but we'll only need a landing party of three."

"You only have one so far, sir," said Jack-in-the-Box.

"Val's got to be in the party," replied Cole. "She'll know what questions to ask."

"That's still only two, sir."

"I'm the third."

"I thought the Captain wasn't supposed to leave the ship in dangerous territory," noted Jack-in-the-Box.

"He's not," said Cole. "And if you can find anyone else she'll obey when things start getting hairy, I'll be happy to stay on board."

Jack-in-the-Box had no answer to that, and he fell silent.

"Pilot, what's our ETA?" asked Cole.

"If the Boratina Wormhole hasn't moved, we'll enter the Cyrano system in eighty-seven Standard minutes," answered Wxakgini.

"And if it has?"

"Then we won't enter the Cyrano system in eighty-seven Standard minutes."

"Thanks for that enlightening answer," said Cole dryly. "Christine, select a replacement for Mr. Briggs. Briggs, go down to the armory and draw a burner, a screecher, and a suit of body armor."

"I hate that stuff," complained Briggs.

"Yeah, well I hate losing officers," responded Cole. "The whole suit doesn't weigh five pounds. I want you wearing it before we get into the shuttle."

"It makes me sweat."

"Just keep telling yourself: corpses don't sweat."

"Yes, sir," said Briggs dejectedly. Then: "Is the Valkyrie going to wear body armor?"

"The Valkyrie can take care of herself better than anyone I've ever met," said Cole. "She can wear what she wants." Briggs opened his mouth to protest, and Cole held up a hand. "And before you complain, the day you can beat her in a fair fight, or even an unfair one, you can wear what *you* want. In the meantime, get into the body armor and stop bitching about it."

"Yes, sir," said Briggs.

"Well?" demanded Cole when Briggs remained where he was.

"I was waiting for my replacement."

"Okay, you get to keep out of the armor for another five minutes," said Cole. "But when he shows up, you go to the armory."

"Yes, sir."

When they were ten minutes from the Cyrano system, Cole contacted Val and told her to join him and Briggs at the shuttle as soon as they braked to sublight speeds. No one could tell whether the ship was going faster or slower than light without reference to a computer that was monitoring the speed, but everyone could always tell when the ship crossed the light barrier in either direction. There was an instant of disorientation that couldn't be ignored or mistaken for anything else.

They left in the *Kermit* a few minutes later, and soon entered Cyrano's atmosphere—and within seconds they were confronted by half a dozen two-man fighter ships.

"What should I do, sir?" asked Briggs, who was at the controls.

"They're just making sure we're not here to blow up something else," said Cole. "You've got your false ID and the false registry for the *Teddy R* and the shuttle. Just answer all their questions. We're here to do business with Muscatel. If they tell you that his base has been demolished, just say that he was holding some goods for us and we want to land and see what became of them."

"They had to know he was a pirate," said Briggs.

"This planet was his headquarters for years," said Val. "That means he paid a lot of people off—and *that* means they'll be looking for someone to replace that money. For all they know, it could be us."

Then the radio came to life, and Briggs spent the next few minutes answering precisely those questions Cole had predicted they would ask. Finally the *Kermit* was cleared to land, and it touched down at a small commercial spaceport about six miles from the remains of Muscatel's warehouse.

"God!" muttered Briggs as they emerged from the shuttle. "I can smell the fumes from here. What the hell did the *Pegasus* do—spray the place with toxic chemicals?"

"Not directly," answered Val. "But Donovan kept a lot of stuff in that warehouse. Doubtless some of it reacted badly to my ship's pulse canons."

They rented an aircar at the small spaceport, and took it to the hole in the ground that used to be Donovan Muscatel's headquarters.

"I told you there wouldn't be anything left of it," said Val, looking at the smoldering remains of the building in the bottom of the newly made basin.

"Would his ships be at the spaceport?" asked Cole. "The ones that aren't off being pirates, I mean."

She shook her head. "He'd never have trusted the port authorities to keep them safe. If they weren't in orbit—"

"They weren't."

"—then they'd have been moored to the buildings here."

"That's too bad."

"Why do you care?"

"Because if we could have found an intact ship, we'd probably have been able to find the communication codes to the other ships and would have been able to find out where they were, and if Muscatel was alive or dead."

"We don't care about him," said Val. "We're after the Hammerhead Shark and my ship."

"So, in all likelihood, are they," said Cole, "and they may have some knowledge concerning where he is."

"If we spread enough money around, we'll find him," Val assured him.

"You're missing the point," said Cole.

"What point?" she demanded.

"Oh, we'll find the *Pegasus* sooner or later, I have no doubt of it," said Cole. He stared at her. "But what if Muscatel's ships find it first?"

"You've got it backwards," said Val. "I told you: The Shark will be after *them*."

"The *Teddy R* is a Republic warship," said Cole. "Lord knows it's not the newest or the best, but it was created to fight in wars. If the *Pegasus* isn't a warship, and if it is you've never mentioned the fact, then whatever you think about the Shark, he's not likely to engage two or three ships at once. Even if he's the most vindictive bastard in the galaxy, he's more likely to choose his spots and pick them off one by one."

"You don't know the first thing about him," protested Val.

"I don't know the *second* thing about him," answered Cole. "The first thing is that he's survived in this business long enough to get a reputation. That implies that he's not suicidal." He paused. "Look, either way we're more likely to find him if we know where Muscatel's ships are. Whether they're chasing him or being stalked by him, sooner or later if we keep an eye on them we're going to find the *Pegasus*."

"Okay, it makes sense," she admitted grudgingly. "Let's get their registration numbers from the port. No sense asking for flight plans; whether they're the pursuers or the pursued, they're not going to stick to any plans."

"The spaceport isn't going to turn the names over to you just because you ask," said Cole.

"I'm not going to ask," she said, placing her gloved hands on the handles of her weapons. "I'm going to demand."

"There are easier ways."

"Oh? Like what?"

"Like I took your advice and removed the stones from the tiara. A couple, placed in the proper hands, will get us what we want just as easily, and we won't be reported to the closest hundred bounty hunters."

She shrugged. "If your way works, fine. If not, we've still got my way. Let's go."

"Not so fast," said Cole.

"Why not?" she asked. "There's nothing to see here."

"We knew it was a hole in the ground before we left the ship. I came down to find some witnesses."

"What can they tell you?"

"If I knew, I wouldn't need to find them, would I?" replied Cole.

"Fine. Where do we find them?"

"We check the police and the hospitals," said Cole. "We're here on legitimate business, remember? Well, legitimate business as far as the authorities of Cyrano are concerned, anyway. We had millions of credits of goods stashed here, goods that we'd paid for and were about to pick up. We have every reason to want to know what happened, who was responsible for it, how many of Muscatel's ships were destroyed and how many survived. You've been thinking like a pirate for too long; we don't have anything to hide."

She stared at him for a long moment. "And the Navy took your ship away?"

"Two of them," said Cole. "Well, three actually, but I got the *Teddy R* back."

"No wonder we're losing the damned war."

"We're not losing it," he said. "Correction: *They're* not losing it. They're just not winning it."

"If they treat all their competent officers the way they treated you, I can understand why."

"Sir?" said Briggs, who had been wandering around the site. "I can't be sure without further data, but I'd be willing to bet that there was only one ship moored here."

"How can you tell?" asked Cole, looking into the crater.

"Not enough radiation for two nuclear piles," said Briggs, holding up a small sensing device. "They're treated to go inert if anything damages them, but even so some trace radiation always escapes."

"But not enough for two ships?"

"I don't think so, sir."

"Well, that's that," said Cole. "I think we can assume that Muscatel's still got three ships." He turned to Val. "I want the truth, now. Can the *Pegasus* outgun three ships at once? And don't tell me it depends on the ships. You know what kind Muscatel has, and I don't."

"No, probably not," she admitted.

"Then it makes more sense that they're pursuing him."

"In a rational universe that makes sense," she said. "But you don't know the Shark."

"I know he's lived this long. That implies at least a certain cunning and a strong sense of self-preservation, if not intelligence."

"Sir," put in Briggs, "it doesn't really matter if they're chasing him or he's chasing them. Sooner or later they're going to meet. Why don't we just sit back and let them destroy each other?"

"You're talking about my ship!" bellowed Val.

"That's one reason," said Cole with a wry smile. "Seriously, we do have an agreement. Also, there's plunder to divide—but only if the *Pegasus* remains in one piece."

"It was just a thought, sir," said Briggs uncomfortably.

"And a good one," said Cole. "It would be practical in ninety-nine out of a hundred situations." Pause. "Welcome to the hundredth." He took one last look at the wreckage. "Well, let's get over to the hospital we passed on the way in. If there are any survivors, or if anyone was close enough to be an eyewitness, that's where we're likely to find them."

They went back to the aircar and skimmed along, some eight inches above the ground, until they came to the hospital. They floated into an underground lot, moored the vehicle, then took an airlift to the registration desk.

"Good afternoon," said Cole to the portly human receptionist.

"Good afternoon," she answered. "How may I help you?"

"I understand you've got some patients who were involved in the tragic attack on Mr. Muscatel's headquarters."

"Wasn't it terrible?" she said. "I don't believe we've ever experienced anything quite like it. I mean, military attacks are what everyone comes to the Frontier to avoid."

"*Was* it a military attack?" asked Cole. "I was told it was a dispute between pirates."

"What's the difference? It was a ship, and it fired on our planet."

"I defer to your judgment," said Cole. "Have you any patients who were involved?"

"Certainly. What names are you looking for?"

"I don't know," said Cole. "I did business with the company, not with any particular person other than Donovan Muscatel himself. Is he here?"

"No, I'd know if he was," she said. "I hope he'd not dead. He donated the east wing of the hospital, you know."

"I hope so too," said Cole. "How many men and women survived the attack?"

"It was more than men and women," said the receptionist. "There was a Pepon as well."

"A Pepon?"

"From Peponi. Well, that's what they call themselves, anyway. I'm sure there's an official name and probably a medical name as well."

"Who else?"

"Two men. There's a woman in surgery, but she's not expected to survive." She glanced at a hidden screen. "Yes, we just lost her about three minutes ago."

"How about any eyewitnesses to the attack?"

"Are you a businessman or a reporter?" she asked suspiciously.

"A businessman. May I speak to the survivors?"

"Let me check." She studied another hidden screen. "All right. They're not tranquilized, and in fact they'll be released before nightfall. They're just here for observation."

"The Pepon too?"

She glanced down again. "Yes."

"Where can I find them?"

"I'll have an orderly escort you there."

"I'd like my friends to come along," he said, gesturing to Val and Briggs.

"Only two visitors are allowed at one time," she replied. "Hospital rules."

"All right," said Cole. He put an arm around Briggs's shoulders and walked him toward an exit, speaking only when they were too far away for the receptionist to overhear. "It's probably a dead end, but hunt up the jail and see if they've got any survivors or eyewitnesses, then report back here."

"Why would they be in jail?" asked Briggs.

"Maybe they were eyewitnesses who were caught looting," answered Cole. "Maybe they were employees with prices on their heads, and their protector is dead or gone. You want a catalogue of all the possible reasons?"

"No, sir. I'll be back as soon as I can."

Briggs left, and Cole returned to the desk. "We're ready," he announced.

A robot rolled up to him. "Follow me, please," it grated in a scratchy metallic voice.

Cole and Val fell into step as it swiveled and rolled to an airlift. They emerged on the fourth floor and followed the mechanical orderly down a corridor until it stopped by an open door. "Humans Nichols and Moyer are in this room. Pepon Bujandi is four rooms farther down. I will post myself by the door to his room."

Cole and Val entered the room. Two men, neither wearing hospital gowns, were sitting on a pair of floating beds, staring at them curiously.

"Which one of you is Nichols and which is Moyer?" asked Cole.

"I'm Jim Nichols," said the smaller of them. "He's Dan Moyer. Who wants to know?"

"I want to know," said Cole. "You work for Donavan Muscatel, don't you?"

"We've got nothing to hide," said Moyer. "Yeah, we work for him."

"How come you're still alive?"

They exchanged looks. "We were returning from town with some supplies when they hit the warehouse. The force of the pulse explosions knocked us off the road and shook us up a little, but we're getting out of here in another hour or two."

"Were the two of you alone in the vehicle?"

"You know we weren't," said Nichols.

"How many were with you?"

"Just the Pepon."

"I'm told a woman from your group just died in surgery."

"That was Wanda," said Nichols. "Obviously she wasn't in the building when they hit it. I don't know what she was doing. They told us they brought her in pretty banged up. That's all we know about it."

"One last question," said Cole. "Is Muscatel alive?"

"No more answers until you tell us who the hell you are and why you're asking all these questions," said Moyer.

Suddenly they were looking down the barrels of Val's burner and screecher. "You can tell us or you can die," she said coldly.

"Put the guns away," said Cole.

She glared at him and didn't move.

"These men aren't our enemies, and they're not likely to answer our questions if you kill them."

"I know you," said Moyer as Val reluctantly holstered her weapons. "At least I've heard of you. Bigger than any man, armed to the teeth, drop-dead gorgeous, red hair—you've got to be her! You've got no name, or a hundred names, no one's sure which, but you're the captain of the *Pegasus*. You've got a reputation from here to the Rim. What the hell are you doing on a little dirtball like Cyrano?"

"Waiting for you to answer the question," said Val coldly. "Is Donovan alive?"

"Yes," replied Moyer. "He's out in the Delphini system somewhere."

"He's not coming back," said Cole.

"How do you know?" demanded Nichols.

"He's got nothing to come back to. That means you're stranded here."

"We'll latch on somewhere else," said Moyer.

"Right," said Nichols. "We've got a score to settle. We lost a lot of friends today."

"Maybe we can help you settle your score," said Cole.

They exchanged looks again. "You talk, we'll listen," said Nichols at last.

"Your warehouse was blown apart by the *Pegasus*."

Moyer frowned. "I thought the *Pegasus* was *her* ship."

"It was, until the Hammerhead Shark stole it from me," said Val.

"The Shark?" repeated Moyer. "I thought he was in the Spiral Arm."

"Not for the last two years," said Val.

"He's the one who attacked you today," added Cole, "and there's every chance that he'll be going after Muscatel and the rest of your organization."

"You said you can help nail the bastard. How?"

"I've got a ship, and we're running with a skeleton crew. Whether you sign on or not, my ship is going after the Shark—but we can use all the crew we can get. If you do sign on, you'll each receive one percent of whatever we take, but I want you to know up front you'll be on a military ship, and military discipline will be demanded of you. That's my offer. Take it or leave it."

"There aren't a lot of military ships out here on the Frontier," said Moyer. "Offhand I can only think of one." Suddenly he grinned. "You bet your ass I'll take it!"

Nichols frowned. "Are you who I think you are?"

"I have no idea who you think I am," said Cole. "Are you in or out?"

"In," said Nichols. "What about Bujandi?"

"I'm going to walk down the hall and make him the same offer."

"When do we leave?"

"One of my officers is at the jail right now. As soon as he comes back we're out of here."

"Once we're on your ship we'll be able to help you contact Donovan," said Moyer.

"I never doubted it," said Cole.

A few minutes later Bujandi agreed to join the crew. Then Briggs returned, and the landing party, with three new crew members, took off for the *Teddy R*.

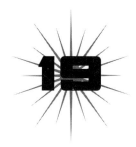

While the three new crew members were being processed, Cole went up to the bridge to see if they'd had any luck tracing the *Pegasus*.

"Captain on the bridge!" announced a young man, snapping to attention and saluting.

"Well, I'll be damned," said Cole. "When did you get back?"

"A few hours ago, sir," said Luthor Chadwick.

"And you're feeling okay?"

"Yes, sir. They gave me two new eardrums, and fixed some laser burns on my rib cage while they were at it."

"Well, we're all glad to have you back. Has anyone filled you in on what's happened since you've been hospitalized?"

"Commander Forrice did, sir."

"I wish I had something positive to add," said Cole. "Carry on, and if you feel you need some bed rest, just tell whoever's in charge of the shift and we'll get you replaced."

"Thank you, sir, but I feel fine," insisted Chadwick. "Really I do."

"Okay. Have you met Crewman Esteban Morales yet?"

"No, sir. I'm not acquainted with the name."

"He choose to join us after we took the *Achilles*."

"Is there some reason why you asked me that, sir?" asked Chadwick.

"Only you and he would know for sure," said Cole, "but there's a possibility that he's the guy who caught you with the screecher. What's your reaction to that?"

"We were on opposite sides then. If we're on the same side now, it's forgotten, sir. And I assume he'll forget that I killed two of his shipmates."

"He assures me that he carries no grudge, that he understands that the situation has changed."

"Then there will be no problem, sir."

"Good. I just wanted to make certain." Cole looked around the bridge, couldn't see any need to remain there, and headed for the mess hall. He wasn't hungry, but he didn't want to go to his room, and the cramped interior of the *Teddy R* didn't offer him that many choices.

When he arrived, he sat down and was joined a moment later by Sharon Blacksmith.

"Welcome back," she said. "You made some interesting new friends."

"What is that supposed to mean?" asked Cole.

"Just that I've been doing my job, part of which is finding out exactly what you've saddled us with," replied Sharon. "Daniel Moyer arrived on the Inner Frontier eleven years ago, just ahead of the Republic's police. There are two outstanding warrants for murder against him, dating back twelve and fourteen years. Do you want to know *who* he murdered?"

"Not unless it was a starship captain."

"James Nichols is even more interesting," she continued. "He was a bounty hunter. He had to find a new profession when the Republic found that they'd paid him for five ringers, innocent men he'd passed off as wanted killers."

"They're pirates," said Cole. "And we're not heading toward any church socials."

"Damn it, Wilson! They're just this side of being psychopaths. We may have chosen to be pirates, but we're a military ship with military discipline. They could be incredibly disruptive, and that's even without the likelihood of their killing someone."

"Have either of them served in the Navy?"

"They came from the Republic," answered Sharon. "Every able-bodied man and woman served in the Navy as soon as they reached their majority. These two are no different."

"Were either of them cashiered out?"

"No."

"Then they can accept discipline and exercise self-control," said Cole. "If we find they can't, we'll set them off at the next oxygen world we come to. But they want the Shark badly enough to behave until we catch him."

"At which point everybody's favorite pirate queen will lop their heads off before she'll let anyone else kill the Shark," said Sharon.

"We'll worry about that when we come to it," said Cole. "These guys worked for Muscatel. They know his communication codes. They know his hideouts. They know how his mind works. They could prove very useful to us. Val knows the Shark, but no one except these guys knows Donovan Muscatel." He paused. "You haven't mentioned the Pepon yet."

"You don't want to know."

"No, I really don't," said Cole. "They start today with a clean slate. If they dirty it, they'll suffer the consequences, but a pirate ship operating with half the crew it needs can't be too fussy about who it recruits."

"They're killers, Wilson."

"So is the young man on the bridge, the one with two new eardrums," responded Cole. "So is Forrice. So are half the men and aliens on this ship."

"The men and aliens on this ship killed the enemy during wartime," said Sharon. "This is different."

"It certainly is," said Cole. "They were drafted. These three volunteered."

"But—"

"The subject is closed. When they start misbehaving, it'll be open again."

"Misbehaving is a hell of a euphemism for murder."

"The only person they want to murder is the Hammerhead Shark," said Cole. "Now let it drop."

"You can't just order me to shut up."

"Of course I can. I'm the Captain."

"Well, you're going to be a lonely Captain tonight."

"I read somewhere that loneliness goes with command," replied Cole.

"It goes with insensitivity."

He smiled. "That too."

Suddenly Val's image appeared next to him.

"What's up?" asked Cole.

"I just remembered something," she said. "The *Pegasus* picked up some Meladotian crystals just before the Shark showed up."

"Okay, I give up. What are Meladotian crystals?"

"They a very rare, very delicate crystal that's found only in the Meladotian system. They use it in jewelry on the Canphor Twins."

"Fine. They use it in jewelry on Canphor VI and VII. So what?"

"Meladotia II is a very inhospitable world," said Val. "A couple of hundred degrees Fahrenheit, and an ammonia atmosphere. Humans almost never go there, even to mine it."

A look of dawning comprehension crossed Cole's face. "You took it from an alien miner."

"A Balimond," she said.

"Let me take a wild guess: for whatever reason, Balimonds don't believe in insurance."

"It's a human institution, and they don't have much use for humans."

"So what you're saying is that the Shark can't sell it to an insurance company."

"Right."

"And he can't dump it on the Twins, because the Canphor system is off-limits to human ships, even though they're sitting out the current war."

She grinned. "You got it."

"So whether he likes it or not, he's *got* to palm the crystals off on a fence—and the biggest fence in this sector just happens to be David Copperfield."

"They tell me you hit it off with him," said Val.

"Well, he let me live, anyway," said Cole. "All right, so sooner or later the Shark is going to try to sell the crystals to a fence, and the likelihood is that he'll choose Copperfield. Biggest fence, most money, best contacts for unloading it in the Canphor system." He paused, lost in thought for a moment. "There's no sense staking the place out. It could be months before he shows up, maybe even longer if he's being chased by Muscatel's three ships—or if he's chasing them. But that doesn't mean we can't make a private arrangement with Copperfield to let us know when the Shark contacts him and when he expects the crystals to be delivered."

"You'd better do it in person," interjected Sharon. "A fence operating just outside the Republic has got to be very careful. He's got to know that the offer's legit, that the cops aren't standing ten feet beyond holo range with some burners aimed at you."

"I agree," said Cole. "Val, have you ever met David Copperfield?"

"Twice."

He fell silent, chin on fist, eyes half-closed.

"What's the problem?" asked Val at last.

"I'm trying to decide whether to bring you with me," said Cole. "I don't know if seeing two pirates he knows will reassure him or set off alarms in his head. He likes me, or at least he seems to, and he's had dealings with you; that's on one side. But when the hell did two pirates ever team up and ask a fence to screw another pirate?"

"Probably more often than you'd guess," said Val.

"I agree," said Sharon. "There are business mergers all the time. This is just another business."

"That's the problem. It's *not* just another business. This is the kind of business that when you run in the red, the red isn't ink. If he helps us, he knows we'll have something we can hold over him forever."

"But he also knows we almost never deal with him," said Val. "He might not see us again for five or ten years."

"We almost never deal with him at five percent," said Cole. "But what if we say: You pay us forty percent or we tell every crew member of the *Pegasus* who informed on them? Or we tell every pirate on the Frontier that David Copperfield sold out one of his clients because another client paid him to."

"You've been to Riverwind," said Val. "You've seen his protection. No one can get to him."

"Bullshit. All I have to do is say I'm Steerforth and I can walk right into his office. Who's to say one of the Shark's men won't announce himself as Pickwick?"

"You can do this either-or shit all day," said Sharon. "I say you take the Valkyrie. If nothing else, she can protect your back better than anyone else."

"All right," agreed Cole. "Maybe I'll take Morales, too. If we have to leave in a hurry, he knows the routes to the spaceport better than anyone else." He paused, then shook his head. "No, bad idea."

"Why, if he knows his way around Riverwind?"

"If Val can't come into Copperfield's study with me, I'm not going to worry about her; she can take care of herself. But if she *can* come to the study, that means Morales will be alone. He's just a kid, and despite what he did to Chadwick in a confused firefight in close quarters, I don't think he can take care of himself under those circumstances. We'll find our way to and from Copperfield's house without him."

"You're too soft, Cole," said Val. "Everyone's expendable."

"Under certain rare and rigidly defined conditions," agreed Cole, "but not every minute of every day. We can accomplish our mission without endangering him, and that means we *should* accomplish it without endangering him."

"You're the Captain," she said. "Just get me back my ship."

She cut the connection, and her image disappeared.

"You know," said Sharon, "we're going to try to track the *Pegasus*, and we're going to quiz Moyer and Nichols and Bujandi until they're dizzy, and we're going to try to find Muscatel's ships, but your red-headed friend just came up with the best idea anyone's had for locating the Shark."

"I told you she was going to prove useful," said Cole.

"Of course, that presupposes that we need to find the *Pegasus*," added Sharon. "If it weren't for her, we wouldn't have to."

"If it weren't for her, I'd still be going into the Republic trying to sell the tiara and the other jewels," said Cole. "She's giving us a post-graduate course in piracy."

"Then why are you trying to help her get her ship back? It's in our best interest not to find it for a few years."

"Because she's not stupid, Sharon. She'll know if we're trying to draw it out, and the day that happens she's gone—possibly leaving a dead Captain behind her."

"What the hell," said Sharon. "Since she's either going to kill you or get you killed, maybe you don't have to be lonely tonight after all."

Cole and Val cleared Customs on Riverwind with a minimum of red
tape, and were soon making their way to David Copperfield's mansion.

"When we get there, let me introduce you," said Cole as they sped
above a local thoroughfare.

"Screw the niceties," said Val. "We're going to make him a proposition, and he's going to say yes or no."

"He's more likely to say yes if you let me do the talking," said Cole.
He looked over at her. "I don't suppose you'd be willing to stop long
enough to buy a period costume, assuming we can find one?"

She growled an obscenity.

"I didn't think so. Besides, they probably don't make nineteenth-
century A.D. dresses for redheaded giants." He paused. "Do you at
least know how to curtsy?"

"What the hell are you talking about?" she demanded. "We're two
pirates on our way to see a fence!"

"You're not much at adapting to situations, are you?" said Cole.

"I make situations adapt to me."

"That's probably why we're trying to get your ship back," he said
wryly.

They rode in silence for the last mile.

"We're here," she announced.

"I meant what I said," Cole told her. "You let me introduce you,
and let me do the talking. I want you to only answer direct questions."
She seemed about to explode with anger, and he held up a hand.

"We're not doing this for *my* ship. If you won't do it my way, you can go in there alone and good luck to you."

She glared at him for a moment longer. "All right," she said at last. "We'll play it your way."

They walked up to the front door. It opened, and Mr. Jones let them in.

"Welcome back, Mr. Smith," he said. "Will you and Mrs. Smith please follow me?"

Val looked annoyed, but said nothing, and she and Cole fell into step behind Mr. Jones, who led them to Copperfield's study. The door allowed them to pass through, then snapped shut.

"My dear Steerforth!" said the alien that called itself David Copperfield. "How delightful to see you again!" He turned to Val. "And this enchanting creature is . . . ?"

"Olivia Twist," said Cole, as Val looked confused.

"What a perfect name!" enthused Copperfield. Suddenly he bowed low. "My house is your house, dear Miss Twist."

"Thank you," mumbled Val, frowning.

"And how may I help you today, Steerforth?" asked Copperfield. "Have you decided to part with your diamonds after all?"

"They're long gone," replied Cole.

"The jewelry, then?"

"Otherwise disposed of."

"Then you've made a new haul," said Copperfield.

"Actually, we're not here to sell you anything," replied Cole.

"Oh?" Copperfield suddenly looked suspicious. "I hope you are not here to steal from me, because if you are, you should know that four weapons are trained on you at this very second."

"Rob a friend I went to school with?" said Cole as Val looked at him as if he was crazy. "Unthinkable."

"I *knew* you were a kindred spirit!" said Copperfield. "May I ask why *you* are here?"

"As I said, I'm not here to sell you anything, but rather to buy something from you."

"Everything I have is for sale, except for the clothes on my back," answered Copperfield. "And if you made the right offer for them . . ."

"The only thing we want to buy is information."

"Ah!" said Copperfield with a smile. "The most valuable commodity of all, and hence the most expensive."

"We don't think you possess the information we need yet, but rather that you will be obtaining it in the relatively near future."

"This sounds intriguing."

"Poor Olivia's carriage was stolen by highwaymen," said Cole.

"Had this carriage a name?"

"The *Pegasus*," said Val.

"A well-known carriage indeed," said Copperfield. "And of course my sources have already informed me of the devastation it caused on Cyrano." He smiled at Val. "You are known by many false names, my deal Olivia, and each of them is said to be more than formidable. How is it that you managed to lose your carriage?"

"I got stinking—"

"She was indisposed," said Cole, speaking over her.

"A sweet young innocent like her?" said Copperfield.

"You left out 'trusting,' and that's what cost her the carriage."

"And you think they'll be contacting me to sell it for them?" asked Copperfield.

"No, but they've got some things they won't be able to unload anywhere else," said Cole.

"Such as?"

"Meladotian crystals," said Val.

Copperfield's eyes widened. "Meladotian crystals?" he repeated.

"Right," said Cole.

"Beloved Steerforth, I am going to ask you a question," said Copperfield. "We are like brothers, you and I. Closer. In all the Inner Frontier, only you are truly family."

"Thank you, David," replied Cole. "I feel exactly the same way."

"But family is one thing, and business is quite another," continued Copperfield. "Why should I help you when your avowed enemy is coming to me with Meladotian crystals?"

"He's going to want five percent for the crystals, possibly more," said Cole. "Help Olivia get her carriage back and *we'll* sell them to you for three percent of market."

"*Hey!*" said Val.

"Be quiet, Miss Twist," said Cole sharply. "Our friend is considering his options."

"Three percent, you say?" asked Copperfield.

"That's right."

"And exactly what do I have to do in exchange for this beneficence?"

"I'm going to give you a scramble code before I leave," said Cole. "The moment you know that they're coming here, I want you to send me a subspace message to that effect, and use the code to hide the contents. It's the latest military technology, and I doubt that the *Pegasus* will be able to do a thing with it."

"They'll know it came from here."

"Send Mr. Jones to the spaceport and have him send it from there," suggested Cole. "It'll just be one more signal among hundreds."

"You were always the brightest boy in school, Steerforth," said Copperfield.

"We'll be waiting for them when they arrive," continued Cole. "They'll be out of the pirating business long before they can reach your house."

"Three percent?" repeated Copperfield.

"Three percent."

"Then it only remains for you to tell me who will be contacting me, so that I will know to alert you."

"He calls himself the Hammerhead Shark."

Copperfield's eyes widened again. "The Hammerhead Shark?"

"That's right."

"I'm sorry, but all deals are off! I had no idea who you were after!" He turned to Val. "And you, Miss Twist, should consider yourself fortunate in the extreme that you are still alive."

"All right," said Cole. "Two percent."

"My dear Steerforth, you could offer them to me for free and it would make no difference. I value my life too much to do anything to offend the Hammerhead Shark."

"He'll never make it this far," said Cole. "I told you: We'll meet him right at the spaceport."

"Because we went to school together, and thus have a bond between us, I will forget you ever came here or mentioned the Hammerhead Shark. Now I must ask you to go."

"That's your final word?"

"No creation of the immortal Charles ever speaks a final word," replied Copperfield. "But that is my decision."

Cole shrugged. "If you change your mind . . ."

"I won't."

Cole turned to Val. "Okay, let's go."

They walked to the door of the study, where Mr. Jones was awaiting them. "Follow me, please," he said, turning and heading toward the front door.

"He sounds like he believes the pair of you stepped out of the pages of the same book," said Val. "All this talk about a bond between you."

"Maybe he does," answered Cole. "As you can see from your surroundings, he's caught up in the fantasy."

They passed an open room with three of Copperfield's henchmen sitting around a table, playing cards. Jones kept walking, but Val instantly pivoted, pulling her burner and aiming it in a single motion.

"Hit the floor!" she yelled, and Cole instantly dropped to the carpet as two of the cardplayers ducked and a third went for his screecher. He was too slow, and he fell to the floor, a bubbling black hole between his eyes.

Cole jumped to his feet, pulled his pulse gun, and trained it on Mr. Jones, while Val kept hers aimed at the two remaining cardplayers.

"What the hell was that all about?" Cole demanded.

"Get the fence out here," she said, never moving.

"David!" shouted Cole. "Come out. It's safe now."

"How do I know?" yelled Copperfield through the heavy wooden door of his study.

"Would Steerforth kill David Copperfield?" said Cole. "Just get out here!"

"In a moment." There was a brief silence. "There are now four weapons trained on you. If you make any sudden movements, if you threaten me in any way, you won't live to reach the front door. You are only alive now because of our shared interest in the immortal Charles."

The door opened and David Copperfield emerged, a weapon of alien design in each hand.

"What has gone on here?" he demanded.

"The man I killed," said Val. "How long has he worked for you?"

Copperfield shrugged. "A week, maybe two. Why?"

"His name is Barak Numika, and he's a crew member of the *Pegasus*. If you don't believe me, tear off his sleeve and check the tattoo on his left arm: it's a waterfall in perpetual motion. Then contact your local police station, have them run a search on the identifying marks of a wanted murderer called Barak Numika and check his last known whereabouts. They'll tell you he was serving aboard a pirate ship called the *Pegasus*." Val paused. "You've had a spy in your employ, Mr. Copperfield."

"Why?" asked Copperfield. "How could the Hammerhead Shark know you'd come here to offer this accommodation?"

"He couldn't know. He has no idea that I've joined forces with . . . Steerforth."

"And if he wasn't put here to watch out for us," added Cole quickly, "that means he was put here to look for weaknesses in your defenses. The Shark's coming here, all right, but not to offer you Meladotian crystals. He's coming to relieve you of everything you've got."

Copperfield seemed lost in thought for almost a full minute. Finally he spoke.

"Put your weapons away." He turned to his own men, and raised his voice for the benefit of his four unseen gunmen. "These two are our friends and allies. They are not to be harmed, now or in the future." He pointed to Numika. "Get that spy out of here and dispose of him." Then to Val. "You put yourself at risk to save my operation and probably my life. I'll need that scramble code, and if you can stop the Shark, I will offer you five percent of market for the crystals."

Cole nodded. "It's a deal."

"Perhaps I can sweeten it," continued Copperfield.

"Oh?"

"There is one thing I covet above all else," he said. "On Picacio IV, out in the Albion Cluster, there is a man named Euphrates Djinn, who is in the same business as I am. I have no idea if that is his real name. I suspect it is not, but it's the name he's gone by for the past fifteen years."

"What about him?"

"He possesses a signed first edition of *A Tale of Two Cities*." A look of rage spread across the alien's face. "He never reads it! He never displays it! And he refuses to sell it! He has no interest in it and no use for it. He keeps it just to drive me crazy!" He began hyperventilating little blue puffs of vapor. "Get it for me, and I will pay you not three percent, not five percent, not thirty percent, but one-half of market value for anything you bring me for two years after that book is in my hands."

"We'll think about it," said Cole.

"We'll *do* more than think about it," said Val. "We'll do it." Cole looked at her questioningly. "I know Euphrates Djinn. It'll be a pleasure to rob him. Hell, I just might cut the bastard open from stem to stern, too."

"You heard the delicate, refined Miss Twist," said Cole. "You've got another deal."

"I don't like it," said Sharon Blacksmith.

"Neither do I," added Forrice.

"The Captain may occasionally have to leave the ship in the course of action—maybe twice a decade," continued Sharon. "But *not* to go planetside and steal a goddamned book!"

"I'm the one who made the deal," said Cole, facing them in his small office. "If something goes wrong, whoever's down there is in deep shit. I can't ask a crew member to take the risk."

"Why not?" said Forrice. "You'll be surprised at how many will volunteer if it means keeping you safely aboard the ship."

"They gave up their careers for me. I won't ask them for any more until it's necessary—and as long as I can go down there, it's not necessary."

"You're getting a little long in the tooth for this kind of stuff," said Sharon. "I don't know what you think you're proving. Bull and Val are both much stronger than you. Slick can go places you can't go. You can't put on as much body armor as Domak was born with. You can't operate in the dark half as well as Jack-in-the-Box. You can't . . ."

"Enough," said Cole. "I'm not going down there because I'm a great warrior or even a great thief. I'm going because I'm the one who agreed to the deal."

"You weren't the only one on Riverwind," said Sharon. "Let Val go."

"She *is* going."

"It takes two of you to steal one book?" asked Forrice.

"It may take one of us to fight off all of Djinn's defenses while the other steals the book."

"At least tell me that you're the thief and not the warrior," said Sharon.

"I'm the thief," said Cole. Suddenly he smiled. "I keep expecting her to pat me on the head and tell me that I'm a cute little feller."

"Let's grant her better taste than that," said Forrice. "Well, I'm off to get something to eat."

"That's it?" demanded Sharon. "You're all through trying to talk reason with him?"

"Do you know anyone who ever talked reason to him and won?" asked Forrice. "Besides, from everything I've heard about Picacio IV, the odds are thousands-to-one that there aren't any Molarian females in season there. Why should I go down to the surface?"

"I'm glad to see you have your priorities straight," said Cole as Forrice turned and spun gracefully to the door.

"Besides," said the Molarian as he stepped out into the corridor, "after they kill you, we'll go on a punishment party, and if there *are* any Molarian females I'll find them then."

"I admire your patience and self-restraint," said Cole just before the door snapped shut behind the First Officer.

"Are you sure you want to take the Valkyrie?" asked Sharon.

"I hope that's an earnest question and not a jealous one."

"I don't have any ownership papers," she responded. "You're a free agent. I'm just concerned that she's neither the most subtle nor the most silent person I've ever met. Maybe Morales . . ."

Cole shook his head. "Morales is just a kid, and he's never been to Picacio or met Euphrates Djinn. Val knows him, knows his layout—and let's be honest: if he's as big a fence as Copperfield says, he'll have layers of protection. No one's sneaking in and out without his knowing it. If you think there's someone on board better capable to cover my back in a situation like that, I'm willing to listen."

She sighed and shook her head. "No, I guess not."

"I *know* not. And don't worry about a budding romance. If she hugged me, she'd break my ribs. I hate to think of what could happen if she wrapped her legs around me."

Sharon chuckled at the thought. "Okay, you can go. But come back in one piece."

"It'll be in one piece or not at all."

"How long should we give you before we figure you're in serious trouble and send down a rescue party?"

"That's a command decision, so either Four Eyes or Christine will make it." He smiled at her. "I'm sure you'll lobby for five minutes."

"We rescued you from the Navy. None of us can ever go back to the Republic. As long as we're outcasts with prices on our heads, it makes sense to keep the reason for it alive."

"I know it's going to come as a shock to you," said Cole, "but I have every intention of coming out of this alive."

They spoke a few more minutes, and then Sharon left to return to the Security Department. Cole promptly walked to the bridge, where Christine Mboya was in command.

"What have you found out so far?" he asked.

"About Djinn or about Picacio?" she replied.

"Take your choice."

"Picacio IV is an oxygen world, with about eighty-four percent Standard gravity. It was first opened up as a hospital world for convalescing heart patients, since the gravity puts much less strain on them and the oxygen content is a little higher than Standard. But after a few years they discovered that one of the three continents was inhabited by huge creatures, rather like Earth's dinosaurs, and a safari industry instantly sprang up. Then they found that the freshwater oceans could produce enough fish to feed a few nearby worlds that were suffering everything from droughts to spontaneous volcanic activity, and suddenly, with fishing, medical, and safari industries all thriving, it became a financial center for a fifty-world section of the Albion Cluster."

"That's a little more than I needed to know," said Cole. "Light gravity, high oxygen content, right?"

"Right."

"How many spaceports?"

"Four. One of them, right by the hospital, services the city that's grown up around it, and that's where Djinn is."

"Okay, now tell me about Euphrates Djinn."

"His birth name is Willard Foss, and over the years he's been Benito Gravia, Marcos Rienke, and simply McNeal with no first name. He's been Euphrates Djinn since he set up shop on Picacio IV fifteen years ago."

"How big is his operation?"

"He's one of the three biggest fences in the Cluster. He's got warehouses on Picacio IV, Alpha Prego II, and New Siam."

"How many men has he got on Picacio?"

She shook her head. "I'm good with a computer, but I'm not that good. He's probably a bigger fence than your friend David Copperfield, but I don't know if that means he has more security forces."

"They're security forces when they're protecting a legal operation. In this instance, we call them thugs and gunmen."

"Just remember that they shoot as straight as security forces," said Sharon's voice.

"Should I write that down, or will you trust me to remember it?" asked Cole sardonically.

"We care about you, sir," said Christine stubbornly.

"I know," replied Cole with a weary sigh. "And I appreciate it. But if I get cared for much more, I just may choose to stay down on Picacio and go to work for Euphrates Djinn."

"I'm sorry, sir."

"Don't apologize. Just tell me if there's anything else I need to know."

"I've been trying to pull up a blueprint of his house, but from what I can tell he's added a number of rooms and levels, and paid off enough bureaucrats so that he didn't have to register the changes. That'll make it harder to figure out where the book is."

"Maybe I'll just let Val ask him," suggested Cole. "She can be pretty persuasive." He paused. "I guess that's everything. I don't imagine he bought his alarm system through the normal channels, or that we can find out what type it is?"

"That was one of the first things I tried to find out, sir," said Christine.

"All right," said Cole. "That's that." He raised his voice. "Pilot, what's our ETA?"

"In normal space, three days and seven hours," answered Wxakgini. "If I can find an entrance to the Gulliver Wormhole, about six hours."

"What's so hard about finding it?"

"Wormholes aren't like highways," said Wxakgini. "They don't stay in one place."

"Well, do your best," said Cole. He turned back to Christine. "How long until white shift is over?"

"About eighty Standard minutes, sir."

"Since there's a possibility we may reach Picacio halfway through red shift, I want Val at her sharpest. Inform her—or if she's sleeping, leave a message to be delivered when she wakes up—that she's relieved of all duties until after we return from Picacio."

"Who do you want to replace her, sir?" asked Christine.

"Who's seen more action—Domak or Sokolov?"

"I'll check their records, sir."

"Whoever it is will be in command during blue shift. If anything goes wrong, I want someone with battle experience in charge."

"It's Lieutenant Domak, sir," said Christine, studying her computer.

"Tell her she's in charge during blue shift until Val gets back to the ship. And tell Four Eyes to stay on call, in case things get hairy. I don't want him putting in sixteen-hour days, but I'll feel a lot safer if he's in command if anyone starts shooting. I'll speak to Domak before we leave and explain that if Four Eyes replaces her, it's on my explicit order. She might as well know who to resent."

"Then why put her in charge at all?" asked Christine.

"Because if we're attacked before Four Eyes can get here, I want someone who's been shot at before giving the orders."

"Who do you think will be shooting, sir?"

"I don't know. But Muscatel had four ships. Why shouldn't a successful fence like Djinn have a few—and if he does, why shouldn't one of them be in orbit, ready to shoot down any intruder who wants to horn in on his operation?"

"Now I see, sir."

"Fine. I'm going off to take a nap, just in case I need all my strength in six hours rather than seventy-two. If we find the wormhole, wake me at 1900 hours."

He went to the airlift, and a moment later was in his cabin.

"What?" he said aloud. "No half-dressed floozie waiting to see me off?"

Sharon's image popped into existence just in front of him. "You need your rest. I have a feeling that this is going to be a more dangerous operation than you're making it sound."

"Now why should you think that?"

"Because you're a contrarian," she replied. "If it was cut and dried, you'd make it sound dangerous just so no one loafed on the job. But I've seen you in serious situations before, and the more dangerous they are, the more you belittle them." A sudden smile crossed her face. "I intuit it's so the floozie and the rest of the crew won't worry too much."

"All right," he said, lying down on his cot. "I'm going to sleep. But when I get back, I expect tons of praise and sexual rewards."

"Would you settle for a soya sandwich?"

"Probably," he said just before he fell asleep.

Picacio IV was one of the few habitable planets Cole had seen that possessed rings—sixteen of them to be exact, though to the naked eye they blended into just one huge ring. The control tower near the hospital took over the ship's controls, and as they entered the stratosphere prior to landing, Cole and Val began making their preparations to leave the *Kermit*.

"I'd wear a wig," she remarked, "but there's not much I can do to hide my size."

"You can't make yourself smaller," agreed Cole. "I suppose you could build up the heels of your boots, or put lifts inside them. They might not recognize you as a seven-footer."

"I'd rather not fall flat on my face if I have to maneuver," replied Val.

Cole tried to imagine her falling *flat* on anything, and couldn't conjure up a picture of it. "As you wish." He picked up a shining item and placed it in a pocket.

"What the hell was that?"

"A ceramic gun," he explained. "It should get past any security devices."

"How many shots does it fire, and with how much force?" she asked.

"Three shots, and I've got two more clips, so I'll have nine shots total. As for force, I don't think I'd trust it to kill anything much larger than you—but I'm using explosive bullets, and that should make up for any lack of force."

"Does it make a bang?"

"These are bullets, not beams or pulses," he answered. "They make a bang."

"I thought we were supposed to be doing this covertly," she noted.

"If I have to use it, we've already been spotted. You're the muscle; I'm just carrying this for emergencies."

"We have landed on Picacio IV," announced the shuttle.

"Keep all life-support systems functioning," ordered Cole. "Open the hatch until the Third Officer and I depart. Then close and lock it, activate all security and defensive systems, and let no one come aboard until I, the Third Officer, or some other crew member of the *Theodore Roosevelt* whose voiceprint is in your memory banks utters the entry code."

"All orders have been logged," announced the shuttle, opening the hatch. Val and Cole stepped through, and it slid shut behind them.

It was nightside where they had landed, but the planet was almost as bright as at high noon.

"My God, will you look at that!" said Cole, awestruck.

Overheard, the rings, forty thousand miles wide, composed mostly of ice, were reflecting the light of the sun that shone on them from the opposite side of the world. They glowed and sparkled with a brilliant shimmering light, the intensity fluctuating as they continued their endless journey around Picacio IV.

"I've seen it before," said Val, unimpressed. "Let's get moving."

"Well, *I* haven't seen it," said Cole. "I want to look for a couple of minutes. I may never have the chance again." He stood and stared, and finally turned back to Val, who was fidgeting impatiently. "Okay, let's go."

An unmanned aircar sensed their movement and approached them. "Please enter from the left side and I will take you to Customs," it announced.

They did as it said, got off a few minutes later at the Customs kiosk, paused while their false IDs were approved, and then entered the main section of the spaceport.

"A lot of airsleds," noted Cole.

"They're all carrying patients to or from the hospital," answered Val. "Medicine's the primary business on this continent." She paused thoughtfully, then added: "Followed by crime."

"Well," said Cole, "we're not here to commit medicine. How do we get to Djinn's place?"

"This way," she said, pointing straight down.

"He lives under the spaceport?"

She smiled. "We catch subterranean transportation here—the whole city is catacombed with it—and ride it out to his estate."

He followed her as she walked to an airlift. They descended about forty feet, got off, and found themselves on a small raised platform. A shuttle—Cole wanted to call it a monorail, but there were no rails and it floated a foot above the floor of the tunnel—immediately pulled up. They got on it, and Cole realized that they were in a single car, not a train. He guessed that there were hundreds, perhaps thousands of cars, and the closest one to sense their motion would instantly respond to it.

"Please indicate your destination," said a mechanical voice as an intricate map of the city popped into view. "If you know the address, please state it. If you do not, then find the section of the map where you wish to go and state the coordinates aloud. If it is a private residence or business, you need only state the name of the owner."

"Euphrates Djinn," said Val.

"I cannot take you to Mr. Djinn's estate without his express permission," said the shuttlecar. "Shall I ask for it?"

Val looked at Cole questioningly.

"Shuttle," said Cole, "kill all systems except life support for two minutes."

"Done," said the shuttlecar, as even the lights died.

"If we announce ourselves, where will we be left off?" asked Cole.

"Every house and business has a subterranean area—they're more than basements—on one of the tracks," answered Val.

"So it'll drop us off inside the house?"

"Well, right at the door, anyway."

"But we'd have to announce ourselves?"

"Right."

"And if he says no?"

"Then the shuttle won't stop at his house, but beyond his property, and he'll know we're here."

"If only you announce yourself and I keep silent, what'll happen if I try to get off with you?"

"If I'm announced, someone will be waiting for me," she said. "Of course, that doesn't mean that I can't kill him or them before they spot you."

Cole shook his head. "No, I don't want his whole security team alerted before we even know where the damned book is." He paused. "You're sure they'll be waiting where the shuttle stops? They won't wait for us to actually enter the house?"

She frowned. "I'm trying to remember." She uttered an obscenity. "I can't recall where they met us, but it makes a lot more sense for a security team to size us up *before* we enter the house."

"What's his exterior security like?"

"Atomizing fence, a few marksmen, the usual."

Suddenly the lights came back on. "Your two minutes have elapsed," announced the shuttlecar.

"All right," said Cole. "Val, what name did Djinn know you by?"

"Cleopatra."

"Shuttle, contact Euphrates Djinn and tell him that Wilson Cole and Cleopatra request the pleasure of his company."

"Sending . . ."

"Are you sure you want him to know who you are?" asked Val.

"He's a criminal. The Republic would like to lock him away. That same Republic wants me dead. My own name ought to buy me a little cachet with him."

"Euphrates Djinn has acknowledged your request, and will allow you access to his estate," announced the shuttlecar.

"Tell him we accept his kind invitation, and we'll be there shortly," said Cole.

The shuttlecar moved forward. Since the tunnels were unlit, Cole couldn't begin to guess their speed. In four minutes it began slowing down, and it came to a halt after another few seconds. The door slid open and they found themselves in a sparsely furnished chamber. Three men were waiting for them.

"Commander Cole?" said one of them.

"Captain Cole," Cole corrected him.

"My mistake," said the man. "And I remember Cleopatra from the last time she was here. Mr. Djinn is waiting for you on the ground level. We'll escort you there as soon as you pass through our security scanners."

"We already passed through some at the spaceport," said Cole.

"Ours are more thorough."

The scanners pinpointed all of Val's weapons, which she removed, but missed Cole's ceramic pistol.

"Your burner, your screecher, and your daggers will be returned when you leave," another of the men told Val.

"They'd better be," she said coldly.

"And now," said the first man, "if you will accompany us into the airlift . . ."

The five of them floated up to the ground floor and stepped out into an ornate foyer. From there they were taken to a large, luxurious parlor where they were told to remain. The three men left, and a moment later a bald, rotund little man with a handlebar mustache entered the room. He waddled over to them and extended his hand to Cole.

"I have heard of your exploits, Mr. Cole," he said. "I knew it was only a matter of time before the Republic found some pretext to rid itself of its greatest hero. That is, after all, the way of governments. I am Euphrates Djinn, at your service." He turned to Val. "And you, my dear Cleopatra—or should I say Nefertiti, or Domino, or Flame, or . . . but why go on?—we both know who you are, if not what to call you. May I offer either of you a drink?"

"Later, perhaps," said Cole.

"Fine. Now, how may I serve you?"

"As you may have heard," began Cole, making it up as he went along, "I came to the Inner Frontier with my ship and most of my crew. As such, there's probably not a ship on the Frontier that can match our firepower." *And if you believe that*, he thought, *the rest will be easy*.

"I've not seen your ship, but there are some pretty powerful vessels out here," said Djinn.

"Not with highly trained military crews," continued Cole.

"I will grant you that," said Djinn. "Have you a point to make?"

"You are a successful fence, Mr. Djinn," said Cole. "Your reputation extends throughout the Inner Frontier. They have even heard of you on the Spiral Arm and out near the Rim."

"I'm flattered."

"But such a reputation can be a two-edged sword," continued Cole. "No one knows what you're worth, but guesses range up to three billion credits."

"Ridiculous," said Djinn.

"I'm not here to argue whether it's one billion or three billion, Mr. Djinn. I'm here because whatever the amount, it is bound to attract the attention of men and aliens who are not bound by the same code of ethics I'm sure that you and I share."

"And you propose to protect me?"

"I know you have a security force, and I'm sure you've got some ships. We're not talking about protecting you from the man who sneaks in here by night, or the lone ship that decides it's worth the risk to attack one of your ships or customers. But there are warlords all over the Rim, and with the Republic's attention focused on its war with the Teroni Federation, they're starting to appear on the Inner and Outer Frontiers. That is the kind of enemy we can protect you from."

"Why am I blessed by your presence?" asked Djinn. "Why haven't you made your offer to David Copperfield or Ivan Skavinsky Skavar?"

"David Copperfield is right next to the Republic. If he needs help, he can call upon the Navy and they'll probably come. The reason I chose you rather than Ivan or the others is standing beside me. She is our one recruit since we reached the Inner Frontier. We chose her for her knowledge of the current situation, and she assures me that you're the biggest and the best. If you reject my offer, I'll make it to the next man or alien in line."

"And what do you want for your services?"

"It may be a week, a month, a year, or a decade before you're attacked by a major force," said Cole. "You and I can determine the proper fee for such an engagement, to be paid only when we have achieved victory. Beyond that, I want only a small annual retainer, which will give you first call on our services."

"And how many millions of credits constitutes a small retainer?" asked Djinn suspiciously.

"I don't want money."

"Jewelry, then? Or perhaps art treasures?"

"What I want is treasure enough for me, Mr. Djinn. I am a collector of ancient books, dating from the days when Man was still earthbound. If you have any, I'll look them over and make my selection."

A smile spread across Djinn's pudgy face. "You had me going for a moment there," he said with an amused laugh. "*He* sent you, didn't he?"

"I have no idea what you're talking about," said Cole.

"David Copperfield. He's been after my signed first for more than a decade. Nice try, Mr. Cole, but my answer to him is the same as always: Never."

"Why should I lie?" said Cole. "Yes, he did make me a handsome offer if I could obtain it for him. But that has nothing to do with my offer to you. If you'll give me the book, my ship and crew will stand ready to defend you from any and all attacks for a period of, shall we say, eighteen Standard months?"

"I know the Albion Cluster far better than you do," said Djinn, "and I know that no warlord is going to assemble a powerful enough force for me to require your services for at least five years. So it really makes no difference to me whether your offer is sincere or not." A smile worked its way slowly across his thick lips. "Now perhaps you'd like to make another offer?"

Cole frowned. "I don't follow you."

"What is it worth for me to let you leave here alive?"

"Oh, you're going to let us leave here alive," said Cole. "And you're going to let us leave with the book."

"I admire your sense of humor, Mr. Cole."

Cole pulled his pistol out and trained it at Djinn. "I hope you admire my taste in ceramics as well."

"Does that toy really work?" asked Djinn.

"There's an easy way to find out," said Cole. "I'm hoping you don't choose it, and just hand me the book."

"Kill him and get it over with," said Val, and Cole couldn't tell if she was trying to scare the fence or if she really meant it. "We'll find the damned book without him."

"You heard the lady," said Cole. "Make up your mind."

Djinn shrugged. "You may have the book for the rest of your life, Mr. Cole," he said, walking to the wall behind him. "Which is to say, I expect to have it back within ten minutes."

He touched the wall a number of times in a precise pattern, and suddenly a small section slid back to reveal the leather-bound Dickens novel. He stood aside, but neither Val nor Cole stepped forward.

"You bring it to us," she said.

"I detect a lack of trust here," said Djinn in amused tones.

"Who do you think you're dealing with?" said Val. "The second a hand that wasn't in your security system's memory banks reached for it, every alarm in the place would go off." She paused. "It might save the book, but it wouldn't save you."

"What the hell has Copperfield offered you to take such risks against a man who never did you any harm?" asked Djinn curiously.

"You wouldn't understand," said Cole. "We're old school chums."

Djinn got the book and handed it to Cole. "Ten minutes," he said. "Maybe twelve if you're lucky. Enjoy them while you can."

"Val," said Cole, "I get the impression that Mr. Djinn would like to take a nap."

Before Djinn could react, Val's hand chopped down on the back of his neck and he dropped to the floor.

"You didn't kill him, I hope?"

"What difference does it make?" she replied.

"We're pirates, not killers."

"Don't get preachy with me," she said. "You killed a bunch of men on the *Achilles*."

"They attacked us."

"And you think Djinn just planned to let you walk away with his book without attacking you?"

"We'll argue about it later," said Cole. "Right now we need to figure a way out of here."

"Only three men brought us up," she replied. "I'll take two, you take one."

"They were all armed," said Cole. "And we don't know how many more are out there."

"All right," she said. "If you don't want to fight them, let's look for Djinn's escape route. I never yet saw anyone this rich and powerful who didn't have an emergency exit hidden somewhere on the premises. This is the room where he does his business, like David Copperfield's study, so it must be accessible from here."

"Who the hell would he escape from?" asked Cole dubiously. "He owns the local authorities."

"The authorities are never a problem, and no rival walks in here without being disarmed. No, men like Djinn have to be able to escape from ambitious lieutenants."

Cole considered her statement, then nodded his agreement. "It makes sense. Let's start looking."

"Not toward the door. All the ambitious underlings are on the other side of it."

"Why aren't they here already?" asked Cole. "You can't tell me the security system's not making half a dozen holos of this."

"I'm sure it was on when we entered. But he's no fool. He would have disabled it before he showed you the book. He wasn't worried about getting it back from you; he thought his men could do that, and maybe they can. He wanted to make sure *they* didn't know where it was hidden."

"You get a hell of an education in the pirate business, don't you?" observed Cole. He looked around the room. "It's probably hidden behind some wall panel, just the way the book was."

"But without knowing the codes, how are we going to open it?" she asked.

Cole lowered his head in thought for a moment, then straightened up abruptly. "I think I know."

"What is it?"

"If he had to make a getaway in a hurry, he wouldn't have time to punch in a code. It'd be more important for him to get out fast."

"So?"

"So there *isn't* any code. The system is programmed to recognize *him*." He walked over to the unconscious Djinn. "Come on, give me a hand lifting him up."

She walked over, and a moment later they had him propped up between them.

"Now let's walk him as close to the walls as we can and see what happens."

They began dragging him, as two friends might drag a drunk, past the wall that held the book, then a second wall, and just as Cole was about to admit he'd been wrong, a panel opened on the third wall, and they stepped into an airlift.

"Bring him or leave him?" asked Val.

"Bring him. Maybe if we run into any of his men, we can use him as a hostage and convince them not to shoot."

"Most of them would probably love an excuse to blow him apart and split the spoils," said Val. "Look what my crew did to me, and I was one hell of a generous captain."

"Bring him anyway. Even if they'd rather kill him than us, it doesn't hurt to have a shield."

The airlift descended to a lower level, but it wasn't the same level the shuttle had used.

"Does it go any farther down?" asked Val, looking into a room filled with stolen art treasures.

"No, this is it," said Cole after checking the controls. "Let's see how high it goes."

"Wait!" she said.

"What is it?" he asked.

"Let's grab some of this stuff before we leave!"

"It'll slow us down," said Cole. "His men aren't going to stay put forever."

"Then you go," she said, stepping out. "I'll be along later."

"We'll go together," said Cole. "Just be quick about it."

She hefted a few small statues, decided they were too heavy, briefly considered a pair of paintings, and finally settled for a handful of alien gemstones on which had been engraved microscopic scenes of exquisite beauty. She tucked them into the top of one boot and rejoined Cole in the airlift.

They ascended all the way to the roof, where they emerged and found a small ship, hidden from the street by the various angles of the roof.

"Fueled and ready for a quick getaway," said Cole.

"How do you know?"

"What's the point of an escape route if you don't keep everything in working order? I'll bet the damned ship gets serviced every week."

"We're going to have a problem," said Val.

"Oh?"

"Take a look. It's a one-man ship."

Cole frowned. "I hadn't noticed." He propped Djinn up against a faux chimney and walked over to the vessel. "Is there any way the two of us can fit into it?"

"Not even if I were a foot shorter and we were locked in a sexual embrace," said Val.

"Okay," he said. "Take it to the spaceport and come back with the *Kermit*."

"The *Kermit* could never land here," she said. "It's too big."

"Then use your initiative and steal a ship that *can* land here."

"Give me your ceramic gun," she said, holding out a hand. "All my weapons are still down at the shuttlecar's level."

He withdrew the pistol and handed it to her, along with the book. "Make it fast," he said. "They may be used to his killing the holo system when he's doing business, but I'll bet he doesn't leave it off for twenty and thirty minutes at a time."

She began getting into the ship.

"One more thing," he said.

"What?"

"Whatever you steal only has to be big enough for you and me."

"You don't want to take him along?"

"What for?" responded Cole. "No one here would pay two credits to ransom him. And Copperfield doesn't want him, just his book. If we take him to Riverwind, they'll just kill him there. And since it's a pretty obvious that we're never going to have any dealings with him again, I can't see that letting him live will cause us any problems."

Her face said she was unconvinced, but she merely shrugged, muttered "You're the Captain," and finished climbing into the ship.

It took off almost instantly, and Cole was left alone on the roof with the unconscious Euphrates Djinn. He spent a few minutes studying the brilliantly reflective rings swirling slowly across the night sky. Then Djinn began groaning, and he turned his attention to the rotund fence.

"Welcome back," he said.

"Where are we?"

"On your roof."

"My roof?" said Djinn groggily. After a moment he looked around. "Where's my ship?"

"My friend borrowed it," answered Cole. "She'll be back with a bigger one, and you can reclaim it at the spaceport."

"You'll never see her again," predicted Djinn. "Take me back down and return my book, and I'll give you safe passage off the planet."

"Possibly you mean it," said Cole. "But I have more faith in her word than in yours."

"Then you're still a dead man, and all you've done is given me a stiff neck and a headache."

"We've also stolen your book and your ship," said Cole. "They may be small accomplishments, but they're ours."

"Spare me your humor," said Djinn, blinking his eyes and rubbing his neck. "By now my men are searching the house and combing the grounds, looking for you."

"Too bad the secret airlift won't open for them," said Cole.

"There are other ways to reach the roof, and other ways to kill you," promised Djinn. He touched his neck gingerly and winced. "What the hell are you doing out here anyway? Why aren't you blowing up military bases all over the Republic? After all, they're the ones who want you dead."

"Being a pirate pays better than being a revolutionary," answered Cole. "And you live longer."

"Some do. You won't."

"Let's hope you're wrong," said Cole. "Because I have no intention of dying alone."

A minute later he saw a low-flying ship approaching Djinn's estate. As it drew nearer, there were shouts from the interior of the house, and he could hear windows opening and men moving beyond his range of vision.

The ship came to a stop about twenty feet above the roof and hovered, motionless. A hatch opened and a ladder swung down. An instant later Val climbed down the first few steps.

"Get moving!" she yelled. "The winds could blow the ship beyond the roof any minute."

Cole took a step toward the ladder and the corpulent Djinn hurled himself at him, knocking him down.

"I've got him up here on the roof!" Djinn shouted into the night. "Get your asses up here quick!"

Two men pulled themselves up over the edge of the roof, about forty feet away from where Djinn and Cole were thrashing about. Val aimed the ceramic pistol and fired off two shots. The first missed. The second hit one of the men and exploded on contact. She quickly aimed at the other man and fired again, and he, too, vanished in a small explosion.

Three more men appeared at various spots along the roof's edge, and Cole realized that he still had the extra clips for the gun in his pocket. Val hurled herself down on top of Djinn, who collapsed like a balloon losing air. A quick kick to his head put him back in dreamland.

"Get up the ladder and steady the ship!" said Val.

"What about you?" asked Cole, climbing to his feet.

"This is what you brought me along for, remember?"

Cole realized that arguing would just waste time, so he raced to the ladder. It was beyond his reach, but the lighter gravity allowed him to leap up and grab hold of it. He started climbing as the three men charged the Valkyrie.

She reached into the top of her boot, right where Cole had seen her place the gemstones a few minutes earlier, and withdrew a pair of knives. A second later one was embedded in one of the men's throats, and the other had buried itself deep in a second man's chest.

"Where the hell did you get those?" yelled Cole as he neared the top of the ladder.

"Ship's galley!" she said with a laugh, then turned her attention to the third man, who either had no weapons or felt no need of them. He charged her, and got a swift, fifty-foot flight to the ground for his trouble.

Two more men appeared. Val dove behind the body of the first man she'd killed, appropriated his pulse gun, and fired at the two. One shot hit dead center between the first man's eyes; the other tore off the second man's leg, and he tottered and fell off the roof.

She looked up, saw Cole had reached the ship, ran to the ladder, leaped up and grabbed it, and began climbing. When she was halfway up, a laser beam missed her head by inches. She turned and fired at a man who stood on the ground in front of the house. At the last second a small gust of wind ruined her aim and she missed, but by the same token his next beam missed her as the ladder swirled around in the wind. She fired once more, and reached the hatch before he could aim and fire a third beam.

"I'm here!" she said. "Get us the hell out of here!"

"Some ship you stole," said Cole. "It's low on fuel, its light drive is inoperative, and two of its gyro-stabilizers are missing."

"I didn't have time to window-shop," she said angrily. "Just take us back to the spaceport and we'll get the *Kermit*."

"This may be trickier than you think," said Cole. "Djinn's men have probably contacted the spaceport already."

"Why?" asked Val. "*They* don't know we can't shift to light speeds or that we've barely enough fuel to get us past the rings."

"Let's hope you're right," muttered Cole.

She *was* right, and a few minutes later they were headed back out of the Albion Cluster to rendezvous with the *Teddy R* and deliver David Copperfield's cherished first edition.

Cole waited patiently until Mr. Jones opened the front door and escorted him inside. He followed the man down the long corridor to the study that was becoming quite familiar to him, then entered.

"Steerforth!" said David Copperfield happily, walking around his desk to greet him. "I never expected you back so soon!" He paused. "Have you begun making plans to get it for me?"

Cole placed a package on the desk. "With the somewhat reluctant compliments of Euphrates Djinn."

David Copperfield stared at the package. "It's really here!" he said softly. "After all these years, it's really here!" He picked it up lovingly. "We'll speak in a moment or two. But first . . ." His alien fingers gently removed the wrapping, revealing the book in all its worn glory. He opened it, then looked up, and though he was an alien Cole thought his face, at that instant, looked exactly like that of a small child who was about to cry. "There's no autograph."

"You're looking at the endpaper," said Cole. "It's on the title page."

Copperfield turned to the title page, and a look of almost human ecstasy crossed his face.

"I don't know how to thank you!" he said.

"Sure you do," said Cole. "Fifty percent of market value for two years, and you'll help us set a trap for the Shark."

"Oh, that!" said Copperfield dismissively. "It's already done. But you deserve even more, and I shall have to find exactly the proper reward for you. You have no idea what this means to me."

"Back up a couple of sentences," said Cole. "*What's* already done?"

"The *Pegasus* will be here in three days," said Copperfield, never taking his eyes off the book. "That should give you ample time to prepare, should it not?"

"Three days is fine," said Cole. "Did the Shark, or whoever you spoke to, mention anything about Donovan Muscatel?"

"Not a word," said Copperfield. "Have they gone into partnership?"

"No," answered Cole. "Muscatel's got three ships out looking for him."

"Ah!" said Copperfield. "Then *he* was the one who hit Cyrano a few days ago. I heard about that, but the details were very vague."

"The Shark hit Muscatel's headquarters, killed a bunch of his men, and destroyed a ship."

"Well, that's one way to eliminate your competition," said Copperfield. "Of course, you must first make sure they're all gathered there in one spot." He finally looked up from the book. "I just noticed: you've come alone. I hope the remarkable Miss Twist is still among the living?"

"She's fine," said Cole. "But now that you and I have an understanding, I decided I didn't need a bodyguard."

"One always needs bodyguards," said Copperfield. "And she is quite beautiful and quite formidable."

"Yeah, it's a pity we're going to get her ship back for her. She makes a good addition to my crew, especially with her knowledge of the Inner Frontier."

"Retrieving her ship might not be as easy as you make it sound," said the alien. "My reading of the Hammerhead Shark is that he'll blow himself and his ship up before he'll surrender them."

"Then we'll take all the billions you're going to pay us and buy her another ship," said Cole.

"You really mean to put her aboard her ship or a substitute?" asked Copperfield.

"Yes."

"Then I take it that you are not emulating Tom Sawyer and Becky Thatcher."

"Wrong author," said Cole. "But no, we're not."

"Perhaps I shall toss my hat into the ring," he suggested. Then he smiled. "Figure of speech, of course. Actually, I never found a hat that could fit my head."

"That's fine with me," said Cole. "Just try not to get her mad, especially in close quarters." He looked around the study. "Have you got a subspace radio around here? My ship's too far away for me to contact it with my communicator."

"Anything for the man who obtained my heart's desire," said Copperfield, making a gesture in the air with his left hand. Instantly a panel atop his desk vanished and a radio was elevated until it seemed to be sitting atop the desk.

"Thanks," said Cole. He walked over, uttered the scramble code and the *Teddy R*'s approximate position on the edge of the Frontier, and waited for a response while Copperfield thumbed through his book.

"Forrice here," said the Molarian. "All I'm getting is audio. You want to go to visual, too?"

"Not necessary," replied Cole. "I'll make it brief. I'm still on Riverwind."

"Are you all right?"

"I'm fine, the *Kermit*'s fine. I want you to bring the *Teddy R* here within a Standard day."

"That close to the Republic?" asked Forrice.

"That's right."

"Just making sure," said the Molarian. "Is there anything else?"

"Yes," said Cole. "Service the weapons and the defensive shields along the way. I want everything in perfect shape when you arrive."

"Will do. Is that everything?"

"That's it."

"See you soon," said Forrice, breaking the connection.

"Who was that?" asked Copperfield. "He didn't sound quite human."

"He'd be unbearable if he was any more human," answered Cole. "He's my First Officer."

"What's his name, in case I need to contact him?"

Cole smiled. "I gave him a code name you'll have an easy time remembering."

"Oh?"

"Sydney Carlton," said Cole.

"I like him already!" exclaimed Copperfield happily.

"I thought you might," said Cole. "Back to business. Where was the *Pegasus* when it contacted you—on the Inner Frontier or in the Republic?"

"Oh, on the Frontier, absolutely. Our friend Olivia Twist has seen to it that every police and military vessel in the Republic is on the lookout for it." The alien looked at Cole. "Suddenly you appear troubled."

"I am," responded Cole. "You're a few light-years from the Republic. Why does the Shark think he's going to get here without being identified and stopped?"

"I never considered that," admitted Copperfield.

"Well, we'd better *start* considering that," said Cole. "If we're going to lay a trap for him, we've got to know how to spot him when he shows up."

Cole had been back on the *Teddy R* for less than an hour before David Copperfield's image appeared in front of him, looking very distraught.

"What is it?" asked Cole. "We're monitoring your system. Nothing's entered it since I left."

"I've been doing some serious thinking," said Copperfield.

"And?"

"And I must have been mad not to have realized the consequences of this agreement."

"We'll protect you," Cole assured him. "I told you when we first discussed it that we'll stop him before he leaves the spaceport. He'll never get through to your house."

"You're not thinking this through, Steerforth," said the alien.

"Enlighten me."

"Like I told you, Olivia Twist has alerted everyone between here and the Republic. The police and the Navy are primed to find and stop the *Pegasus*."

"So?" said Cole, wondering where the alien was leading.

"Don't you understand?" said Copperfield, his face agitated, his voice shaking with desperation. "If the Shark makes it to Riverwind with everyone on the lookout for him, either he's not in the *Pegasus* or he's disguised it so well that it got past the Navy. And if they can't spot it, how can you?"

"He's still on the *Pegasus*," said Cole with more certainty than he suddenly felt. "He's got three of Muscatel's ships on his tail. He couldn't take the time to change ships. Besides, there's no way he'd give up its armaments."

"Then it doesn't look like the *Pegasus* anymore!" yelled Copperfield. "It's got a new exterior, or new ID, or new *something!*"

"We'll spot it," persisted Cole. "I've got Olivia Twist here. Believe me, she'll know how to identify her own ship."

"Steerforth, we've been friends since boarding school, but I don't trust your judgment on this."

"You can't call it off," said Cole. "If you contact him to stay away, he'll figure out that you were selling him out and then lost your courage."

"Why should he? I'll tell him I just heard of a plan to ambush him."

"You'd do that to Olivia Twist?" said Cole. "If so, then we'd have no choice but to explain to the Shark that you betrayed us all—first him, then Olivia and myself."

"You'd really do that, wouldn't you?" demanded Copperfield.

"Only if I had to. Believe me, we'll stop him at the spaceport."

"But I *don't* believe you! I want to come up to your ship until this is over!"

Cole shook his head. "You can't. We need you there or the Shark will know it's a trap. You have no other reason not to be there to meet him."

"Can't I come up to the ship and just throw my image down to my office, much the way I'm speaking to you now?"

"Let me check on that," said Cole. "I'll get back to you in a couple of minutes."

He killed the connection, then contacted Val.

"Let me guess," were her first words. "He's lost his nerve already."

"Good guess," said Cole.

"You told him he had to go through with it, of course."

"Of course. But he asked if he could come up to the *Teddy R* and just cast his holo down to the office. I didn't think so, but I thought

I'd check with you first. I assume the *Pegasus* has portable sensors that can tell the difference?"

"Just about every ship does," said Val. "Maybe not this ancient thing we're on, but *real* ships do. More to the point, the Shark doesn't need them. He's got a couple of extra senses that Men don't have. A holographic image will never fool him."

"That's what I thought."

"So are you going to let him come up anyway?"

"No."

"Good," said Val. "I should have figured it. You seem polite and you seem soft, but no one commands a starship by *being* soft." She paused and stared at him curiously. "Did you really win all those medals they talk about?"

"They ought to be through talking about them by now," said Cole. "It's ancient history."

"And they say you were demoted twice," she continued. "Now, *that* shows character."

"You really think so?"

"Absolutely."

"Let me give you a gentle hint," said Cole. "If you ever give up the pirating trade, don't enlist in the Republic's Navy."

"It's not real high on my list of priorities," she assured him.

"Okay, I'd better get back to David Copperfield and give him the bad news." Cole broke the connection and contacted Copperfield again.

"Well?" said the alien anxiously.

"Out of the question," replied Cole.

"I don't like this, Steerforth. If you don't spot the ship, you're no worse off than before."

"Think it through," said Cole. "If we don't spot the ship, you'll do your business with the Shark and he'll leave Riverwind none the wiser."

Suddenly Copperfield's alien eyes widened. "That's right, isn't it?" He smiled. "I trust you don't mind if I hope he sneaks past your defenses?"

"They're *your* defenses too," Cole reminded him. "And no, I don't mind."

"Good," said Copperfield, obviously relieved. "I was about to rename my mansion Bleak House."

"That's what I like—confidence in an ally."

Cole broke the connection and wandered up to the bridge, where Forrice was in command.

"Anything enter the system in the last few minutes?" he asked.

"Three freighters and a one-man ship," answered the Molarian.

"Damn it!" muttered Cole. "We can't stay here forever. The Navy doesn't want the *Pegasus* half as bad as it wants the *Teddy R.* We're bound to be spotted before long."

"Excuse me for interrupting," said Sharon Blacksmith as her image appeared between them, "but do you really think he had time to give the *Pegasus* much of a makeover? After all, we know that it was clearly identified as the *Pegasus* when it hit Muscatel's headquarters, and we can assume it's been on the lookout for Muscatel's ships ever since. I don't know how long it takes to disguise a ship, but it's got to be longer that he had."

"Let's make sure of it," said Cole. "There's one way he could do it without touching down. In fact, he could even do it in hyperspace."

He contacted Val.

"What now?" she asked.

"Your crew on the *Pegasus*—were they all human?"

"Yes."

"What about the Shark's?"

"He had a couple of Lodinites, and I think there was an Atrian."

"But no Tolobites?"

"What the hell's a Tolobite?"

"Our crew member Slick is a Tolobite."

"No, he's the first I've ever seen."

"Thanks." He closed the connection. "All right, if they didn't have a Tolobite who could work in the cold of space with no protective equipment, they couldn't have disguised it. I'll grant them one hour to get rid of its insignia—if it still had any after Cyrano; it'd make sense not to advertise who it is. Then, if the Shark is an even more skilled pirate than Val, and we have to assume he is or he couldn't have stolen her ship, either he or someone who works for him could change the registration and ID codes before they ever had to approach a planet."

"You're probably right," agreed Forrice. "That means if we can get a visual, that might be enough for Val to identify it."

"It won't work," said Sharon.

"Why not?" demanded the Molarian.

"I'm the one who questioned her when she came aboard, remember?" said Sharon. "The *Pegasus* is a class-M300 vessel. You know how many of them are zipping around the Inner Frontier? She's added all kinds of defenses and armaments, but its basic structure is that of a cargo ship." She paused. "I just checked my sensors. You know how many M300 ships there are in the system at this very minute? Five. Are you going to blow them all out of the ether?"

"All right, all right," said Forrice. Then: "How do we know that one of them isn't the *Pegasus*?"

"While you've been discussing the problems of the universe, I've been monitoring the spaceport. Nothing resembling Val's description of the Hammerhead Shark has shown up, so we've still got some time."

"But it does imply that we'd better post some people down there, since we're not certain to spot him before he lands," said Forrice.

"*Will* he land?" asked Cole. "Won't he send down a shuttle?"

"Cargo ships aren't like starships, Wilson," said Sharon. "They're built to enter atmospheres and land. How else would they load and unload their cargo?"

"Then we'd better organize a party to wait for them at the spaceport," said the Molarian. "We'll need Val to identify them, and—"

"Val stays here," said Cole. "If there's a way to spot the *Pegasus* before it lands, we can't spare her."

"We could send some bodyguards down to David Copperfield's house," suggested Sharon.

"Yeah, I suppose it couldn't hurt," said Cole thoughtfully. "But they're only part of the solution. The Shark's not going to take his whole crew to David's place, even if he manages to sneak past us—and we don't want to eliminate just some of his muscle, or even the Shark himself. We need to take out his entire crew before anyone else can find out what's happened here, or who's responsible for it. Even if we don't, how long do you think David Copperfield can stay in business if word gets out that he sold one pirate out to another?"

"So Val stays on the ship," said Forrice. "She'd damned well better be able to spot the *Pegasus* when it shows up."

"My sentiments precisely," agreed Cole.

"So who do we send?" asked Forrice.

"Well, it can't be you or me," said Cole. "Or Sharon, or Christine, or Val. I suppose Bull Pampas and—"

"You're not thinking clearly, Wilson," said Sharon.

"Oh?"

"There are three crew members who should have first refusal about going down there to face the Shark if he gets by us," she continued.

"Of course!" he said. "Bring me the two Men and the Pepon we picked up on Cyrano."

A moment later he was facing Jim Nichols, Dan Moyer, and Bujandi.

"I've summoned you here to offer you an assignment," said Cole. "The Hammerhead Shark is on his way to Riverwind. We have every intention of stopping him before he lands, but he may have disguised his ship, and if he has an inkling that we're waiting for him, he may have arranged some distractions. So I want some people waiting down there if he gets by us. You have carte blanche to take whatever action is necessary to see to it that he doesn't get out alive. But I want you to be aware of the fact that there's a chance that the local authorities or even the Navy may confront you before you have a chance to return to the *Teddy R.* Therefore, this is not an assignment. I need volunteers, and I thought given what happened back on Cyrano you should have first crack at it."

All three volunteered, and he told them to take the *Alice* and depart for the planet after drawing their weapons from the armory.

"Now what?" asked Forrice.

"Now we wait."

"That's all? Just wait?"

"My experience of war is that it's ninety-nine percent waiting—and when that other percent comes along you wish you were still waiting," said Cole.

Hours passed.

"Captain," said Christine Mboya, as she checked her sensors again, "there's a lot more traffic moving into the system."

"Military?" asked Cole.

"Not as far as I can tell, sir."

"No sign of the *Pegasus*?"

"None, sir," she replied. "But I've been told that it may not resemble the Valkyrie's description of it."

"Are you monitoring all the spaceport's transmissions?" asked Cole.

"Incoming and outgoing, yes, sir."

"All right. Get me David Copperfield again."

An instant later Copperfield's image appeared on the bridge. "Have you changed your mind, Steerforth?" the alien asked hopefully.

"No, David, I haven't," said Cole. "But I have a couple of questions for you. First, how corruptible are your spaceport officials?"

"What a silly question!" said Copperfield, laughing in spite of himself. "If they weren't corruptible, how could I remain in business on Riverwind?"

"Second question," continued Cole. "Is there any other spaceport on the planet that can accommodate an M300 ship?"

"There isn't another spaceport on the planet, period," answered Copperfield. "Oh, some of the smaller one-man and two-man jobs might be able to land at a local airstrip, though it almost never happens, but certainly something the size of Olivia Twist's ship won't be able to."

"Thanks, David. That's what I wanted to know."

"I don't suppose you know where it is yet?" asked Copperfield glumly.

"Not yet," said Cole. "Don't look so unhappy. Along with your own muscle, you've got three motivated Muscatel crew members with you."

"Most of my own men have deserted me," complained Copperfield. "As for your three, they're proper and polite and saying all the right things, but you know and I know that if it's a choice between protecting me and killing the Shark and his men, they're going to choose the latter."

"We're doing our best to see to it that it doesn't come down to that choice," Cole said reassuringly. He stared at the alien. "Put that pistol away or hide it better."

"Pistol?"

"In the pocket of what passes for your waistcoat."

"That's not a gun," said Copperfield. "It's the book you brought back for me. If I have to exit in a hurry, it's coming with me."

"What about the rest of your Dickens books?" asked Cole. "I saw a shelf of ancient ones in your study."

"None of them are signed."

"Cargo ship landing on Riverwind," announced Briggs from his station across the bridge.

"I'll talk to you later, David," said Cole, breaking the connection before Copperfield could ask panicky questions about the ship in question. "What have we got there, Mr. Briggs?"

"It's not an M300, but it's the same size. Could he have somehow changed its outline?"

"Not with three of Muscatel's ships hot on his trail," said Cole. "Keep on it and tell me what you find out." He turned to Christine. "Has the *Alice* finally been moved into a hangar?"

"Yes, sir."

"Good. No sense letting him know there's a military shuttlecraft on the planet. The registration papers say it was sold to a private party. That may satisfy the local authorities, but it'll never fool the Shark."

"But why would it worry him, sir?" she asked. "The *Pegasus* has ten times the firepower."

"Because its presence implies the existence of a mother ship," said Cole. "Admittedly the *Teddy R* isn't going to give our opponents nightmares, but on the other hand, until they locate us, they don't know that the *Alice* didn't come from Fleet Admiral Marcos's flagship."

"Sir?" said Briggs.

"Yes, Mr. Briggs?"

"The ship is transporting refrigeration units for a new housing complex. It's unloading them, and is due to take off in about ten minutes."

"If it's here for more than twenty minutes, let me know," said Cole. Suddenly he raised his voice. "Hey, Sharon!"

"You don't have to yell," she replied as her holo popped into view. "Someone from Security is always monitoring the bridge."

"Bully for them," said Cole. "Is Val asleep?"

"Let me check." She looked at some monitors. "No, she's not in her cabin."

"Where is she?"

"Not in the mess hall. Not in the officers' lounge. Ah! Got her! She's working out with Bull Pampas in that tiny exercise room."

"She's working out?" he persisted. "She's not . . . ah . . ."

"She's lifting weights," said Sharon. "And before you ask, *dead* weights."

"Okay, thanks. Go back to being a Peeping Tom."

"Thomasina, please," she replied with mock dignity, but he was already on his way to the airlift.

A moment later he entered the cramped confines of the exercise room, and instantly made a face. "Stinks of sweat," he noted.

"Just means we've been working hard," replied Val, as Pampas jumped to attention and saluted.

"Relax, Bull," said Cole. "I just want to talk to Val for a minute."

"I'll leave, sir," said Pampas. "We were just about done anyway."

"It won't take long," said Cole. "Stick around."

"I'll take a quick Dryshower and be back in fresh clothes in about ten minutes," said Pampas, walking out into the corridor.

"What is it?" asked Val.

"Did you ever disguise your ship before?" asked Cole.

"Once the *Pegasus* developed a reputation I always disguised it," she answered.

"How?"

"I programmed a number of false registrations, names, and IDs into it."

"Good," said Cole. "You'd recognize them if you saw or heard them?"

"Yes."

"I'm going to have Christine run the ID of every ship that's entered the system. Let me know if any of them could belong to the *Pegasus*."

"Happy to."

He looked around for a holo lens. "I don't think we can transmit them to the exercise room. The infirmary is right down the corridor; let's go over there and contact the bridge."

She accompanied him to the small admissions room, where he contacted Christine. She listed thirty-two ships that had entered the system in the past Standard day. When she was done, Cole looked at Val questioningly.

"No, I don't recognize any of them."

"Oh well, it was worth a try. We'll run any new ones by you every few hours."

"Fine," she said, heading back to the exercise room.

Cole returned to the bridge, though he had no idea what he planned to do there. He was getting nervous. The *Teddy R* hadn't been bothered yet, but it was only a matter of time before a police or military ship noticed its configuration and started putting two and two together. He was too close to the Republic to feel comfortable, and he had no idea how long he'd have to stay here before the *Pegasus* showed up. What if the Shark sensed a trap, or simply changed his mind? The *Teddy R* could be stuck here, waiting for a ship that never came, a target for the Navy ships that he knew would inevitably come.

There had to be *something* he was overlooking, something he could do. He was sure of it, but it was just beyond his mental grasp, and that frustrated him.

Finally he stalked off to the mess hall in a foul mood. Three crew members, one human and two Mollutei, nodded a greeting to him, saw that he was in no mood to socialize, and managed to finish their meals and leave within three or four minutes. He sat alone in the mess hall, glowering at his untouched coffee, until Sharon Blacksmith showed up and sat down opposite him.

"One of us does not look happy," she remarked.

"One of us is wondering how much longer he can stay in this system without endangering the entire crew beyond the limits of acceptability," he replied. "What if the son of a bitch doesn't show up for a week?"

"Then we'll leave," said Sharon. "And he's a son of a shark."

"Don't make light of this," said Cole. "If we leave, we're putting David at his mercy."

"I didn't know you were that fond of David."

"I'm fond of fifty percent of market value for two years." He paused. "The hell I am. To tell you the truth, I'm not fond of the whole damned pirate business. We're a military ship and a military crew. We should be doing military things."

"We are. We're going to war with pirate ships."

"It sounds good, but so far we've destroyed one pirate ship, we're trying not to destroy another, we've robbed one fence, we're helping another, and here we are, risking our ship and our lives—and for what? For fifty percent of market value."

"Get used to it, Wilson," she said. "They're never going to take us back. You know that."

"I don't want to go back," he said. "I just want to feel like something more than a thief on a grand scale."

She stared at him long and hard. "This has nothing to do with the current situation," she said at last. "Hell, you *like* David Copperfield. I can tell whenever you speak about him. And everyone likes Val—even you."

"I told you: I didn't spend my whole life training to be a thief, and a pirate by any other name . . ."

"All right, I believe you. So what?"

"So nothing. We've set this situation up. We have to go through with it. I made a promise to Val. I made another to David Copperfield. I've got two men and an alien who trust me sitting on the planet just waiting to be attacked. We'll see it through. Then we'll consider what comes next."

"Whatever you decide, you know we're behind you," she said, then noticed that he was paying no attention to her but was staring at some fixed point in space. "What is it?"

"I'm an idiot," he said suddenly.

"We all love you anyway," she said lightly.

"It was staring me in the face."

"What was?"

"The three crewmen I sent down to protect David Copperfield," he replied.

"I haven't got the slightest idea what you're talking about," said Sharon.

He touched his communicator, and instantly Christine's image appeared.

"Yes, sir?" she asked.

"Contact Moyer and Nichols and whatever the hell the Pepon's name is," said Cole. "There are three Muscatel ships pursuing the *Pegasus*, or at least we have to assume they are. They have to communicate with each other. Have the crewmen give you any access codes they can remember. I don't want you to try to contact them. I don't even care if you monitor them. I just want you to identify them and their positions."

"Yes, sir."

The holograph vanished.

"*That's* what I was missing!" he said, his depression forgotten. "If we can't identify the *Pegasus*, at least we can identify the ships that are tracking it. Once we pinpoint their positions, we should be able to figure out where the *Pegasus* is and how soon it'll get here."

"Always assuming they *are* tracking the *Pegasus*."

"Wouldn't you, if it had killed most of your men and destroyed your headquarters?"

"I might think I was lucky to be alive and decide I didn't want any more of the Hammerhead Shark."

He shook his head. "Donovan Muscatel didn't get to be one of the biggest pirates on the Frontier by ducking his enemies. He'll be in hot pursuit, and when we find *him*, we'll have a pretty good idea of where to find the Shark." Suddenly his appetite returned. He ordered a sandwich and a beer, finished them both quickly, remembered his coffee and finished that too, and then hurried back to the bridge.

"Well?" he said as he approached Christine Mboya.

"They're just giving me the codes now, sir," she said.

"What the hell took so long?"

"They didn't want to do it in front of Mr. Copperfield, and he didn't want to leave his study. I don't know why he feels safer there than anywhere else, especially when he's still got his bodyguards stashed around the place, but that was the problem. There were computers in every room, of course, but all of them were security-coded. He finally found one in the pantry, of all places, that would let him contact the ship without passwords or security codes. I gather Mr. Copperfield uses it when he's willing to be monitored by the police or whoever." She glanced down at her monitors. "The codes are all in, sir."

"And the police might know them?"

"It's possible," she answered. "Do we care?"

"No, not really. They don't know what the codes are for, and even if they did, the Muscatel ships haven't broken any laws. The police can't act on what they've got." Cole paused. "Okay, let's get to work."

She tried a code, with no response, then a second and a third.

"It's not working, sir," she announced.

"Keep going," he said. "How many more codes did Moyer send up?"

"Only four more, sir. The fourth doesn't work."

"Damn it! Something's got to work!" said Cole. "If the Shark is on his way here, so is Muscatel!"

"The fifth doesn't work, sir." Pause. "Neither does the sixth."

"Shit!" said Cole. "I hate it when I get a great idea and it doesn't work!"

"Wait a minute, sir!" said Christine. "The seventh code *is* working." She paused, frowning. "Well, I'll be damned!"

It was the first time Cole had ever heard even so inoffensive an expletive as "damn" pass Christine Mboya's lips. "What is it?" he asked.

"They're headed for this system, sir," she said. "They'll reach it in about seven minutes. And they're not coming together, but triangulating on it. That means the *Pegasus* has *got* to be here, sir." She looked up, puzzled. "But all of my sensors say it isn't."

"That's impossible," said Briggs, staring at his own monitors. "It *must* be here!"

"It is, or they wouldn't be converging on Riverwind," said Cole.

"Maybe so, sir," said Christine. "I think they've managed to cloak it somehow. At any rate, I can't spot it."

Cole seemed lost in thought for a moment. Then he looked up.

"Maybe you won't have to," he said.

"Sharon," said Cole, "did Val give you any contact codes for the *Pegasus* when you first debriefed her?"

"A handful of them," replied Sharon Blacksmith's image. "Why?"

"Start using them. Let me know if anything you send gets a response."

"You don't really think it will, do you?"

He shook his head. "Not much sense cloaking your ship, however the hell they did it, if you're going to answer your subspace radio. Still, it's a first step."

"What if they *do* respond?" asked Sharon.

"Talk to them."

"About what?"

"Sports. Sex. The weather. I don't much care. Just keep them talking."

"So the Muscatel ships can pinpoint them?"

"Right. Now go do it."

"It's not going to work," said Christine as Sharon's image vanished.

"Probably not. But like I said, it's our obvious first step. Mr. Briggs, I want you to plot the courses of the three Muscatel ships and see exactly where they converge—and when."

"Yes, sir," said Briggs, going to work with his computers.

"Val," said Cole, "I need some input."

"What is it?" asked the Valkyrie as her image popped into existence on the bridge.

"You didn't tell me that the *Pegasus* had a cloaking device," he said.

"I told it to Security. *You* never asked."

"Is it any good? Most of them aren't worth the powder to blow 'em to hell."

"I never use it," she said. "It's an enormous drain on the power. The Shark would be crazy to use it for more than five or six hours unless he knew he could refresh his nuclear pile tomorrow." She paused. "I assume from your question that he's activated it?"

"Yes."

"Then it's obvious he smells a trap."

"Maybe he's just playing it safe. After all, he's a pirate and he's very near the Republic—and they love the notion of hot pursuit."

She took her head adamantly. "Not a chance. The Republic wants us a lot more than it wants him, and no one's bothering us, are they? If he's using the cloak, it's not the Republic he's afraid of."

"Okay, next question. We can't spot him. How are Muscatel's men able to track him?"

She shrugged. "I don't know. Maybe from neutrino activity or some emissions."

He frowned. "That doesn't make sense. Why could they find it if we can't? Either it's camouflaged or it isn't."

"Different technologies specialize in different things," she answered. "You know that. Donovan Muscatel bought his ships from the Vapines of Romanitra II. They're humanoid, but they have different senses than we do. What's standard for their sensors might be impossible for the *Teddy R*'s."

"Thanks for nothing," he muttered.

"I know how to cloak a ship," she said defensively. "I've never had to track one that was cloaked."

"Sorry to interrupt," said Sharon, her image appearing right next to Val's, "but the *Pegasus*, if it's there, doesn't respond to any of the codes Val gave me."

"Well, of course it wouldn't, not if they're trying to stay undetected," said Val. "You need my Captain's code."

"What the hell is a Captain's code?" asked Sharon. "I never heard of it."

"Every Starship Captain has one," said Cole. "Or at least every Captain *should*. Let's say that the enemy boards the ship and takes it over. The ship is approaching the fleet, or just your fellow pirates as the case may be. You've got to be able to override the enemy's commands or they'll kill your friends and allies. Every captain knows how."

"It's not in my records," said Sharon. "Come to think of it, neither is yours."

"It's the one code that's never written down or locked in a data bank, for obvious reasons," said Cole. "If the enemy, or a turncoat, can find it, it's no damned use." He turned to Val. "What will the *Pegasus* do if you transmit your code?"

"Nothing," said Val.

"Nothing?" he persisted.

"You're just talking about sending the code, not giving it any orders?" she said.

"Right."

"Then I stand by my answer," she concluded. "Nothing."

"How will you know the message got through?"

"The ship will acknowledge receipt of the code."

"By subspace radio?"

"By whatever means the message was transmitted," said Val.

"So if you radio it from the *Teddy R*, it'll send its acknowledgment back to the *Teddy R*?"

Her eyes widened in comprehension. "Yes."

"Give that code to Sharon."

"Not Christine?" asked Val. "She's at the main transmitting station."

"No, she's going to be too busy tracking the three Muscatel ships."

"But you want to send it right now?" asked Val.

"Hell, no. We're about to hightail it out of the system. We'll send it in about four more minutes."

"I don't understand," said Val angrily. "Are you going to help me take my ship back or not?"

"Not when we've got three other ships that are going to do it for us," said Cole. "Sharon, when you get the code, send it on a tightbeam to Moyer. I don't want it reaching the *Pegasus*, wherever it is, and triggering a response to us."

"Got it," replied Sharon.

"Then tell him to make contact with the Muscatel ships—we already know which code will work—identify himself, feed them the code on a tightbeam, and have their ships get the *Pegasus* to respond to *their* signal."

"Tightbeam or not, if it passes near the *Pegasus*, she'll respond," said Val.

"Then have him break the code in half, and transmit the second half first, kill the connection, and then send the first half in another message to a different Muscatel ship. That way whether the *Pegasus* reads the message or not, the two halves aren't going to jell in the right order." Cole walked over and glanced at the various monitors in front of Christine. "All right, let's get going. The Muscatel ships will enter the system in less than two minutes. I want that code on the planet in one, and I want us safely away before the shooting starts."

Val's and Sharon's images vanished as the former gave the codes to the latter.

"Pilot," said Cole, "get us the hell out of here."

"Where to?"

"Take us out three light-years, then stop and hold that position."

Wxakgini grunted an assent and set the ship in motion.

"Christine, keep monitoring the three ships. If this works, they're going to start shooting in the next couple of minutes. I want to be able to call them off before they totally destroy the *Pegasus*."

"That's cutting it awfully close, sir," said Christine. "One properly aimed shot could destroy it."

"Not likely," said Cole. "Val installed all kinds of defense mechanisms. One-on-one it could probably win a battle with any of Muscatel's ships, but I think three of them ought to at least cripple it." He turned to Briggs. "Mr. Briggs, the instant the first shot is fired, I want you to open a channel to Moyer, Nichols, and the Pepon. Make sure they keep in constant touch with their three ships, and that they call them off once the *Pegasus* is disabled. I don't want our Third Officer going after Muscatel for destroying her ship."

Next he contacted Forrice, who was in his cabin.

"Sorry to wake you up," said Cole, "but I need you."

"I wasn't sleeping," answered the Molarian. "You'd have to be a corpse not to know what was going on here."

"I haven't made any of the transmissions private," acknowledged Cole. "The crew has a right to know what's happening."

"So what do you want me to do?"

"I need someone I can trust down in the Gunnery Section. And take Bull Pampas with you. He's still the best weapons mechanic we've got."

"You sure you don't want me on the bridge?"

"The bridge is going to have too damned many people on it," answered Cole. "I'm transferring control of the weapons down to Gunnery."

The Molarian nodded an acknowledgment. "What are your orders? Are we shooting the *Pegasus* or the three other pirate ships?"

"Neither," said Cole. "They're going to be too busy fighting each other to pay any attention to us."

"Then who *are* we expecting?"

"Hopefully no one," answered Cole. "But we're going to send some easily traced transmissions down to Riverwind. If the police or the military picks them up and traces them to us, it could be a problem."

"I don't think any police ships can stand up against us," offered Forrice.

"I don't think so either," said Cole. "But they're just cops doing their job. They're not the enemy unless they fire on us. While I'm in command, you'll fire on my orders only. If anything happens to me, use your judgment—and do what you can to avoid a conflict with the police."

"And if a military ship traces our messages back to us?" asked the Molarian.

"Blow it to hell and gone," said Cole. "Don't even wait for my orders. The second you identify it, fire. You can bet your ass they'll do the same to us as soon as they figure out who we are."

"Got it. Anything else?"

"Yeah," said Cole. "Don't miss."

The Molarian hooted his distinctive laughter.

"Now contact Pampas and meet him down there."

"I'm on my way," said Forrice, breaking the connection.

"Pilot, what's our position?" demanded Cole.

"Two and a half light-years out from Riverwind, sir," said Wxakgini.

"Sharon, does Moyer have the code?"

"Yes."

"Christine, has he sent it?"

"I can't pick up a transmission, sir, but one of the three Muscatel ships just made a minor course adjustment." She leaned forward, staring at her monitors. "They got it, sir! A second ship just changed course. Only a few degrees, but that's enough."

"Sir," said Briggs, "one of the Muscatel ships is transmitting a code every ten seconds—and a ship we can't spot is responding automatically."

Cole grinned. "The poor sonofabitch is probably searching high and low, trying to find a way to disable the response."

"I'd guess that the *Pegasus* is about halfway between the twelfth planet—the outer one—and Riverwind," said Christine, still studying her monitors.

"He's not going any closer to Riverwind," said Cole. "He's either going to make a break for deep space or he's going to turn and fight."

"Why do you think so?"

"Because everyone can read that response. Any police or military vessels in the area are going to want to know why he's cloaked, and he's already got his hands full with the three pirate ships. He doesn't want to have to protect his flanks and back too, especially since a Navy ship can outgun him."

"There it goes!" said Christine.

"What's happening?"

"He's fired a pulse cannon at the closest Muscatel ship."

"Did he hit it?"

"It's beyond his range," said Christine. "It's just barely entered the system."

"Okay, that's it," said Cole. "He's heading out."

"No, sir, he's firing."

"Christine, if *you* know it's beyond his range, don't you think *he* knows it?"

"Sir?" she said, puzzled.

"He's just trying to make them slow down and approach him a little more cautiously," said Cole. "That buys him a little maneuvering room. If they spread out and try to surround him, he'll only have one retreat route open. This way he's got half the galaxy—at least for another thirty seconds or so."

"There he goes," confirmed Christine.

"I thought we couldn't spot him."

"We can't—but the three pirate ships just increased their speeds."

"Deeper into the Frontier, of course?"

"Yes, sir."

"All right," said Cole. "Now we can sit back and enjoy the show."

"I beg your pardon, sir?"

"He's got to deactivate the cloak. It consumes too much power. If he's going to go at multiples of light speed, maneuver against three pursuers, and bring his guns into play, he can't keep the cloak on."

"Maybe he's just running, sir," suggested Briggs.

"Sooner or later he's got to face them," said Cole. "It might as well be sooner." He paused. "This isn't an act of piracy on Muscatel's part. It's a punishment party, and they're not going to call it off after what he did on Cyrano."

"Besides," added Val, her image popping into existence once again, "he's the Hammerhead Shark. He doesn't run."

"He's running right now," said Briggs.

She shook her head. "He's just choosing the battlefield. Believe me, I know that bastard."

"Can he take the three Muscatel ships?" asked Briggs.

"*I* could," said Val.

"What the hell kind of firepower do you have on the *Pegasus*?"

"Firepower's just half of it," said Val. She tapped her temple with a forefinger. "The rest of it's up here. If I could take them, *he* can take them."

"Let's hope they at least soften him up a bit for us."

"Well," said Val without much conviction, "you can hope."

Donovan Muscatel's three ships slowed down when they were a light-year out of the system and began adjusting their positions.

"What's going on?" asked Briggs.

"The *Pegasus* has either slowed down or stopped, and they're trying to encircle it," said Val, who had just come up to the bridge.

"It can't be done," said Briggs.

"They're doing it."

He shook his head adamantly. "That's one of the basic rules we learned at the Academy. You can't englobe an enemy with less than six ships, and twelve is optimum."

"They're not englobing him," said Val. "They're just making him work a little harder to get everyone in his sights, and giving one of them a head start if he makes a break for it." Her face reflected her contempt. "Fools. As if the Shark would run from the likes of them."

"So where is he?" asked Cole. "He can't fire while he's hidden. He'll shred the cloak and probably burn out half his systems."

"He's just watching and waiting," said Val. "If he's stopped dead in space, they can't track him through any neutrino activity."

"What's to stop them from firing where they think he is?" asked Christine.

"Those aren't the biggest ships around," answered Val. "He'd love to make them use up their ammunition."

"Besides," added Cole, "all he'd have to do is jettison some junk, and if he stays still, sooner or later they'll assume they hit him. Eventually they'll approach closer to make sure, and then he'll blow them away." He paused and shrugged. "At least, that's what I'd do."

For ten minutes there was no further movement, no radio signals, nothing. Then one of Muscatel's ships began moving again, approaching the spot where the three ships would intersect if they were all approaching at the same speed.

"He's too anxious," said Cole. "He's going to get himself blown to bits. He can't outgun the *Pegasus*, and he's sure as hell not trying to outthink it."

"He's got his screens and shields activated," said Christine, studying her monitors.

"They won't do much good if he gets a lot closer," said Cole. "A pulse cannon will tear right through them at eighty thousand miles."

"And it'll cripple him at two hundred thousand," added Val. "There's not a pirate ship on the Inner Frontier with better weapons. Well, except this one."

A second ship moved forward.

"He's going to kill them all," said Cole. He turned to Val. "I trust you told Sharon the full range of each of your weapons?"

"Yes."

"You'd better be right," said Cole. "I have a feeling we're going to have to face the *Pegasus* before too long." He sent his image down to the Gunnery Section. "How's it going? Everything ready?"

"Everything's primed," answered Forrice. "Bull and I have it all under control."

"Good. Get Morales down there to help."

"We don't need any help."

"Until one of you gets shot or one of the cannons goes haywire."

"But he's just a kid, Wilson."

"This is how kids grow up."

"You're the boss," said Forrice. "At least, until I take over the ship."

"You can have it."

"That's right," said the Molarian. "Wait until we're facing not one enemy but four of them, and then give it to me."

"Can I go back to the battle, or do you want to bitch some more?" asked Cole.

"Go. I'll summon the kid."

Cole broke the connection. "I see the third ship is moving. We ought to be able to pinpoint the *Pegasus* right now. Why aren't they firing at it?"

"Beats me," said Val.

Suddenly Cole frowned. "You don't suppose that asshole wants to take his revenge personally, do you? Make the Shark suffer physically rather than just blow him out of space?"

"I wouldn't put it past him," said Val.

"He's going to get all three ships killed for his trouble," said Cole. "The closer he gets, the better chance the *Pegasus* has of penetrating his defenses."

"Who knows what he lost on Cyrano?" said Briggs. "Maybe a wife or lover, maybe a kid who was going to take over the business, maybe some treasure he'd spent his whole life trying to get. He might not care about the risk."

"Well, he'd better *start* caring," said Cole. He turned to Christine. "How close are they getting to the spot?"

"The spot, sir?"

"The point they're converging on."

"The closest ship is about fifty thousand miles, the farthest is just over ninety, sir."

"If sound carried in space, I'd tell you to cover your ears," said Cole. "It won't be long now."

And suddenly, as the words left his mouth, the closest of the three Muscatel ships opened fire. Soon all three were firing pulse and laser cannons—and then the *Pegasus* became visible. It was clearly undamaged. It fired one cannon, and a huge ball of raw energy engulfed the closer ship. There was no explosion, no flare of light, nothing. One instant the ship was there, firing its weapons, and the next it was gone.

"That's some cannon you've got there," commented Cole.

"You've seen bigger, I'm sure," answered Val.

"On dreadnaughts," he acknowledged. "Never on a refurbished cargo ship."

"It cost me three years' loot to arm that ship the way I wanted it," she said proudly.

"Don't look so pleased with yourself," said Cole. "It's going to make our job that much harder."

The second ship was hit and vanished.

"Captain, I'm getting a transmission from the third ship," said Christine. "I'll put it on audio."

"How about visual, too?"

She shook her head. "They're not sending any visual signal."

"To the Captain of the *Pegasus*," said a voice. "This is Jonathan Stark, in command of the *Silver Demon*. You have killed our commander, Donovan Muscatel, who was in command of the second ship you destroyed. He was the one with the grudge against you; we were just following orders. We wish to terminate hostilities."

And then came the Shark's voice—incredibly deep, incredibly threatening. "You cannot end the battle that easily. Approach us under a signal of truce, allow us to board you, turn over all your weapons, let us take whatever we find of value, and we will let you live."

There was a long silence.

"We agree to your terms," said Stark.

"Good," boomed the Shark. "Then approach."

"They're fools," said Val.

"They can't outgun him," said Cole.

"They should turn around and get the hell out of here while they still can," she said. "I *know* the Shark. He doesn't honor truces."

"Maybe we can warn them," said Cole. "Christine, you're the expert. Is there some way we can send them a signal that the *Pegasus* can't intercept or read?"

"I'll see."

It became a moot point a minute later. When the *Silver Demon* got within sixty thousand miles of the *Pegasus*, the Shark blew it apart.

"Well, so much for that," said Cole. "It looks like it's up to us."

"We shouldn't have any trouble taking it, sir," said Briggs.

"We won't have any trouble *destroying* it," said Cole. "The trick is to disable it and then disarm the crew, so that Val can repossess it."

"That'll be a little harder," agreed Briggs.

It's starting to look like it'll be fucking impossible, thought Cole. *Just how much am I willing to endanger my own ship to help Val get hers back?*

"Sir!" said Christine excitedly. "I've got a message from the Shark!"

"For *us?*" asked Cole, surprised. "I'd have sworn he didn't even know we were here."

"No, sir. For David Copperfield."

And suddenly Cole got his first look at the Hammerhead Shark. His first impression was that the Shark was big. His second was that he was huge. The Shark's eyes extended far out from his head on bony stalks, just like the long-extinct hammerhead shark of Earth's oceans. His face seemed to be in a perpetual snarl as he glared into the camera. His chest and arms were massive and scale-covered, his belt held half a dozen hand weapons that seemed totally unnecessary, and his legs reminded Cole of smooth tree trunks. He did not wear a T-pack, the translating device that enabled most aliens to speak and understand Terran. Like many on the Inner Frontier, where T-packs were both rare and expensive, he'd learned the language himself, and spoke it in a frighteningly deep voice with very little trace of a sibilant accent.

"You betrayed me!" he bellowed, extending a clawed forefinger toward the hidden holo camera. "You tried to set me up!"

They could hear a near-hysterical David Copperfield denying it, but he'd forgotten to add his holograph to his message—and then Cole remembered: it wasn't Copperfield who'd turned off the camera. He had three crewmen stationed there. If the Shark landed, they were going to be outnumbered and outgunned; their only advantage would be the element of surprise.

"I'm coming to get you!" continued the Shark. "You like the writings of the humans that you imitate, you sorry piece of filth? Very well. I shall turn you into covers for the books you worship, piece by piece. That is my solemn pledge to you!"

The transmission ended.

"Pleasant guy, isn't he?" said Cole dryly.

"I told you what he was like," replied Val.

"Well, David did this at our instigation. We can't let him suffer for it. Four Eyes, are you ready?"

"Ready and locked on," said the Molarian's image.

"Remember: You're just disabling it."

"You'd better give me the order to fire or I won't even be able to do that," said Forrice. "He's approaching light speed."

"Fire," said Cole.

At first they couldn't see anything. Then Briggs's sensors picked it up, created an image, and flashed it on the bridge's largest viewscreen.

"Nice shot, Four Eyes," said Cole. "He looks to be in some distress, but he's still functional. Now we'll step in and finish the job."

"What do you mean, finish the job?" demanded Val.

"I don't mean destroy the ship," said Cole. "I mean, empty it of bad guys."

"I'll take the Shark myself," she said. "Nobody else on this ship could handle him."

"He's all yours."

And then the Shark's image appeared on the bridge. It looked from face to face, paused at Val's and smiled grimly, then continued looking until it came to Cole.

"Commander Cole," said the Shark. "I might have guessed. I recognize you from your holos. The Navy wants you almost as badly as I now do."

"It's Captain Cole, and you and the Navy are both destined to be disappointed."

"Captain?" repeated the Shark. "That won't last. It never does, not with you."

"It lasted long enough for us to meet. Your ship is disabled. You can't escape us, and you must know that we can outgun you. If you will surrender and turn the *Pegasus* over to its rightful owner, we will set you down on an uninhabited oxygen world to live out your lives. That's the best offer you're going to get, and it's not going to stay on the table forever."

"You dare to offer terms to *me*? I'm the Hammerhead Shark! I *make* offers, I don't accept them."

"Then you'd better learn to *start* accepting them," said Cole. "I'm withdrawing it in five Standard minutes."

"A lot can happen in five minutes," said the Shark, pulling his thin lips back to expose his pointed fangs in what seemed to be a very alien grin.

"Raise all our defenses, Mr. Briggs," said Cole softly. "I don't know what he's getting at, but he looks too damned confident."

"But if I am to choose an uninhabited oxygen world," continued the Shark, "I choose Riverwind."

And with that, the *Pegasus*'s cannon disgorged another huge pulse of energy, headed right for Riverwind.

"It's your choice," said the Shark. "Board my ship or save Riverwind. You can't do both in the five minutes it will take the energy pulse to hit."

He bellowed his laughter and cut the connection.

"Pilot, catch up with that damned thing!" ordered Cole.

"Which damned thing, sir?" asked Wxakgini. "The ship or the pulse?"

"The pulse, damn it!" Then: "Mustapha!"

The chief engineer's image appeared. "Yes, sir?"

"I assume you've been following this. Once we get within range, what the hell do we use?"

Mustapha Odom frowned. "It has no mass, sir, so we probably can't knock it off course. You'll have to find some way to dissipate it. Give it something to hit before it reaches the planet—and something explosive would be even better. Have we any explosives in the armory?"

"Four Eyes—how about it?"

"Just pulse, laser, and sonar," answered the Molarian. "We've got a thermite bomb in the cargo area, but no way of delivering it."

"This is the Captain!" shouted Cole. "I assume you're all listening in. Whoever's closest to the cargo area, get that bomb and move it to a shuttle. Tell Briggs which shuttle you've chosen. He'll pilot it from here."

"That's me, sir!" said Esteban Morales.

"I thought you were in the Gunnery Section," said Cole.

"I'm still closer than anyone else," he said, and they could hear his feet pounding down a corridor.

"Four minutes, sir," said Christine.

"If there's one thing I don't need right now," said Cole irritably, "it's a countdown."

Another minute passed.

"Done, sir," said Morales. "It's in the *Archie*."

"Okay. Mr. Briggs, open the shuttle hatch and send the *Archie* after that pulse at as many multiples of light speed as it'll take."

"It's off," said Briggs. "It's not built for these speeds, sir. It'll shake apart in a couple of minutes."

"A couple of minutes is all we need. Then it's going to blow up anyway."

"What should I do now, sir?" asked Morales.

"Get back to the Gunnery Section," said Cole.

"Gunnery?" asked Morales.

Oh, shit! thought Cole. *Don't tell me what I know you're going to tell me.*

"I'm on the *Archie*, sir. That's what I thought you wanted."

"Get into a protective suit, Mr. Morales," said Cole. "Fast!"

"Where the hell do we keep—? Ah! I see them!"

"As soon as you're in it, I want you to jettison."

"It'll kill him, Wilson," said Sharon Blacksmith's voice.

"Let's hope it doesn't."

"Don't you understand? Even if he lives through it at light speeds, he's going to be in terrible shape. In case it's slipped your memory, we're still not carrying a doctor!"

"It's not a choice between the kid and the ship, damn it!" said Cole. "It's between him and a city filled with people!"

"Ready to jettison, sir," announced Morales.

"Oh, Jesus! Did you hear all that?" asked Cole.

"It's okay, sir. I've always wanted to be a hero like you."

Heroes like me live, thought Cole bitterly. "All right, son. I don't know what advice to give you, because no one I know except Slick has ever been outside a ship at light speeds. Try to keep in a fetal ball to protect your vital spots. We'll pick you up less than thirty seconds from now."

"Here I go, sir."

Then there was silence.

Briggs was tracking the *Archie* on his sensor monitors. "Contact in about fifteen seconds, sir," he announced. "Providing there *is* contact and the shuttle doesn't melt first, or pass right through it."

"Don't worry about that. If we destroy it, it'll be on every screen in the ship. Concentrate on finding the kid."

"Got him, sir!"

"Any movement, any sign of life at all?"

"No, sir."

Suddenly all the screens turned a blinding white for a few seconds.

"That's it," announced Briggs. "No more energy pulse."

"And the kid?"

"We won't know until we pull him in."

Getting Morales aboard took more than the thirty seconds Cole had promised. More than two minutes. And it was clear before they pulled him out of his spacesuit that he had died instantly.

"Wrap him up," said Cole. "I'll read over him, and we'll give him a burial in space."

"Then what?" asked Forrice.

"Then we're going fishing," said Cole grimly.

Cole finished reading from the beat-up copy of the Bible he kept in his office, and Morales was jettisoned into space.

"He got his wish," said Forrice. "He died a hero."

"Fools die for their causes," replied Cole grimly. "Heroes live."

"You could have saved him."

"True," agreed Cole.

"But at the cost of a city."

"Also true."

"I've changed my mind," said the Molarian. "I guess I don't want to be Captain after all."

"I don't blame you," said Cole.

The two of them took the airlift up to the bridge, where Val and Domak had relieved Christine and Briggs. Cole turned to Forrice. "You're not on duty for a few hours yet. Why don't you get some sleep?"

"Molarians don't need that much sleep."

"The hell they don't."

"All right. I want to be here when we catch up with the Shark."

"I'll wake you as soon as we spot him. But if it takes a few hours, I want you fresh when you come back up here."

"All right," said Forrice reluctantly. "But you'd damned well better let me know when we find him."

"I will."

The Molarian went off to the airlift.

"All right," said Cole. "Has anyone got any idea where he is?"

"I haven't been able to find any trace of him, sir," said Domak.

"Me neither," said Val.

"He can't have gone that damned far," said Cole. "Lieutenant Domak, I want you to capture the images we have of the hit we made on the *Pegasus*. Enhance them as much as possible, and then have Mr. Odom look at them."

"Yes, sir."

"I still want first crack at him," said Val.

"I don't see anyone racing to fight him ahead of you," said Cole. "Just how tall is he, anyway?"

"Maybe a foot taller than me."

"And he must be three times as broad," said Cole. "How the hell do you beat something like that?"

"By spending your whole life training to beat something like that," she responded.

"Good answer." *Meaningless*, he thought, *but good.*

Cole found himself feeling hungry, and it occurred to him that he hadn't eaten in more than twelve hours, so he went to the mess hall and ordered a sandwich and a beer. As he was sitting at his table, Mustapha Odom approached him.

"May I sit down?" asked the engineer.

"Please do."

Odom pulled up a chair. "I've studied the images of the *Pegasus*."

"You're our expert," said Cole. "How far can it go in the condition it's in?"

"You've done some damage to its light drive and its stabilizers," answered Odom. "My best estimate, and it's only an estimate, is that it can't go more than about ten or eleven light-years before the drive gives out. They're going to have to set down for repairs, or that ship's going to be dead in space."

"Thanks," said Cole, getting to his feet. "That's what I needed to hear."

"Excuse me, sir," said Odom, "but if you're not going to eat the other half of your sandwich . . ."

"Help yourself," said Cole, walking to the airlift. A moment later he was back on the bridge. "Lieutenant Domak, how many star systems are there within a dozen light-years of Riverwind?"

"Four, sir."

"How many of them have oxygen worlds?"

She checked her monitors. "None, sir."

"That's encouraging," said Cole. "Pilot, take us by each world in the four closest star systems. Skip the gas giants."

"Yes, sir," said Wxakgini from his pod atop the bridge.

"Lieutenant, scan each world we come to. If Mr. Odom is right, and he usually is, the *Pegasus* is going to be on one of them."

"What do I do when I find it?" asked Domak.

"Take no action at all. Just let me know."

He noticed Val examining each of her weapons, making sure they were in perfect working order.

"You know, there's every likelihood that he's going to fire on us when he sees us, and that you'll never get close enough to use those."

"Maybe," she said. "But I plan to be ready."

"Very commendable. I'm just warning you that if he stands and fights, we may have no choice but to destroy the *Pegasus*."

"Just offer him the chance to fight me personally," she said. "He'll jump at it."

"Do you really think you can beat him?" asked Cole. "He looks awfully formidable."

"I can beat him."

He stared at her, and while he'd seen her in action and knew her skills, he couldn't imagine any way that she could hold her own against the Hammerhead Shark.

"Don't you look at me like that!" snapped Val. "I deserve the chance to take him!"

"All right," said Cole. "If he talks before he shoots, I'll make the offer." He turned to Domak. "I'll be in the lounge. Let me know when you find it."

He left the bridge and went to the cramped officers' lounge, where he tried to relax by watching a holographic entertainment featuring singers, dancers, magicians, and statuesque naked ladies, but he couldn't concentrate and he turned it off after twenty minutes. A few minutes later Domak's image appeared.

"Yes?" he said, suddenly alert.

"We examined the Priminetti and Vasquez systems, sir. Four planets in the first, seven in the second, excluding gas giants. No sign of the *Pegasus*."

"Keep looking. Either the *Pegasus* is on a planet in one of the next two systems, or Mr. Odom's never getting another one of my sandwiches."

"Yes, sir," she said as her image vanished.

He was restless, but didn't want to be seen pacing the bridge nervously, because that nervousness might spread to the crew. He considered stopping by Security, just to visit with Sharon, anything to take his mind off the waiting so that when it ended he'd be fresh and alert. He was about to leave the lounge when Domak's image appeared again.

"We've found it, sir."

"Good! Where is it?"

"The fifth planet of the Hamilton system, sir. I checked, and none of the planets have been named, so I guess it's just Hamilton V."

"Tell Pilot to hold our position," said Cole. "And wake Four Eyes. I'll be right over."

He left the lounge, walked down the corridor to the bridge, and was soon looking at the image the sensors had constructed of the *Pegasus*, sitting atop a flat, featureless plain.

"Is anyone working on it?"

"Two Men are outside in protective gear, sir," said Domak.

"Can you tell for sure that they *are* Men?" he asked.

"Neither of them is the Shark," she replied. "He gives off a different reading."

"So he's definitely inside the ship?"

"Yes, sir."

"Good. Let's let him know we're here."

"I'm not at the transmission console, sir," said Domak.

"Let's send something more interesting. Who's in Gunnery?"

"Idena Mueller and Braxite, sir."

"Idena, can you read me?"

"We can read and see you, sir," said Idena as her image appeared on the bridge.

"I want you to fire a laser beam toward the *Pegasus*," said Cole.

"*What?*" yelled Val.

"Shut up," said Cole harshly. He turned back to Idena's image. "I want you to miss it by one hundred yards. Then I want you to miss it a second time, by seventy-five yards. Can you do that?"

"Yes, sir."

"Okay, line up your shot and fire at will." Cole turned back to Val. "I'm trying to get your ship back. If you contradict me or challenge my orders again, I'll blow the damned thing to hell and gone. Do you understand?"

He could see her struggling with her self-control. Finally the tension seemed to ooze out of her and she nodded her head. "I understand. And I apologize."

"You don't have to apologize," he said. "Just don't do it again."

"There it is!" said Domak, as the first laser beam melted the rocky ground one hundred yards from the ship.

"Val, get our defenses up," ordered Cole. "If he thinks we're attacking rather than trying to get his attention, he may fire back."

"Done," said Val.

"And there's the second shot," announced Domak.

"All right," said Cole. "He should know that we wouldn't miss him twice, not after we hit him from long range near the Riverwind system. Now it's his move."

Nothing happened for almost a minute. Then the Hammerheead Shark's holograph appeared on the bridge, glaring balefully at Cole.

"Have your say," said the Shark harshly. "Then the battle commences."

"It won't be much of a battle," said Cole. "You're grounded and outgunned."

"I know it. You know it. Surely you didn't attract my attention just to tell me that."

"You know, you're a really unlikable character," remarked Cole.

"I take great pride in it."

"Somehow I'm not surprised."

"What have you to say?" demanded the Shark.

"We both know that I can destroy your ship and everyone on it— and near it—whenever I choose," said Cole. "The problem is, it's not *your* ship. It's *hers*." He gestured to Val. "And she'd like it back."

"What she wants doesn't interest me."

"I never thought it did. But we'd still like it back, so I'm willing to make you an offer." The Shark stared at him, but didn't say a word. "Same as before. If you and your crew will surrender your weapons and become our prisoners, we'll drop you off at the first uninhabited oxygen world we come to. I won't return your weapons, and I won't give you any means of reporting your plight or your position to any passing ships or nearby worlds, but at least you'll be alive. Have we got a deal?"

"I would rather die fighting than live a prisoner, even in a jail the size of a world," said the Shark.

"I was afraid you were going to say that," said Cole. "Very well. I have another proposition for you." Again the Shark said nothing. "The former Captain of the *Pegasus*—I'd give you the name she's currently using, but I'm sure it's not the one you know—is willing to give you the chance you want: to die fighting."

"Explain."

"She'll come down to the planet and fight you, one-on-one. If she wins, your crew gives up the *Pegasus* and everything in it, and surrenders to me."

"And if I win?"

"We give up all claim to the *Pegasus* and you go free."

"Wilson!" said Sharon's disembodied and outraged voice.

"If he kills her, what the hell do we want the *Pegasus* for?" Cole responded. He stared at the Hammerhead Shark. "Do we have a deal?"

"In principle," replied the Shark. "Only one detail must be changed."

"Which detail?" said Cole suspiciously.

"It occurs to me that your side is putting up nothing of value," said the Shark. "The woman is not a member of your crew, so surely you don't care if she lives or dies. And you just admitted that you have no interest in the *Pegasus*. So if I win, you've lost nothing. We have to sweeten the pot."

"With what?"

"I accept your proposition—provided that I fight *you* rather than her."

Cole stared at the Hammerhead Shark's grinning image for almost a full minute without speaking.

"Well?" demanded the Shark.

"You're on," said Cole.

"Wilson!" shouted Sharon.

"Are you crazy?" demanded Forrice.

"Be quiet, all of you. He challenged me. I accepted. That's the end of it."

"Oh, no, Commander Cole," said the Shark with a malevolent smile. "The end of it will come two seconds after our combat begins."

"It's Captain Cole. What weapons do we use?"

"I offer you your choice," said the Shark. "And they needn't be confined to government-issue. I'd dearly love to battle to the death with broadswords."

"I don't doubt it," replied Cole. "But we don't happen to have any."

"Pulse guns, burners, screechers, you name it," said the Shark. "Whatever it is, I accept it."

"Screechers."

"Very well. Screechers it shall be."

"One more thing," said Cole.

"What?"

"I'm not fighting where someone from the *Pegasus* can backshoot me."

"I don't need any help," the Shark assured him.

"Nevertheless."

"Doubtless you have something in mind."

"There's a ridge about two miles west of where your ship is located," said Cole. "I'll fly a shuttle down and land on the far side of it. The *Pegasus* doesn't have anything that can shoot through the ridge without killing both of us."

"How do I know you won't bring an entire party down with you?" demanded the Shark.

"I'll land before you walk to the ridge, and transmit holographs of the interior and exterior of the shuttlecraft to the *Pegasus*. We can speak during the transmission, so you'll know it's current and not canned. When you're satisfied that I'm alone and armed with nothing but a sonic pistol, come on over and take your chances."

"It's a deal!" said the Shark enthusiastically. "I'll be known as the one who killed the famous Wilson Cole!"

"It's 'infamous' these days," said Cole dryly. "The shuttle will depart the *Theodore Roosevelt* in the next five or six minutes. Keep an eye out for it—or in your case, maybe I should suggest that you keep an eye in for it."

But the Shark had already broken the connection.

"He's inside the *Pegasus*," reported Domak.

"Wilson," said Sharon's image, "sonic weapons won't work on an airless world. You know that."

"Yeah, I know it," said Cole. "But the Hammerhead seems to have overlooked it. I get the feeling he's not the brightest shark in the water."

"But he's the strongest, and you're going down there without any functioning weapons."

"Then I'll just have to improvise, won't I?" He turned to the Valkyrie. "Walk down to the shuttle with me."

"Val, not me?" demanded Sharon, half angry, half hurt.

"That's right," said Cole.

"You're going to let me fight in your place, right?" said Val eagerly as she walked with him to the airlift.

"No, I gave him my word."

"But I'm the only one with a chance against him!" she protested.

"We're short of time," said Cole, "so just for once stop arguing with me and listen, all right?"

She stared at him curiously as they exited the airlift and walked to the shuttle bay. "Go ahead and talk."

"That's better," said Cole. "As soon as I leave, I want you to go back to the bridge and monitor the Shark. When he sees me touch down, he's going to leave the *Pegasus*."

"Now tell me something I don't know."

"I'm about to."

He gave Val her instructions, boarded the *Kermit*, and took it down to the surface, landing on the west side of the ridge, as he had said he would do. He was sure the shuttle was being watched from the *Pegasus*, but he shot off a pair of chemical flares, just to make doubly certain they knew he was there.

"Let me see the interior of your shuttle," demanded the Shark.

Cole attached his helmet to his protective suit, then stepped outside and let the holo cameras show every inch of it.

"Now respond to me so that I'll know this image wasn't prepared a long time ago," said the Shark.

"I am responding to you so you'll know this image wasn't prepared a long time ago," replied Cole. "I have touched down west of the ridge I mentioned, and I set off two flares. Satisfied?"

"I'm on my way," said the Shark. "It should take me twelve Standard minutes to get there. Say a twelve-minute prayer to your god, Commander Cole, because in less than thirteen minutes you will be dead."

"I keep telling you, it's *Captain* Cole."

"Soon it will be the late Captain Cole."

"Save your breath," said Cole. "I don't want anyone to say I beat you because you were too tired to fight or that you used up all your oxygen getting here."

The Shark muttered what Cole assumed was an obscenity in its native tongue and stopped transmitting.

Cole went back into the *Kermit*, closed the hatch, took off his helmet, and sat down at the command console. He waited until seven minutes had passed, then activated his subspace radio.

"Okay, Val," he said. "It's time. I'll listen in if you don't mind."

"Right," she said. "This is the *Teddy R*, calling the *Pegasus*. Take a good look at my image. I want to make sure you know who's contacting you." A short pause. "I know every one of you backstabbing bastards, and you know me. And since you know me, you know it's not an empty threat when I tell you that if you don't take off within one minute and head two hundred miles due east, I'll blow you apart where you sit. If you obey my orders, you will be taken prisoner and set down on an oxygen world, but at least you'll be alive. If you're still on the ground in forty-five seconds, I guarantee you won't be."

A longer pause.

"If you try to leave the planet, there'll be pieces of you in orbit for the next million years."

A final pause.

"All right, Captain. They're airborne and heading east."

"Let them see that you're tracking them from above," said Cole. "It'll encourage them to land where they're supposed to land."

"Yes, sir."

"Well, I'll be damned," said Cole.

"What is it?" asked Val.

"In all the time you've been aboard the *Teddy R*, that's the first time you've ever said 'Yes, sir' to me. It's going to be a shame to lose you."

He cut the transmission, then contacted the Shark.

"You still on your way here?" he asked.

"Where else would I be?"

"Well, I'm afraid I've got some disappointing news for you," said Cole. "I've changed my mind."

"What do you mean?" demanded the Shark suspiciously.

"I don't feel like fighting anymore," said Cole, firing up the *Kermit*. "Perhaps some other time."

"I always knew you were a coward, despite all your medals," said the Shark. "When I get the *Pegasus* repaired, I'm coming after you, and next time you won't be able to run away."

"That could pose a problem," said Cole. "How much oxygen do you have in your suit?"

"Enough."

"Enough to walk two hundred miles?" said Cole. "I doubt it."

"What are you talking about?" shrieked the Shark.

"You'll figure it out," said Cole as the *Kermit* took off.

He returned to the *Teddy R* five minutes later. Val, Sharon, and Forrice were waiting for him in the shuttle bay.

"Not bad," said Val with a smile.

"I still want to know: Why the screecher?" asked Sharon.

"If something had gone wrong and I'd had to fight him, it made more sense to face an enemy who was armed with a pistol that didn't work on this world than one that did," replied Cole, starting to climb out of his protective suit.

"I guess you were right," said Forrice.

"What about?" asked Cole.

The Molarian throw a heavy arm around Cole's shoulders. "Fools die. Heroes live."

"Shit!" said Val, standing in the cargo area of the *Pegasus*, hands on hips. "Shit!"

She was staring at a small open container that was totally empty.

"What the hell happened to my Meladotian crystals?" she demanded.

"He sold them," said one of the cowering crew members.

"To whom?"

"We don't know. He went down to a planet with them and came back with money."

"All right, he came back with money," said Val. "Where is it?"

"He hid it."

"On the ship?"

"No, he didn't trust us."

"Well, he was right about that, anyway," she said disgustedly. "Now, where is it?"

"He had caches all over the Frontier."

She turned to Cole, who had been silently observing her. "Damn it! I can't afford a new light drive without those fucking crystals!"

"I hope you don't think the *Teddy R* can pay for one," he replied.

She glared at him, then at her former crew. "All right, you bastards!" she snapped. "Get busy disconnecting the pulse cannon and the cloak."

"What do you want us to do with them?"

"Move 'em to the *Teddy R*," she said. "This smug-looking bastard" —she indicated Cole—"will tell you where to put them. Don't cause any trouble and we'll put you off on a colony world instead of an uninhabited one."

"We appreciate this, of course," said Cole. "But why are you giving them away?"

"I'm not giving them away," she said. "I'm taking them with me."

Cole looked around the area. "Where can we talk alone?" he asked her.

"This way," she said, leading him to an empty storage chamber. The door irised to let them in, then snapped shut behind them.

"Val, I don't want to argue with you in front of your former crew, but we can't just carry tons of weaponry in the cargo hold for an indefinite period of time."

"You're not hauling them," she said. "Install them."

"I thought you said you were taking them with you," said Cole, puzzled.

"I am," she said. "I'm the Third Officer of the *Teddy R*, remember?"

"That was just temporary, until we got the *Pegasus* back for you."

"Without the crystals, I can't afford to fix it."

"Then you'll find a smaller ship."

"Forget it."

"What changed your mind?" he asked.

"I've been doing some thinking," said Val. "Your crew gave up their careers to follow you. Mine sold me out. I'm a damned good Captain, but maybe it's not a bad idea for me to stay with the *Teddy R* until I'm a little better at being a leader."

"You're welcome to," said Cole. "But you're under no obligation to."

"If I aimed a pulse gun at you, there'd be a fight between Forrice and Sharon and all the others to take the blast in your place." She jerked a head toward the crew of the *Pegasus*, hard at work moving weaponry on the other side of the door. "Every one of those bastards would fight to be the first to fire the pistol at me. I'm staying with you until I learn why."

"We're happy to have you," said Cole. "The subject is closed."

He turned to the door, waiting for it to iris, stepped through, and led the crew into the *Teddy R.* It took them half a day to move the weaponry that he wanted, while Val collected the few things of value that the Shark had not sold or traded. Then they landed the *Pegasus* on the planet against the day they could refurbish it, secured it so no one could steal it, dropped its crew off on an agricultural world, and headed back to Riverwind.

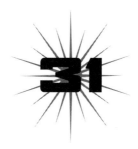

"We're in orbit around Riverwind now," announced Forrice. "We'd better not linger too long. We were lucky last time, but the police and the Navy can't be expected to overlook us again. Someone on this damned planet had to see the *Pegasus* take out those three Muscatel ships."

"Tell Moyer and the others to get back here," said Cole. He paused. "You know, this ship had four shuttlecraft just a few months ago. Then we lost the *Quentin* when Captain Fujiama died, and we lost the *Archie* right here. All we've got left are the *Kermit* and the *Alice*. I think once we accumulate a little loot, the first thing we'd better do is replace those shuttles."

"Sounds reasonable."

"Didn't Teddy Roosevelt have six kids? Which two haven't we used?"

"Let me check," said Sokolov, who was manning the computer console. He looked up a moment later. "Edith and Theodore Junior."

"Okay, we need an Edith and a Junior. At fifty percent of market value, maybe we can get them relatively soon."

He made a face.

"What's the matter?" asked Forrice.

"Listen to me," said Cole. "I'm a military officer, and I'm talking about percentages of market value. I sound like an insurance appraiser."

"You're neither," said the Molarian. "You're a pirate."

"Same thing. What I'm not is a businessman, and I don't like sounding like one."

"One of us is not in a good mood," noted Forrice.

"One of us is in a goddamned foul mood," said Cole. "When you and I were serving on the *Sophocles* all those years ago, did you ever think we'd be choosing our targets based on what percent of market value we could get for their goods?"

"Wilson, go get a drink or whatever it is that affects your metabolism," said Forrice. "You're depressing me."

"If I can't depress my oldest friend, who *can* I depress?"

"There's always me," said Sharon's voice.

"Don't you ever get tired of listening in on private conversations?" asked Cole.

"If they're being held on the bridge, they're not private," she shot back. "I second Forrice's request. Start acting more like a hero and stop depressing the First Officer."

"All right," he said. "Meet me for a drink and I'll depress you instead."

"The mess hall?"

"I wouldn't want to depress all the diners," replied Cole dryly. "Come on over to my office."

"All right," she said. "I hope you're not thinking of having sex on that tiny desk of yours."

"I'm not thinking of having sex at all."

"You *are* in a foul mood," she said. "I'll be there in five minutes."

Cole went down to his office, puzzled by his mood. At first he thought it was Morales's death that was bothering him, but he knew it wasn't. He'd hardly known the young man, and it had been a painful but easy decision to make. It certainly wasn't the Shark's death, or the destruction of the *Pegasus*. But something was bothering him, and he had spent most of the day trying to figure out what it was.

"Hi," said Sharon, entering the office and setting a bottle down on his desk. "Here, make a pig of yourself. You're among friends."

He stared at the bottle and made no attempt to reach for it.

"I'm past the age where I look good dropping grapes in reclining gentlemen's mouths," she continued, "but if you ask politely, maybe I'll pour some of this stuff down yours."

"Later," he said. "I'm not thirsty."

"What is it?" Sharon asked seriously. "I've seen you tense, mad, frustrated, even frightened, but I've never seen you looking so morose. I'd like to think it's because Val made a pass at you, but I don't see any wounds."

He couldn't help smiling at that, but the smile vanished as quickly as it had appeared.

"I don't know," he said. "When I was a kid, I watched all the adventure holos. Pirate stories were my favorite. So now I'm a pirate, and what the hell have we accomplished? We've destroyed the *Achilles*, we killed its crew, we killed the kid, we killed a bunch of men on Picacio IV, we killed the Shark, we killed the *Pegasus*, we arranged for the three Muscatel ships to get killed." He sighed. "And what did we get for all this death and destruction? A higher percentage of market value." He stared at her. "Do you think it was worth it?"

"The question isn't was it worth it, but rather did we have a choice?" she replied. "You might view it as a cosmic joke."

"I don't follow you," said Cole.

"Look at it this way," said Sharon. "You saved five million lives, and got court-martialed for your trouble. You killed all these people and ships, and increased our percentage by a multiple of ten." She smiled. "Don't *you* think God's got a twisted sense of humor?"

"You know," he said, some of the tension finally leaving him, "when you put it like that . . ."

"You see?" she said. "It's all in how you look at it. Some people look at Forrice and are terrified; you look at him and see your closest friend. Some people look at Val and see a sex object; you look at her and see a killing machine. Everything depends on perspective."

"You know something?" said Cole, finally opening the bottle. "I'm damned glad I met you."

"If push comes to shove, I'm damned glad of it too," said Sharon. "And despite what I said about that wildly uncomfortable desk, if you really want to do a little pushing and shoving . . ."

He was about to answer when Sokolov's image appeared to the right of the door.

"I'm sorry to bother you, sir, but David Copperfield insists on speaking to you personally."

"Right now?"

"Yes, sir."

Cole sighed. "All right, put him through."

Copperfield, elegantly dressed and clearly distressed, appeared a second later.

"Hello, David," said Cole.

"Steerforth, you can't desert me!" cried the alien.

"No one's deserting you," said Cole. "You're our favorite fence. Olivia Twist's crystals didn't pan out, but we'll be back soon with more booty for you." He paused. "I doubt we'll be back in the *Teddy R.* There's no sense pushing our luck. But we'll be back in some ship or other."

"You don't understand!" said Copperfield, his face a mask of desperation. "When your three crew members return to the ship, I've got to come up with them! It's a matter of life and death!"

"Whose life and whose death?"

"*Mine!*" yelled Copperfield.

"Calm down, David, and tell me, slowly and succinctly, what the problem is," said Cole.

"I betrayed the Hammerhead Shark!"

"Relax," said Cole soothingly. "It's over. He's dead."

"But he sent messages to five or six other pirates that I set him up, and they've told their friends. I can't stay here, Steerforth! There must be a dozen contracts out on my life by now! You've got to take me with you!"

"How do you know he passed the word?" asked Cole.

"I've already received messages from two of them, threatening to kill me! You got me into this, Steerforth, you and Olivia! You've got to get me out!"

"All right," said Cole. "You can come aboard with Moyer and Nichols and the Pepon. But what about your help? And more to the point, what about your warehouse? If you leave it behind, you're out of business—and if you leave *them* behind, they're going to know what ship you're on and they're probably going to plunder your goods. We can drop you off on any planet you choose, but I'll be perfectly frank—an alien who thinks he's a Charles Dickens character and dresses the part isn't going to be too hard to spot."

"Take my staff too!" said Copperfield. "I know you're shorthanded. They're loyal, they're fearless, and I can't leave them here. The people who want me dead are as likely to demolish my house and warehouse from orbit as to come looking for me personally."

"How many have you got working for you?"

"Fourteen."

"All human?"

"Ten Men, a Lodinite, two Mollutei, and a Bedalian."

Cole looked questioningly at Sharon, who nodded her approval. "All right. If they pass our security check, they can stay on the ship."

"Security check?" repeated Copperfield in panicky tones. "They're all criminals! You know that, Steerforth."

"It won't be a standard check," said Cole. "I want to know what crimes they've committed, and who they've committed them against. And I especially want to know if any of them have killed their employers." Copperfield looked undecided. "It's that or they stay on Riverwind," added Cole.

"I agree," said Copperfield at last. "And probably not all of them will want to join you anyway. I imagine a few will stay behind and find other employment, here or elsewhere." He paused. "They'll have to come in a different ship. Your crewmen assure me they won't all fit on the shuttlecraft."

"It'll be a tight squeeze, but they'll fit."

"Not after I load my Dickens collection onto it."

Cole frowned. "Just how the hell many books do you think Dickens wrote?"

"I have over six hundred editions of *The Pickwick Papers* alone."

"We'll come back for them."

Copperfield shook his head vigorously. "I'm never coming back. Who knows what traps they'll lay for me? And that's assuming they don't blow everything up from space. My collection comes with me. My men will avail themselves of another ship."

"I don't like that word 'avail,' David," said Cole. "If they steal it, the police could follow them to the *Teddy R*, and while I've got all kinds of fake IDs and registrations, sooner or later someone's going to recognize the ship for what it is."

"What are you saying?" asked Copperfield. "I'm not entirely clear about it."

"I'm saying that they hire or buy a ship," said Cole. "If they steal it, I won't let them on board. You can afford it. You're a rich man. Or whatever."

"That was cruel, Steerforth," said Copperfield reproachfully. "You cut me to the quick."

"I apologize, David. But I'm adamant—they can't steal a ship and lead the authorities to us."

"Agreed."

"I'm sorry the Shark couldn't keep his mouth shut," said Cole. "It looks like you're going to be out of business."

"Nonsense," said Copperfield. "I've got warehouses all over the Republic."

"Not to put too fine a point on it, David, you're about to board the most wanted ship in the galaxy. The second the *Alice* is safely back in the shuttle bay, we're heading farther into the Inner Frontier—and we're not coming back this way."

"Then I will find another way to meet my meager needs."

"I've been to your mansion," said Cole. "There isn't much meager about it."

"That was for my help and my clientele," said Copperfield. "I myself can make do on as little as six million credits a year."

"Well, I'm sure glad we don't have to worry about you," said Cole sardonically. "David, we've made our agreement. It time to start moving out with my crewmen, and passing the word to your hired help. The longer the *Teddy R* stays in orbit, the greater the chance that someone's going to put two and two together and figure out who we are."

"Certainly, my dear Steerforth," said Copperfield. "I shall see you shortly." He paused. "Oh. I'll need one room for myself, and three for my collection. And by the way, I forgive you for debauching poor innocent little Emily."

"*What?*" demanded Sharon.

"It took place in England three thousand years ago," explained Copperfield. "And he was very young and impetuous."

He broke the transmission.

"Well, it looks like we've just added to our crew and our library," said Cole. "Any comments?"

"Just one."

"Oh?"

"We'd better use your desk before it's covered with Dickens books."

The *Teddy R* headed deeper into the Inner Frontier for the next two days. It had picked up seven crew members from Copperfield's staff—five Men and two Mollutei—and he'd turned their training over to Bull Pampas and Idena Mueller. The pulse cannon had been installed. The cloak had reluctantly been jettisoned when it proved incompatible with the ship's computer system.

And Wilson Cole was still feeling morose without quite knowing why.

He was on the bridge, being briefed on the current situation by Christine Mboya and Malcolm Briggs. This pirate ship had been spotted along the trade route from Binder X to New Rhodesia, that one was lurking in and around the Volaire system, a new fence just twenty light-years into the Republic on Bienvenuti III was said to be offering seven percent of market value. Gold was up, diamonds were down, machinery was still in demand. A pirate with the unlikely name of Vasco de Gama had declared the Silversmith and Naraboldi systems off-limits to all other pirates and was willing to back his claim up with a fleet of five ships.

Finally Cole felt his eyes glazing over, excused himself, and went off to the mess hall, where he ordered a beer and then didn't touch it when it arrived. He was still sitting motionless, a troubled frown on his face, when David Copperfield entered the small room, saw him, and walked over to his table.

"You look unhappy, my dear Steerforth," said Copperfield, sitting down opposite Cole.

"I've been happier."

"I hope you're not worrying about me," said Copperfield. "I assure you I'll find ways to replace my losses."

"I'm not the least bit worried about you," replied Cole, "and I never doubted that you'd recover your losses."

"Then what *is* troubling you?" persisted Copperfield. "Perhaps I can be of some help."

"I doubt it."

"Try me, my old school chum."

"You really want to know?" said Cole. "I'm looking ahead to thirty or forty years of piracy, and I find it terminally depressing. It's not the career all those novels and holos made it out to be. Most of the time I feel like a goddamned accountant."

"Well, of course you do," said Copperfield. "Consider it a defense mechanism. After all, if you didn't feel like an accountant, you'd feel like a thief, and honorable men like you and I don't like to feel like thieves."

"I don't want to insult you, David," said Cole wearily, "but you are neither honorable nor a man. You're a fence."

"Of course I'm a fence," said Copperfield with some dignity. "The alternative was to become a pirate, and we both know that piracy is no job for the likes of us. I'm surprised that wasn't apparent to you from the beginning."

Cole stared at him curiously. "Go on."

"Look at you. You were the pride of the Republic's navy . . ."

"Never that," said Cole. "But continue."

"You came here with the most valuable members of your crew loyal to you and with a powerful ship in perfect working order. There are ships on the Inner Frontier that can challenge the *Theodore Roosevelt*, but you haven't encountered one yet. And what have you accomplished in the time you've been here? You've destroyed some ships, you've killed some men and creatures that needed killing, and you've accumulated some stones that we both know were barely worth taking. That is the nature of the profession, my dear Steerforth. Even once you learn the ropes, you are forever going to be paid a tiny fraction of what your plunder is worth. And while it's true that you can negotiate with the insurers, how often can you go into the Republic before you're identified and captured? In fact, I have been informed that you've made only two attempts to deal with insurance companies and, even so, one went very wrong."

"We're still learning the ropes," said Cole defensively.

Copperfield shook his head. "You don't understand, Steerforth. You've pretty much *learned* the ropes. What you have been doing is living the typical life of a pirate." He smiled. "Why do you think I avoided piracy and became a fence instead?"

"So you're saying that I was right, that this is the life we have to look forward to until we're caught or killed."

Copperfield smiled again, an inscrutable alien smile this time. "Steerforth, Steerforth," he said, "how can you be so foolish when you are so smart?"

"It takes skill," replied Cole wryly. "I assume you're going to explain what the hell you're talking about?"

"Who says you have to be a pirate?" said Copperfield. "You're not suited to it, none of you, by experience or training."

"In case it's escaped your notice the first hundred times you were told: the Navy doesn't want us back, except in front of a firing squad."

"Whose navy?" asked Copperfield.

"We're not joining the Teroni Federation!" said Cole decisively. "We've been fighting against them all our lives!"

"Except when you were fighting the Republic."

"You've been misinformed. We didn't betray the Republic. We *served* it."

"Until they jailed you," noted Copperfield.

Cole sighed deeply. "Until they jailed me."

"We're getting off the topic."

"The topic was piracy," said Cole.

"The topic was alternatives to piracy."

"Joining the Teronis is out of the question."

"I was never about to suggest it," replied Copperfield.

"Then I'm not following you at all," said Cole. "What's left?"

"Who says that the Republic and the Teroni Federation are the only games in town?" continued Copperfield. "You've all trained to serve aboard a military vessel. I see that you're even training *my* employees to function as part of a military crew. Don't you think it's time you remember who and what you are, and stop pretending to be pirates?"

Cole stared at him, trying to see what he was driving at.

"There are warlords springing up all over the Inner Frontier," said Copperfield. "They need battleships. There are pirates all over the Inner Frontier. Their victims need someone to protect them. There are worlds rich in natural materials that are ripe for plundering. They need someone to patrol them. I don't know anyone who won't pay to protect their safety and their possessions, or to further their ambition. Do you see what I'm saying?"

"Mercenaries?" said Cole, considering the notion.

"You're a military ship with a military crew," said Copperfield. "What possible position could better suit your talents?"

"It's a tempting thought," admitted Cole. "But who would hire us? How would we find them?"

"You wouldn't," answered Copperfield. "Your business agent would."

"You?"

"Who else?" He extended his knobby hand. "Shall we shake on it?"

"You know, David," said Cole, feeling free for the first time in days, "Charles Dickens could have done a lot worse."

EPILOGUE

Cole was on the bridge when David Copperfield stepped out of the airlift and approached him.

"Well?" said Cole.

"We have three offers so far," reported Copperfield. "And I anticipate more almost every day. We're not in the Republic, so there was no reason to hide the identity of the ship or its captain."

"I don't know if that was a good idea," said Cole. "Officially I'm still a mutineer."

"Most people out here consider that a plus," said Copperfield with a smile.

"What kind of pay are they offering?"

"It varies, but the least attractive offer is still more than you would ever have made as a pirate."

"That's a definite comfort," said Cole.

"Stick with me, my dear Steerforth," said David Copperfield. "Before we're through we could end up owning this damned Frontier."

"I suppose I could live with that," admitted Cole.

APPENDIXES

Appendix One

THE ORIGIN OF THE BIRTHRIGHT UNIVERSE

I t happened in the 1970s. Carol and I were watching a truly awful movie at a local theater, and about halfway through it I muttered, "Why am I wasting my time here when I could be doing something really interesting, like, say, writing the entire history of the human race from now until its extinction?" And she whispered back, "So why don't you?" We got up immediately, walked out of the theater, and that night I outlined a novel called *Birthright: The Book of Man*, which would tell the story of the human race from its attainment of faster-than-light flight until its death eighteen thousand years from now.

It was a long book to write. I divided the future into five political eras—Republic, Democracy, Oligarchy, Monarchy, and Anarchy—and wrote twenty-six connected stories ("demonstrations," *Analog* called them, and rightly so), displaying every facet of the human race, both admirable and not so admirable. Since each is set a few centuries from the last, there are no continuing characters (unless you consider Man, with a capital *M*, the main character, in which case you could make an argument—or at least, *I* could—that it's really a character study).

I sold it to Signet, along with another novel, titled *The Soul Eater*. My editor there, Sheila Gilbert, loved the Birthright Universe and asked me if I would be willing to make a few changes to *The Soul Eater* so that it was set in that future. I agreed, and the changes actually took less than a day. She made the same request—in advance, this time—for the four-book Tales of the Galactic Midway series, the four-book Tales of the Velvet Comet series, and *Walpurgis III*. Looking back, I see that only two of the thirteen novels I wrote for Signet were *not* set there.

When I moved to Tor Books, my editor there, Beth Meacham, had a fondness for the Birthright Universe, and most of my books for her—not all, but most—were set in it: *Santiago*, *Ivory*, *Paradise*, *Purgatory*, *Inferno*, *A Miracle of Rare Design*, *A Hunger in the Soul*, *The Outpost*, and *The Return of Santiago*.

When Ace agreed to buy *Soothsayer*, *Oracle*, and *Prophet* from me, my editor, Ginjer Buchanan, assumed that of course they'd be set in the Birthright Universe—and of course they were, because as I learned a little more about my eighteen-thousand-year, two-million-world future, I felt a lot more comfortable writing about it.

In fact, I started setting short stories in the Birthright Universe. Two of my Hugo winners—"Seven Views of Olduvai Gorge" and "The 43 Antarean Dynasties"—are set there, and so are perhaps fifteen others.

When Bantam agreed to take the Widowmaker trilogy from me, it was a foregone conclusion that Janna Silverstein, who purchased the books but had moved to another company before they came out, would want them to take place in the Birthright Universe. She did indeed request it, and I did indeed agree.

I recently handed in a book to Meisha Merlin, set—where else?—in the Birthright Universe.

And when it came time to suggest a series of books to Lou Anders for the new Pyr line of science fiction, I don't think I ever considered any ideas or stories that *weren't* set in the Birthright Universe.

I've gotten so much of my career from the Birthright Universe that I wish I could remember the name of that turkey we walked out of all those years ago so I could write the producers and thank them.

Appendix Two

THE LAYOUT OF THE BIRTHRIGHT UNIVERSE

The most heavily populated (by both stars and inhabitants) section of the Birthright Universe is always referred to by its political identity, which evolves from Republic to Democracy to Oligarchy to Monarchy. It encompasses millions of inhabited and habitable worlds. Earth is too small and too far out of the mainstream of galactic commerce to remain Man's capital world, and within a couple of thousand years the capital has been moved lock, stock, and barrel halfway across the galaxy to Deluros VIII, a huge world with about ten times Earth's surface and near-identical atmosphere and gravity. By the middle of the Democracy, perhaps four thousand years from now, the entire planet is covered by one huge sprawling city. By the time of the Oligarchy, even Deluros VIII isn't big enough for our billions of empire-running bureaucrats, and Deluros VI, another large world, is broken up into forty-eight planetoids, each housing a major department of the government (with four planetoids given over entirely to the military).

Earth itself is way out in the boonies, on the Spiral Arm. I don't believe I've set more than parts of a couple of stories on the Arm.

At the outer edge of the galaxy is the Rim, where worlds are spread out and underpopulated. There's so little of value or military interest on the Rim that one ship, such as the *Theodore Roosevelt*, can patrol a couple of hundred worlds by itself. In later eras, the Rim will be dominated by feuding warlords, but it's so far away from the center of things that the governments, for the most part, just ignore it.

Then there are the Inner and Outer Frontiers. The Outer Frontier is that vast but sparsely populated area between the outer edge of the Republic/Democracy/Oligarchy/Monarchy and the Rim. The Inner Frontier is that somewhat smaller (but still huge) area between the inner reaches of the Republic/etc. and the black hole at the core of the galaxy.

It's on the Inner Frontier that I've chosen to set more than half of my novels. Years ago the brilliant writer R. A. Lafferty wrote, "Will there be a mythology of the future, they used to ask, after all has become science? Will high deeds be told in epic, or only in computer code?" I decided that I'd like to spend at least a part of my career trying to create those myths of the future, and it seems to me that myths, with their bigger-than-life characters and colorful settings, work best on frontiers where there aren't too many people around to chronicle them accurately, or too many authority figures around to prevent them from playing out to their inevitable conclusions. So I arbitrarily decided that the Inner Frontier was where *my* myths would take place, and I populated it with people bearing names like Catastrophe Baker, the Widowmaker, the Cyborg de Milo, the ageless Forever Kid, and the like. It not only allows me to tell my heroic (and sometimes antiheroic) myths, but lets me tell more realistic stories occurring at the very same time a few thousand light-years away in the Republic or Democracy or whatever happens to exist at that moment.

Over the years I've fleshed out the galaxy. There are the star clusters—the Albion Cluster, the Quinellus Cluster, a few others. There are the individual worlds, some important enough to appear as the title of a book, such as Walpurgis III, some reappearing throughout the time periods and stories, such as Deluros VIII, Antares III, Binder X, Keepsake, Spica II, and some others, and hundreds (maybe thousands by now) of worlds (and races, now that I think about it) mentioned once and never again.

Then there are, if not the bad guys, at least what I think of as the Disloyal Opposition. Some, like the Sett Empire, get into one war with humanity and that's the end of it. Some, like the Canphor Twins (Canphor VI and Canphor VII), have been a thorn in Man's side for the better part of ten millennia. Some, like Lodin XI, vary almost daily in their loyalties depending on the political situation.

I've been building this universe, politically and geographically, for a quarter of a century now, and with each passing book and story it feels a little more real to me. Give me another thirty years and I'll probably believe every word I've written about it.

Appendix Three

CHRONOLOGY OF THE BIRTHRIGHT UNIVERSE

Year	Era	World	Story or Novel
1885	A.D.		"The Hunter" (*Ivory*)
1898	A.D.		"Himself" (*Ivory*)
1982	A.D.		*Sideshow*
1983	A.D.		*The Three-Legged Hootch Dancer*
1985	A.D.		*The Wild Alien Tamer*
1987	A.D.		*The Best Rootin' Tootin' Shootin' Gunslinger in the Whole Damned Galaxy*
2057	A.D.		"The Politician" (*Ivory*)
2988	A.D. = 1 G.E.		
16	G.E.	Republic	"The Curator" (*Ivory*)
264	G.E.	Republic	"The Pioneers" (*Birthright*)
332	G.E.	Republic	"The Cartographers" (*Birthright*)
346	G.E.	Republic	*Walpurgis III*
367	G.E.	Republic	*Eros Ascending*
396	G.E.	Republic	"The Miners" (*Birthright*)
401	G.E.	Republic	*Eros at Zenith*
442	G.E.	Republic	*Eros Descending*
465	G.E.	Republic	*Eros at Nadir*
522	G.E.	Republic	"All the Things You Are"

588	G.E.	Republic	"The Psychologists" (*Birthright*)
616	G.E.	Republic	*A Miracle of Rare Design*
882	G.E.	Republic	"The Potentate" (*Ivory*)
962	G.E.	Republic	"The Merchants" (*Birthright*)
1150	G.E.	Republic	"Cobbling Together a Solution"
1151	G.E.	Republic	"Nowhere in Particular"
1152	G.E.	Republic	"The God Biz"
1394	G.E.	Republic	"Keepsakes"
1701	G.E.	Republic	"The Artist" (*Ivory*)
1813	G.E.	Republic	"Dawn" (*Paradise*)
1826	G.E.	Republic	*Purgatory*
1859	G.E.	Republic	"Noon" (*Paradise*)
1888	G.E.	Republic	"Midafternoon" (*Paradise*)
1902	G.E.	Republic	"Dusk" (*Paradise*)
1921	G.E.	Republic	*Inferno*
1966	G.E.	Republic	*Starship: Mutiny*
1967	G.E.	Republic	*Starship: Pirate*
1968	G.E.	Republic	*Starship: Mercenary*
1969	G.E.	Republic	*Starship: Rebel*
1970	G.E.	Republic	*Starship: Flagship*
2122	G.E.	Democracy	"The 43 Antarean Dynasties"
2154	G.E.	Democracy	"The Diplomats" (*Birthright*)
2275	G.E.	Democracy	"The Olympians" (*Birthright*)
2469	G.E.	Democracy	"The Barristers" (*Birthright*)
2885	G.E.	Democracy	"Robots Don't Cry"
2911	G.E.	Democracy	"The Medics" (*Birthright*)
3004	G.E.	Democracy	"The Policitians" (*Birthright*)
3042	G.E.	Democracy	"The Gambler" (*Ivory*)
3286	G.E.	Democracy	*Santiago*

3322	G.E.	Democracy	*A Hunger in the Soul*
3324	G.E.	Democracy	*The Soul Eater*
3324	G.E.	Democracy	"Nicobar Lane: The Soul Eater's Story"
3407	G.E.	Democracy	*The Return of Santiago*
3427	G.E.	Democracy	*Soothsayer*
3441	G.E.	Democracy	*Oracle*
3447	G.E.	Democracy	*Prophet*
3502	G.E.	Democracy	"Guardian Angel"
3719	G.E.	Democracy	"Hunting the Snark"
4375	G.E.	Democracy	"The Graverobber" (*Ivory*)
4822	G.E.	Oligarchy	"The Administrators" (*Birthright*)
4839	G.E.	Oligarchy	*The Dark Lady*
5101	G.E.	Oligarchy	*The Widowmaker*
5103	G.E.	Oligarchy	*The Widowmaker Reborn*
5106	G.E.	Oligarchy	*The Widowmaker Unleashed*
5108	G.E.	Oligarchy	*A Gathering of Widowmakers*
5461	G.E.	Oligarchy	"The Media" (*Birthright*)
5492	G.E.	Oligarchy	"The Artists" (*Birthright*)
5521	G.E.	Oligarchy	"The Warlord" (*Ivory*)
5655	G.E.	Oligarchy	"The Biochemists" (*Birthright*)
5912	G.E.	Oligarchy	"The Warlords" (*Birthright*)
5993	G.E.	Oligarchy	"The Conspirators" (*Birthright*)
6304	G.E.	Monarchy	*Ivory*
6321	G.E.	Monarchy	"The Rulers" (*Birthright*)
6400	G.E.	Monarchy	"The Symbiotics" (*Birthright*)
6521	G.E.	Monarchy	"Catastrophe Baker and the Cold Equations"
6523	G.E.	Monarchy	*The Outpost*

6599 G.E.	Monarchy	"The Philosophers" (*Birthright*)
6746 G.E.	Monarchy	"The Architects" (*Birthright*)
6962 G.E.	Monarchy	"The Collectors" (*Birthright*)
7019 G.E.	Monarchy	"The Rebels" (*Birthright*)
16201 G.E.	Anarchy	"The Archaeologists" (*Birthright*)
16673 G.E.	Anarchy	"The Priests" (*Birthright*)
16888 G.E.	Anarchy	"The Pacifists" (*Birthright*)
17001 G.E.	Anarchy	"The Destroyers" (*Birthright*)
21703 G.E.		"Seven Views of Olduvai Gorge"

Novels not set in this future

Adventures (1922–1926 A.D.)

Exploits (1926–1931 A.D.)

Encounters (1931–1934 A.D.)

Stalking the Unicorn ("Tonight")

The Branch (2047–2051 A.D.)

Second Contact (2065 A.D.)

Bully! (1910–1912 A.D.)

Kirinyaga (2123–2137 A.D.)

Lady with an Alien (1490 A.D.)

Dragon America: Revolution (1779–1780 A.D.)

Appendix Four

RULES FOR THE GAME OF BILSANG

Created by Mike Resnick and Alex Wilson

Players

Two

The Board

Any flat surface

The Pieces

Twenty roughly similar tokens (coins, pebbles, candies, etc.)

Setup

The twenty tokens, called Floats, are arranged on the flat surface in 4 rows of 5. The complete set of Floats is called the Known Universe.

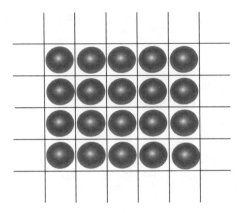

Play

On a player's turn, he or she moves two Floats in opposite directions either horizontally or vertically. Players alternate orientations, so if Player 1 moves Floats horizontally, Player 2 must move Floats vertically. Players may move Floats toward each other or away from each other.

Examples of initial move:

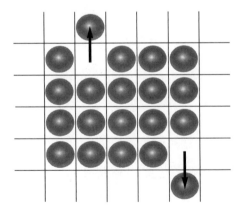

or

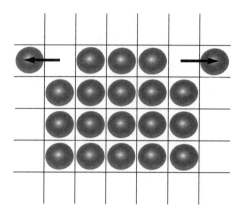

Illegal Moves

Players may not move both Floats just played by the previous player, though players may combine one of the two Floats just moved with another Float.

The moves must also not separate any Float(s) from the Known Universe. All Floats must be connected, at least diagonally. So a move from this:

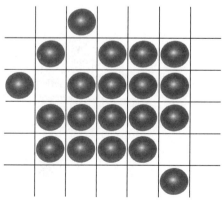

to this:

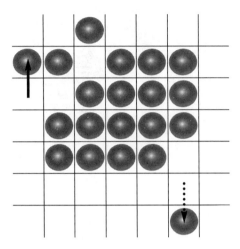

would be illegal because the bottom Float is no longer a part of the Known Universe.

Penalties

Should a player decide he cannot move two Floats in the required orientation, he may switch orientations to that of the other player. As a penalty to the switching player, the nonswitching player moves only one Float instead of the normally required two.

(Example: Player 1 moves two Floats horizontally and Player 2 cannot move two Floats vertically, so Player 2 switches and moves his Floats horizontally as well. Player 1 is required to move his Floats vertically now, but only has to move one Float up or down instead of the normally required two.)

Should a player be unable to move two Floats in any orientation (without using an illegal move described above), that player must remove a Float from the Known Universe. This Float is now Lost and the player must keep a pile of all of his Lost Floats. The removal of the Lost Float must not separate or divide any remaining Float from the Known Universe.

Object

Bilsang ends when only one Float remains in the Known Universe. The player with the fewest Lost Floats in his pile at the end is the winner.

Strategy

A veteran *bilsang* player will know how to use his own penalties to his advantage, to switch orientation when it is advantageous—instead of only when required—and to wisely choose which Floats he removes as Lost.

Alex Wilson (www.alexwilson.com) is a writer and actor from northern Ohio, now living in Carrboro, North Carolina. He has published RPG materials in *Dragon Magazine* and fiction in *Asimov's*, and runs the audiobook project Telltale Weekly.

Appendix Five

RULES FOR THE GAME TOPRENCH

Created by Mike Resnick and Mike Nelson

D eep in the reaches of the outer rim, two space stations shared a wary truce across a narrow band of space barely 140,000 miles wide. Toprench Station and Tri-Yangton Station had been at war for hundreds of years over the strip of space known as the Ori Channel, one of the few places on the Rim where thousands of freighters passed each cycle—owing to the delicate gravitational balance needed between neighboring systems.

Over the years of truce, the laser-gunnery engineers developed a game utilizing the ten barrels of the blast cannons (set to single mode, of course). As each gunnery engineer came on shift, his prime duty was to ensure the proper operation of his cannon. Each shift, the gunny tested and retested each barrel in single mode to ensure continuance should the wary truce end abruptly. He did this by cycling through the prismatic colors on the barrels (when light passes through a prism it can be separated into its component parts) following the ages-old cipher of ROY G BIV—Red, Orange, Yellow, Green, Blue, Indigo, and Violet. The other job he (or she, for many of the best engineers were female) had was to keep an eye (and scanners) on the cannons of the other station, in case the truce came to an abrupt halt during his shift. Each station cycled through its test patterns on all ten barrels, watching as the other station did the very same thing.

The only variety in the position was the test pattern, since each barrel could be set to any color with the addition of white (combination of all colors), black (the absence of all colors), and ultraviolet (which could not be perceived by the human eyes of the opposing station, but could be read on the scanners), giving each barrel a maximum of ten settings. These barrels were set in a circle, and each barrel had to be tested on each setting, and those barrels that failed any one of the settings would be immediately replaced—thereby ensuring the integrity of the blast cannon. Soon, a game developed as each engineer watched the opposing engineer cycle through the prismatic patterns, testing settings on each barrel. At the beginning of his (or her) shift, the engineer would devise a test sequence. He would write this sequence down. The opposing gunnery engineer had two goals: to "Capture" the ultraviolet position—guessing which of the ten barrels would hold the most important (and most lethal) setting—and guessing the setting arrangement of all nine other barrels. The engineer who completed both of these objectives in the fewest "moves" would win.

The game took a long time to play; often the engineers were on twelve-hour* shifts. The game progressed with each engineer devising his or her test pattern, then trying to guess the other gunny's test pattern (the actual pattern never being run, since most times all combinations were run through each of the barrels). One of the barrels was always set to black (or off, since it was often being replaced), one white (or all), one would be ultraviolet (death), and the other bar-

---

*Many times the shifts lasted much longer than twelve hours owing to Toprench play.

rels would be some combination of ROY G BIV—all colors being used, and none being used twice.

The game came to be called Toprench, since after many years of winning (and cheating*) Toprench Station won the game the most times and after discovering the opposing engineers' patterns were able to end the truce and blow Tri-Yangton Station to the Abilene Cluster.

Object of the Game

1: To "Capture" the gold piece in the correct position
2: To guess the pattern of the opposing player's pieces.

Materials

Each player will need 20 multicolored pieces: 2 each of Red, Orange, Yellow, Green, Blue, Indigo, Violet, Black, White, and Gold.

The Board

Can be premade, drawn, designed, or software. Can be set in a line or a circle. You need a place to "hide" your design.

---

*Toprench Station cheated by planting a spy into the opposing gunnery engineers—Edita Petrick, a person who could be male, female, neither, or both. Edita brought about the end of the conflict by transmitting the test patterns of the gunnery engineers back to Toprench so they could win. Later, Toprench Station realized this information was helpful not only in a playing sense but also a strategic one and Toprench used the information to end the conflict.

Ten Slots arranged in a circle or a line.

| | | | | | | | | |

An indicator square in the center (circle) or beside the ten slots.

To Start the Game

Each Player sets a Pattern. Frex:

GN | O | Y | V | I | BU | GD | BK | W | R |

This pattern is hidden from the opposing player.

One player begins by setting the other pieces out in a pattern as a guess. Any number of pieces can be set out at a time, or all pieces can be set out.

FREX: Guess 1
GD | | | | | | | | | |

The first player indicates the number of CORRECT guesses in the box to the side. In this example it would be zero.

Play switches to the second player, with the first player setting a guess. The same procedure is followed. When a guess is correct, the guessing player leaves the piece(s) in the correct position and only changes those pieces he/she feels are not correct.

When the Gold piece is guessed, the defending player must say "Gold" and the game is half won. Toprench can be played in the short term by just guessing where the Gold piece is in the opposing player's design.

Winning the Game

Toprench is won when the same player captures the Gold piece *and* correctly guesses the pattern of the other player's barrels. If one objective is met by one player and the other objective is met by the other, then the game is a draw and another game begins with both players setting a new design.

Mike Nelson is the Director of Technology for a public school district on the Navajo Reservation. He has a wife and three kids and has no other professional publishing credits, although he is forever hopeful.

Appendix Six

TECHNICAL SCHEMATICS OF THE *THEODORE ROOSEVELT*

Created by Mike Resnick and Deborah Oakes

The *Teddy Roosevelt*

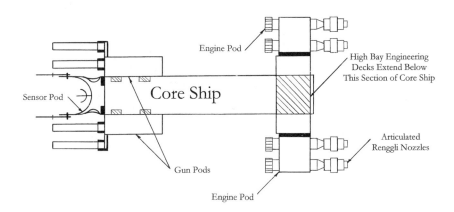

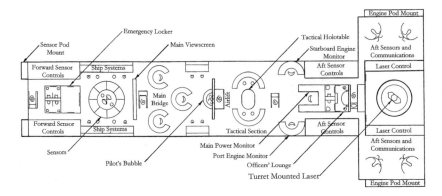

Level One – Core Ship
Sensory/Bridge Deck

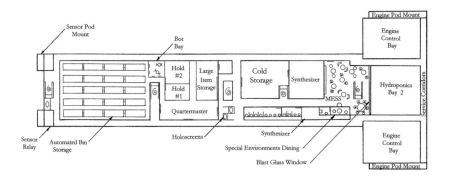

Level Two – Core Ship
Quartermaster/Mess Deck

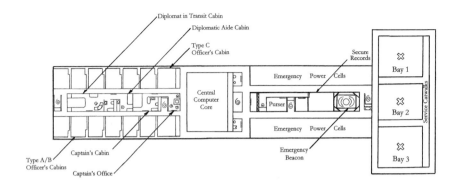

Diplomat in Transit Cabin

Diplomatic Aide Cabin

Type C
Officer's Cabin

Secure
Records

Bay 1

Emergency   Power   Cells

Central
Computer
Core

Purser

Bay 2

Emergency   Power   Cells

Type A/B
Officer's Cabins

Captain's Cabin

Emergency
Beacon

Bay 3

Captain's Office

Level Three – Core Ship
Purser/Officers Quarters Deck

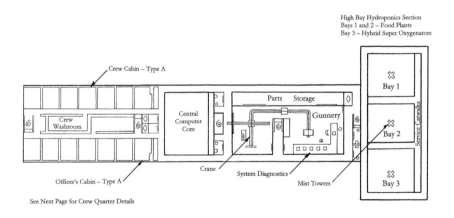

High Bay Hydroponics Section
Bays 1 and 2 – Food Plants
Bay 3 – Hybrid Super Oxygenators

Crew Cabin – Type A

Bay 1

Parts   Storage

Central
Computer
Core

Gunnery

Crew
Washroom

Bay 2

Crane

System Diagnostics

Officer's Cabin – Type A

Mist Towers

Bay 3

See Next Page for Crew Quarter Details

Level Four – Core Ship
Gunnery/Quarters Deck

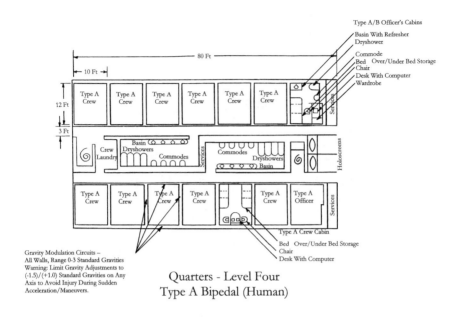

Type A/B Officer's Cabins

Basin With Refresher
Dryshower

Commode
Bed Over/Under Bed Storage
Chair
Desk With Computer
Wardrobe

80 Ft

10 Ft

12 Ft

3 Ft

Type A Crew (×6, top row)

Services

Holoscreens

Crew Laundry
Basin
Dryshowers
Commodes
Services
Commodes
Dryshowers
Basin

Type A Crew (×5), Type A Officer

Type A Crew Cabin

Bed Over/Under Bed Storage
Chair
Desk With Computer

Gravity Modulation Circuits –
All Walls, Range 0-3 Standard Gravities
Warning: Limit Gravity Adjustments to
(-1.5)/(+1.0) Standard Gravities on Any
Axis to Avoid Injury During Sudden
Acceleration/Maneuvers.

Quarters - Level Four
Type A Bipedal (Human)

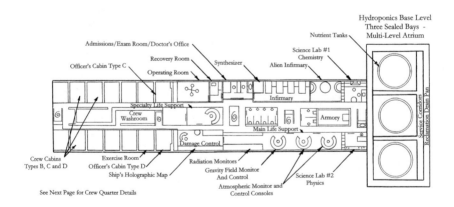

Hydroponics Base Level
Three Sealed Bays -
Multi-Level Atrium

Nutrient Tanks

Admissions/Exam Room/Doctor's Office

Science Lab #1
Chemistry

Recovery Room
Synthesizer
Alien Infirmary

Officer's Cabin Type C
Operating Room

Infirmary

Specialty Life Support
Crew
Washroom

Armory

Main Life Support

Damage Control

Crew Cabins
Types B, C and D

Exercise Room
Officer's Cabin Type D
Ship's Holographic Map

Radiation Monitors
Gravity Field Monitor
And Control
Atmospheric Monitor and
Control Consoles

Science Lab #2
Physics

Service Corridors
Reclamation Drain Pan

See Next Page for Crew Quarter Details

Level Five – Core Ship
Life Services/Quarters Deck

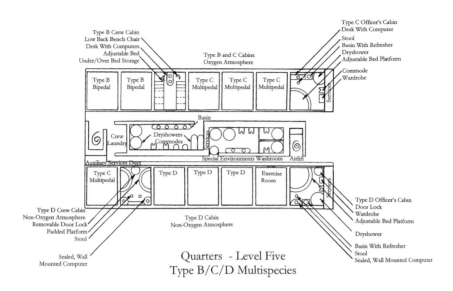

Quarters - Level Five
Type B/C/D Multispecies

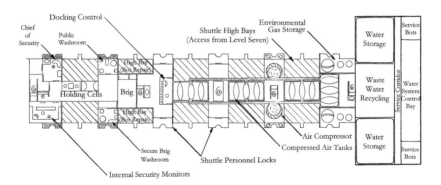

Level Six – Core Ship
Security/Utility Deck

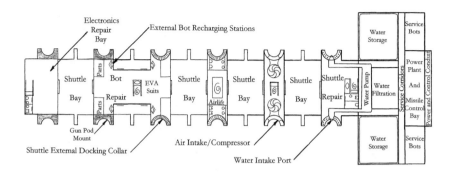

Level Seven – Core Ship
Maintenance/Cargo Deck

Note: Power and Control Circuits Bypass
Shield Layer Between Decks E-8 and E-9

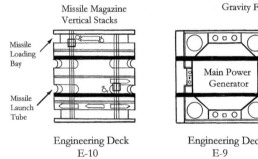

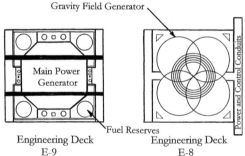

Note: All Engineering Pod Decks
Are High Bay Areas, Equivalent
in Height to Two Normal Decks.

Engineering Decks

Deborah Oakes is an aerospace engineer, a lifetime science fiction fan, and the secretary/treasurer of the venerable Cincinnati Fantasy Group.

ABOUT THE AUTHOR

Locus, *the trade journal of science fiction, keeps a list of the winners of major science fiction awards on its Web page. Mike Resnick is currently fourth in the all-time standings, ahead of Isaac Asimov, Sir Arthur C. Clarke, Ray Bradbury, and Robert A. Heinlein.*

* * * * * *

Mike was born on March 5, 1942. He sold his first article in 1957, his first short story in 1959, and his first book in 1962.

He attended the University of Chicago from 1959 through 1961, won three letters on the fencing team, and met and married Carol. Their daughter, Laura, was born in 1962, and has since become a writer herself, winning two awards for her romance novels and the 1993 Campbell Award for Best New Science Fiction Writer.

Mike and Carol discovered science fiction fandom in 1962, attended their first Worldcon in 1963, and fifty sf books into his career, Mike still considers himself a fan and frequently contributes articles to fanzines. He and Carol appeared in five Worldcon masquerades in the 1970s in costumes that she created, and they won four of them.

Mike labored anonymously but profitably from 1964 through 1976, selling more than two hundred novels, three hundred short stories, and two thousand articles, almost all of them under pseudonyms, most of them in the "adult" field. He edited seven different tabloid newspapers and a pair of men's magazines, as well.

In 1968 Mike and Carol became serious breeders and exhibitors of collies, a pursuit they continued through 1981. (Mike is still an AKC-licensed collie judge.) During that time they bred and/or exhibited twenty-seven champion collies, and they were the country's leading breeders and exhibitors during various years along the way.

This led them to purchase the Briarwood Pet Motel in Cincinnati in 1976. It was the country's second-largest luxury boarding and grooming establishment, and they worked full-time at it for the next few years. By 1980 the kennel was being run by a staff of twenty-one, and Mike was free to return to his first love, science fiction, albeit at a far slower pace than his previous writing. They sold the kennel in 1993.

Mike's first novel in this "second career" was *The Soul Eater*, which was followed shortly by *Birthright: The Book of Man*, *Walpurgis III*, the four-book Tales of the Galactic Midway series, *The Branch*, the four-book Tales of the Velvet Comet series, and *Adventures*, all from Signet. His break-through novel was the international best-seller *Santiago*, published by Tor in 1986. Tor has since published *Stalking the Unicorn*, *The Dark Lady*, *Ivory*, *Second Contact*, *Paradise*, *Purgatory*, *Inferno*, the Double *Bwana/Bully!*, and the collection *Will the Last Person to Leave the Planet Please Shut Off the Sun?* His most recent Tor releases were *A Miracle of Rare Design*, *A Hunger in the Soul*, *The Outpost*, and the *The Return of Santiago*.

Even at his reduced rate, Mike is too prolific for one publisher, and in the 1990s Ace published *Soothsayer*, *Oracle*, and *Prophet*, Questar published *Lucifer Jones*, Bantam brought out the *Locus* best-selling trilogy of *The Widowmaker*, *The Widowmaker Reborn*, and *The Widow-maker Unleashed*, and Del Rey published *Kirinyaga: A Fable of Utopia* and *Lara Croft, Tomb Raider: The Amulet of Power*. His current releases include *A Gathering of Widowmakers* for Meisha Merlin, *Dragon America* for Phobos, and *Lady with an Alien* for Watson-Guptill.

Beginning with *Shaggy B.E.M. Stories* in 1988, Mike has also become an anthology editor (and was nominated for a Best Editor Hugo in 1994 and 1995). His list of anthologies in print and in press totals more than forty, and includes *Alternate Presidents*, *Alternate Kennedys*, *Sherlock Holmes in Orbit*, *By Any Other Fame*, *Dinosaur Fantastic*, and *Christmas Ghosts*, plus the recent *Stars*, coedited with superstar singer Janis Ian.

Mike has always supported the "specialty press," and he has numerous books and collections out in limited editions from such diverse publishers as Phantasia Press, Axolotl Press, Misfit Press, Pulphouse Publishing, Wildside Press, Dark Regions Press, NESFA Press, WSFA Press, Obscura Press, Farthest Star, and others. He recently agreed to become the science fiction editor for BenBella Books.

Mike was never interested in writing short stories early in his career, producing only seven between 1976 and 1986. Then something clicked, and he has written and sold more than 175 stories since 1986, and now spends more time on short fiction than on novels. The writing that has brought him the most acclaim thus far in his career is the Kirinyaga series, which, with sixty-seven major and minor awards and nominations to date, is the most honored series of stories in the history of science fiction.

He also began writing short nonfiction as well. He sold a four-part series, "Forgotten Treasures," to *The Magazine of Fantasy and Science Fiction*, was a regular columnist for *Speculations* ("Ask Bwana") for twelve years, currently appears in every issue of the *SFWA Bulletin* ("The Resnick/Malzberg Dialogues"), and wrote a biweekly column for the late, lamented GalaxyOnline.com.

Carol has always been Mike's uncredited collaborator on his science fiction, but in the past few years they have sold two movie scripts—*Santiago* and *The Widowmaker*, both based on Mike's books—and Carol *is* listed as his collaborator on those.

Readers of Mike's works are aware of his fascination with Africa, and the many uses to which he has put it in his science fiction. Mike and Carol have taken numerous safaris, visiting Kenya (four times), Tanzania, Malawi, Zimbabwe, Egypt, Botswana, and Uganda. Mike edited the Library of African Adventure series for St. Martin's Press, and is currently editing *The Resnick Library of African Adventure* and, with Carol as coeditor, *The Resnick Library of Worldwide Adventure*, for Alexander Books.

Since 1989, Mike has won five Hugo Awards (for "Kirinyaga," "The Manamouki," "Seven Views of Olduvai Gorge," "The 43 Antarean Dynasties," and "Travels with My Cats") and a Nebula Award (for "Seven Views of Olduvai Gorge"), and has been nominated for twenty-eight Hugos, eleven Nebulas, a Clarke (British), and six Seiun-sho (Japanese). He has also won a Seiun-sho, a Prix Tour Eiffel (French), two Prix Ozones (French), ten HOMer Awards, an Alexander Award, a Golden Pagoda Award, a Hayakawa SF Award (Japanese), a Locus Award, two Ignotus Awards (Spanish), a Xatafi-Cyberdark Award (Spanish), a Futura Award (Croatia), an El Melocoton Mechanico (Spanish), two Sfinks Awards (Polish), and a Fantastyka Award (Polish), and has topped the Science Fiction Chronicle Poll six times, the Scifi Weekly Hugo Straw Poll three times, and the Asimov's Readers Poll five times. In 1993 he was awarded the Skylark Award for Lifetime Achievement in Science Fiction, and both in 2001 and in 2004, he was named Fictionwise.com's Author of the Year.

His work has been translated into French, Italian, German, Spanish, Japanese, Korean, Bulgarian, Hungarian, Hebrew, Russian, Latvian, Lithuanian, Polish, Czech, Dutch, Swedish, Romanian, Finnish, Chinese, and Croatian.

He was recently the subject of Fiona Kelleghan's massive *Mike Resnick: An Annotated Bibliography and Guide to His Work.*